I0628880

FINDING CHING HA

FINDING CHING HA

A novel by
Maya Fleischmann

Although inspired by true events, this book is a work of fiction. Names, characters, places, and events are either the product of the author's imagination or are used fictitiously, and any resemblance to actual persons, living or dead, events, places or locales, is entirely coincidental.

Copyright © 2021 by Maya Fleischmann

All rights reserved. Printed in the United States of America. No part of this book may be used or reproduced in any manner whatsoever without written permission except in the case of brief quotations embodied in critical articles and reviews. For information, email hello@mayafleischmann.com.

An Imprint of Turquoise Maya Publishing

ISBN-13: 978-0-9986459-2-6

For my children.
May you always have
lessons to learn
and wisdom to share.

For Tai Poh Poh and Ling.
See you tomorrow,
between memory and dreams.

FOREWORD

What is true?

For so many inter-country adoptees, this is the central and ever-evolving question of our lives — a search for that which is true about who we were when we were born, how we came to be separated from our families of birth and adopted by strangers in another country and of another race, the identities that are assigned to us by others, and the identities we claim for ourselves.

What is true?

I suppose this is the central question of all human life. But inter-country adoptees struggle with this question in ways that often thoroughly permeate the length and breadth of our lives.

The names and details of our birth parents, siblings, and relatives are shrouded, if not entirely and carefully concealed, by decades-old secrets. Shame forever separates birth mothers and fathers from their children. Abandonment, outdated rules, shoddy practices, honest mistakes, and outright lies obscure the most basic of facts, like our date of birth.

Inter-country adoption often seems
systematically calibrated to deny us any
knowledge of how we came to exist in the world.

Of course, even if information is revealed,
there is the far more complicated and nuanced
nature of our *experiences* as adoptees. When
everything we've been told about our birth and
adoption has been edited and spun to further
the comforting narratives of rescue and
compassion and being chosen, what then is true?
In the years far beyond our childhoods, are we
supposed to continue parroting these themes
with unquestioning appreciation and gratitude?
Are we to live our lives, never acknowledging
the circumstances of our births, the family
that once was ours, the very real life, no
matter how short, that was lived before our
institutionalization and adoption?

What is true?

I believe that stories help us make sense out
of our lives. And for most people, self-
identity is deeply rooted in family stories. I,
myself, have never felt part of my own family's
stories — generations going back to the early
American colonies, war heroes, preachers,
farmers, boozy philanderers, beatnik uncles,
singers, rocket scientists, the short-ish men

on my father's side, and the hook nose on my mother's.

My adoptive family's stories do not explain my existence. They do not provide a foundation for my identity. They are, in fact, largely irrelevant to my own life experiences as an inter-country, transracial adoptee, as a child and adolescent, as a teenager and young adult, and to my 60-plus years of living and working as a Korean American in a predominantly white society and culture.

My always strange face in the mirror, the face of a 60-something Korean man, bears no resemblance to anyone I know. I do not have anyone else's eyes, or hands, or smile, or laugh. I do not know the names of my biological parents, or whether they're alive or dead. I'll never know their stories, or how I was born in Korea, looking like them.

So what is true *about me*?

For most of my life, I could not escape this feeling that I came from nowhere. While I had no vocabulary to fully describe this sense of alienation, I eventually told my wife, years ago, that I felt like an island. I got no further than that, really. I had no words. I couldn't describe what it was like being the only Asian kid in my school, or hating being Korean from a very early age. I didn't understand that I simply didn't *know how* to be me, and there was nobody to teach me. As an adult, I couldn't articulate how I felt compelled to invent an identity for myself based on everything *but* those things most intrinsically true about me — my race, ethnicity, and adoption out of Korea.

Is it true that I was the lucky baby, chosen out of many by my adoptive parents, rescued from a dismal fate? My parents told me that. My parents' friends told me that. People I just met at dinner parties have told me that.

But nothing about this feels true.

What feels true?

Eight years ago, my wife and I began working on a documentary film project with the goal of better understanding inter-country, transracial adoption out of South Korea, setting the precedent for nearly a million inter-country adoptions over the last 70 or so years.

Our plan was to film adult adoptees, to give them a venue to tell their stories simply and

honestly, and to faithfully present those
stories with minimal impact by us as
filmmakers. And so we did. We filmed women and
men, born between 1944–1995, now living in
sixteen cities and seven countries, speaking
six languages. We filmed 100 stories in all.

By creating an archive of Korean adoptee
stories unprecedented in geographic and
chronological scope, as well as an astonishing
diversity of outcomes, people around the world
have come to a far deeper and truer
understanding of this subject.

But, really, the greater impact may have been
on me. Over the course of the last eight years,
I came to more clarity and more honesty than
ever before, as to what is true for me. I've
come to terms with the color of my skin, the
shape of my eyes, and my life experiences as an
Asian American. I've come to claim my place in
the Asian American community, and to reject the
honorary whiteness I lived for so many years.
I've come to be open about my sadness and anger
and a lifetime of enduring and observing
America's culture of racism.

One hundred stories have helped me make sense
out of my life. I have filled my own emptiness
with others' stories of Korean families,

tragedy and displacement, undeserved shame and rejection, bigotry and caste, memories of separations from birth mothers, orphanages and foster care, adapting to new families and languages and places, searches for birth parents and biological families, and reunions that are, all at once, tragic and traumatic and loving and joyful. Time and time again, I was behind the camera or editing or attending one of our own screenings, and there has been an unforgettable moment when I've felt my heart literally skip a beat. And I have wept, knowing beyond all doubt that I have received something that has allowed me to feel more real and honest than I could have ever imagined. All of this is now true for me. Sad and painful? Sometimes. But true is better. And true is hopeful.

I said all of that, to say this:

This novel is true for me. Even as a work of fiction, it is true to the stories I have now heard from hundreds of adult adoptees around the world, no matter how different their circumstances. It is true to the pain and hurt adoptees feel for their entire lives. It is true to the emptiness where stories should be.

It is true for my own story, my own origin in

Korea, my own adoption and adoptive family. It is true to the way I lived for so many years. It is true to the always strange face I see in the mirror, and the less than honest voice in my head.

It is true to my imaginings, my wishes, and my unlived lives.

How do I know it's true for me? In the midst of reading, my heart skipped a beat, and I felt an unmistakable and fresh stab of grief. I wept for everything and everyone I will never know. And I knew.

Glenn Morey

FINDING CHING HA

Prologue

July 1967
Hong Kong

Mrs. Wong walked through the maternity ward of Canossa Hospital to visit her granddaughter. Save for the cry of a baby, and whisperings of cooing voices, the hallway was silent, serene. She stopped in front of a private room and knocked softly. As she opened the door, a breeze cooled her skin, dewy from her short walk from the bus stop to the hospital in the humidity of Hong Kong's long summer. Her daughter, Mei Hua sat in a rattan rocking chair by the open window. At the far wall, there was a white metal bed.

"How is she today?" Mrs. Wong stepped towards the bed where Ling, her sixteen-year-old granddaughter, rested in a medicated slumber. The thin, cotton sheet lay loose over her flabby belly. Her body was still and quiet, except for her chest that rose and fell steadily, pushing out heavy breaths.

"She is better." Mei Hua moved to stand next to her mother. Mrs. Wong touched Ling's hand and kissed her forehead before taking Mei Hua's place in the chair. She pulled a sandalwood fan out of her handbag and leaned her chin against it for a moment before opening it. She looked at her daughter. "Mei Hua, I saw the baby," she said, fanning the side of her cheek.

Mei Hua turned toward her mother, a frown replacing a look of surprise. "Why, Ma?"

"Because that baby is my great-granddaughter." The

1

crick that the chair made each time Mrs. Wong leaned back became louder and more frequent.

"It will make it harder for you to forget her."

"I don't want to forget the baby." Mrs. Wong said slowly.

Mei Hua approached her mother. "Ma," she said, kneeling down and placing her hand on her mother's with gentle firmness. "We already decided that we have no choice--"

"No." Mrs. Wong stopped rocking and removed her hand from Mei Hua's. "You and your husband decided this for yourselves and for Ling. I have decided not to give up Ling's baby." She snapped her fan closed. "I will keep Ching Ha."

The Origin of Ching Ha

August 1970
  Hong Kong

Ching Ha lay in bed waiting for her grandmother to tell her a bedtime story. Twirling her three-year-old fingers around strands of her black, chin-length hair, she yawned. She sat up and leaned towards the foot of her bed, craning her neck to see out the bedroom door. The fan on her bedside table clicked with each rotation to the right and paused silently before resuming the rhythmic sounds as it turned left. Its blades faced upwards, whirring, inviting the curtains to take turns dancing in the warm, summer air. Music played from the other bedroom, its high tones and modulations harmonizing with Ching Ha's great-grandmother's velvety voice. Arms with arrows pointed at the numbers on the round wall clock.

"Ten o'clock," Ching Ha called out a random time and flopped back onto her pillow with a noisy exhale. "You're late, Tai Poh Poh."

"I'm coming now."

The music stopped and Tai Poh Poh's slippered feet shuffled into the room. Strands of silver streaked her black hair and peeked out of a thin hair towel. "It's not ten o'clock," she said, her smile bright against her smooth skin that was shiny with rose oil. "It's only seven o'clock."

Ching Ha sniffed the air. She could smell the roses of the face oil and the minty-herbal smell of Tiger Balm that Tai Poh Poh put on her shoulders

3

each night.

"I know. I heard the record playing," Ching Ha teased.

Tai Poh Poh sat at the edge of the twin size bed.

"Tonight, I want to hear my story," the little girl said as she pulled the pink and white sheets up to her neck.

Tai Poh Poh began her story with a clearing of her throat, followed by a deep breath as if preparing for an operatic performance.

"A long time ago, on an island in the middle of the sea, there was a Chinese princess named Ning Nuan. She was going to the home of her cousins in the next province. They were going to travel together to a faraway land as part of their royal duties. Ning Nuan was in her palanquin, reading her book about a strange world in the clouds when she heard a noise. 'Wah, wah, wah.' It sounded like a small animal, or a big bird."

Ching Ha rolled on her side and listened intently.

"She slid open the window. 'Stop, please,' she told the carriage carriers. They stopped. She listened and she heard the noise, again. 'Do you hear that sound?' she asked her guards and palace lady. The palace lady was old — she had taken care of Nuan Ning's mother when she had been a child — but still wise and her senses sharp. She stood very still and turned her head slowly.

"'Yes, Princess.' She pointed to a large plum blossom tree. 'The sound is coming from there.'

"A breeze swept through the valley at that moment and small, purple flowers floated in the air and over the princess's head, as if guiding her to a magical place. Led by her palace lady and guards, Nuan Ning walked to the base of the beautiful Mei Hua plum blossom tree. In a hollow created by its thick and winding roots, Ning Nuan saw a bundle of cloth and linen. Two small arms stuck out from the flowers that had fallen from the tree and were helping to keep the baby warm. Ning Nuan knelt and pushed aside the material. She saw a small face with rosy cheeks, dark brown eyes staring at her. The baby was no longer crying, but sputtering ragged

4

breaths and shaking. It was spring, and the air was still cool.

"'We must warm her up,' Ning Nuan said. She never had children or little brothers or sisters, but every child knows to pick up a small animal with care and love. As she lifted the bundle, brushing away twigs and leaves, she admired the baby.

"The palace lady looked over the princess's shoulder and around the fields, path, valley, and mountaintops. Only their royal party was present. No herd of cattle, no person, no indication that anyone was nearby. They looked at one another.

"'Do you think someone will come back for her?' Nuan Ning asked, as she rocked the baby from side to side.

'"Even if they come back, it will be too late. This baby will be sick and die from cold and hunger or be eaten by animals,' the palace lady said, looking over the baby's body."

Ching Ha gasped and put her hands to her face, imagining a wolf or bear running through a forest, carrying the bundle in its mouth.

"'She is not injured, but we must feed her and warm her up. Let's continue on our journey.'

"As the palanquin swayed and bumped on its way, Ning Nuan fed the baby drops of congee and mashed plums. She spoke to the baby in a confident, but soft, voice. 'I will make sure you have a life filled with fortune and family. Don't worry, Little One.' But Ning Nuan knew that she would not be able to take this baby on the journey with her cousins. She looked at her palace lady and said,

"'I'm sorry, but you cannot go with me on my long journey.'

"The palace lady looked up, her lips parted, head tilted. 'Why Princess?' she asked. 'Have I upset you?'

"'No.' The princess took her hand. 'It is because I trust only you to take care of this baby. If you are her guardian, perhaps there is a chance I will see her again one day.'

"The palace lady's eyes became glossy with tears. 'I will love this child as I have loved and cared for you.' She bowed deeply to her princess then looked at the baby, who silently stared back at them.

"'What will you call her?'

"'I will call her "Ching Ha because she is so quiet and because she will grow up to be a noble woman.'

"When the princess reached the home of her cousins, she and her cousins had two days to be with Ching Ha while they continued preparations for their travels. On the third day, Ning Nuan held Ching Ha, whose cheeks had become rounded and pink from the good food and nurturing from those around her. She gave the baby girl a kiss on her forehead and felt the ache of missing this child even though she had not known her long. She knew this child was special.

"The palace lady took Ching Ha, and they waved to the princess, who was a baby herself when the palace lady had started taking care of her, almost two decades earlier. When the princess and her cousins were far along the mountain road, the palace lady set off in the other direction, according to the princess's instructions. They were carried towards the far edge of the island, where Ching Ha would be safe and loved for the rest of her life."

Ching Ha sat up and clapped. Tai Poh Poh stood up and bowed at the waist, her arms each gracefully brushing across her one at a time.

"Is that really true?" Ching Ha asked, pushing covers back, as though she were going to climb out of bed.

Mrs. Wong tilted her face towards the ceiling as if pondering this question that always came at the end of the story. Ching Ha copied her, looking for the answers on the ceiling.

"It's as true as some other stories I have told you, and not as true as others."

Her great-grandmother gave her the same answer she always did. Ching Ha didn't know what that meant, but she didn't really want an answer anymore. The story and question were just part of their game.

"Good night, Ching Ha," Tai Poh Poh said, kissing her on the forehead.

"Good night, palace lady," said Ching Ha as she opened and closed her hands like a little baby.

Tai Poh Poh turned off the light by the bed and walked out of the bedroom, her smooth slippers making a pat-pat sound, as she walked along the hardwood floors. There was silence; then Ching Ha heard the crackle shush, crackle shush, as Tai Poh Poh's record started playing again, this time more softly than before. Ching Ha lay on her pillow. She watched the colourful, shape-changing light from the building signs and street lamps sneak in through the top of the curtain and dance on the ceiling, lulling her into a peaceful slumber.

To Market, to Market

Ching Ha yawned and squinted dark brown eyes against the morning light. It was Wednesday, so she and her great-grandmother were on their way to Wanchai Market. Her almost-three-year-old belly gurgled, still hungry after her congee breakfast. But Ching Ha said nothing to her great-grandmother because she knew she would get a tasty treat on the walk home.

They stepped away from their building into the lines of people moving along the pavement like ants and joined the city's symphony of street traffic. The rattling of trams along the tracks and the ding ding of their brass warning bells created an irregular syncopation with squeaky car brakes and the beep beep of buses.

Ching Ha and her great-grandmother sidestepped window shoppers, crossed with the throngs of people weaving through cars and dodged pedestrians moving against foot traffic until they entered Southorn Playground. The whole concrete park, encircled by towering residential buildings, burbled with activity and pools of different energies.

Men moved chess across stone tables. Near them, birds chirped and hopped in small, wooden cages that hung in trees. Men and women, wearing loose-fitting pants and baggy tee shirts, swayed their bodies and circled their arms around imaginary shapes, gathering and moving chi. Girls in white and blue pinafores and boys in white shirts and blue shorts darted past, their backpacks bouncing up and down on their backs. Aromas wafted from the food carts lined up on the other side of the park. Ching Ha touched her belly, imagining the rich taste of fish in green peppers drenched in black bean sauce and a plate of smooth, white rice noodles drizzled with hot chili sauce. She tugged on her great-grandmother's arm but Tai Poh Poh continued to walk away from the food.

Although her great-grandmother slowed down so Ching Ha could see a display of windup toys whirring and clinking in a big, plastic bucket on Tai Yuen street, they did not stop. They walked purposefully towards the cobblestone steps leading into the wet market.

The noises here were again different from the streets Ching Ha had been on earlier. Chickens squawked over the loud cries of hawkers selling their wares, and wheels of pushcarts rumbled and clacked across the bumpy road. Ching Ha walked through white, yellow, green and pink splashes of flowers, bolts of shiny blue and red silk and stacked tanks of black and orange fan-tailed goldfish. She stretched out her hand, brushing it against the multilayers of the different shaped petals, the frictionless fabric and the weave of wicker baskets.

The market hosted a variety of smells. As Ching Ha and her Tai Poh Poh walked through the market, the perfumed fragrances of flowers became the pungent bitterness of fresh herbs. A chemical smell wafted in the air of the tiled area, where the workers who wore white coats and high rubber boots hosed away the blood of butchered animals.

This part of the market, filled with animals, made Ching Ha's chest feel tight and unhappy, but her eyes could not look away from the creatures — some alive, some dead or nearly dead. She stared at the pigs, their rear legs hanging from long hooks in the ceiling of the white-tiled stalls. They hung by their toes, their front legs almost touching the ground. They were as tall as the men who were cutting off pieces of their flesh. Their skin was pale and each half of their bellies were round, even though their split-open bodies were empty. Her throat twisted, as though a finger was poking into it. She looked at her great-grandmother who was talking to the fishmonger as they pointed at a fish in one of the tanks stacked in a wall at the edge of his shop. Ching Ha glanced at the pig once more, then looked away with a shudder.

A man in the middle of the cobbled path sat on a short stool, next to two piles of moving netted bags. It took a moment for Ching Ha to hear croaking and see the large frogs clambering to get on top of each other. A woman with a plastic shopping basket stopped in front of him and pointed to the bag. He lifted it up, so she could peer in. She held up three fingers and handed him some coins. The frog man reached into a netted bag and pulled out a slimy, green amphibian. It kicked furiously before hanging limp in defeat. Ching Ha's sense of wonder did not allow her to turn away. She watched him stick a small knife into the base of its neck. He then stuck his finger into the incision and peeled the skin off the frog's writhing body, leaving behind its smooth, pale pink body. Was the frog still alive? Did it feel pain? She sniffled, wanting to buy all the frogs and set them free the next time she went to the beach.

"Look at the fish that I chose," Tai Poh Poh said as she leaned in towards Ching Ha. The fishmonger had his finger hooked under the gills of a thin, silver fish that was angling its shivering tail to the left and the right with decreasing speed and flexibility.

"You see how clear its eyes are?"

Ching Ha nodded quickly, wanting to end the fish's display. She gasped when the fishmonger gripped the fish's tail, swung it and whacked its head onto the wood board. She had seen this many times before, but the instance between life and death shocked her each time. The shimmering creature stopped writhing, and the fishmonger put it in a bag carelessly, as though the creature had been a rolled-up newspaper. He handed the large, clear bag to the girl. She brought the bag close to her face. Her belly filled with fascination and nausea once more. Its dark, watery eyes were still clear and shiny. The centers were as black as her hair; yet she thought she could see herself in them. She wondered how she could be so sad for this now-dead fish, yet so excited to eat it for lunch.

They moved farther down the street until they reached sellers with wide, round baskets filled with greens, crisp capsicums and sweet-smelling oranges and mangos. Tai Poh Poh poked around the pile of long, leafy Chinese vegetables before choosing the brightest leaves and the yellowest flowers. She picked up the bunch and held it to her nose, then placed it near Ching Ha's face. "Smell this choy sum."

She took a deep breath, her nose touching the cool leaves. "It smells so good."

Tai Poh Poh scanned a heap of scallions and chose a group of stalks that had large, bright white bulbs. She sniffed them and handed them to the stall owner to be weighed. The ginger root's beige unblemished skin was smooth and tight. It looked like the head and body of a round, stubby person. At the fruit stand, Tai Poh Poh bought two palm-sized, bright yellow mangos, a branch of speckled brown lychees and three small oranges.

At the end of the street, Tai Poh Poh stared into the basket. We are almost done. She's making sure she has everything, Ching Ha told her belly, as it gurgled for a fresh, warm stick of yau char kwai. When Tai Poh Poh looked up, Ching Ha looked to her like a dog anticipating a command and clapped when Tai Poh Poh nodded.

They hurried back through the market and down a small alley until Ching Ha stood in front of a metal case filled with sticks of deep-fried dough that smelled like oil and sugar. She swallowed the saliva in her mouth. The owner greeted Tai Poh Poh and Ching Ha as he ladled rice soup from a big pot into a large bowl. He topped the white, thick, soupy rice with slices of duck egg and bright green scallions. He walked past Ching Ha and placed the steaming bowl in front of a young lady sitting at a low table. He returned to the metal case and, with a toothy grin, handed Ching Ha a piece of parchment paper. She reached into the case and pulled out the most symmetrical fried dough stick with the smoothest surface and placed it into the waxy bag that he held.

As they walked home, Ching Ha relished the warm treat--each bite breaking through a thin layer of airy crispness that melted into a chewy texture, oozing with the flavour of plain bread.

Tai Poh Poh watched her great granddaughter's contented consumption and chuckled. She stepped on a flattened box. Ching Ha saw the soaked cardboard disintegrate under her great-grandmother's shoe, and the next motions had played out slowly with her great-grandmother's leg slowly moving forward and up into the air, forcing her to let go of the basket and fall backwards, arms stretched out into the air as if reaching for something. Trapped in a dreamlike state, a hand still clutching the greasy bag, Ching Ha froze in place with Tai Poh Poh's slurred cry echoing in her head. When Ching Ha snapped out of her daze, the slow-motion playback vanished and the sound of the streets returned. Three people moved forward to help Ching Ha's great-grandmother, bombarding her with questions. As a woman set the wicker basket upright, an orange slipped out and began to roll away. Ching Ha scampered after it.

As her fist closed around the thin rind of the round fruit, she heard, "Ching Ha. Ching Ha." Her great-grandmother's voice — usually soft, even and firm — sounded fast, broken and high-pitched.

"I'm here, Tai Poh Poh," Ching Ha said, pushing through the gathering crowd until she sat in front of her great-grandmother. She held out the orange. "It rolled away," she said as she dropped it into the basket. Ching Ha looked at the wrinkle forming between her great-grandmother's eyebrows and gently pressed it. "Don't cry." She wrapped her arms around Tai Poh Poh's neck. "I'm here. I'll take care of you."

Nourishing Wisdom

Thin, iridescent flakes scattered into the air as Mrs. Wong scraped her cleaver across the fish. Though she was back in her kitchen, with Ching Ha safely seated at the dining table in front of her, the memory of the taxi ride home from the market was all-consuming. Ching Ha had patted Tai Poh Poh's shoulder and kissed her trembling hand while softly repeating, "Things will be better soon.You will see."

Although Mrs. Wong had told this to Ching Ha, and herself, so many times about scraped knees, colds and disappointments in life, Mrs. Wong wasn't sure now if things really would get better for this child. Perhaps she was not the best person to take care of Ching Ha. She pushed away unhappy wonderings about what might have happened if her fall had been more disastrous.

"Do you feel better, Tai Poh Poh?" Ching Ha sat on her high stool at the kitchen table. The dough stick was in front of her, but she had not touched it since dropping it in the basket after the fall.

"Yes, thank you, Ching Ha." Mrs. Wong sprinkled salt over the fish's body before rubbing it along its silvery body. Water streamed over the fish, making it look like it was writhing in Mrs. Wong's hands. She wiped the water off it and placed it on a chopping board.

Ching Ha stared at the fish. Its eyeballs gleamed at her as Mrs. Wong sliced the fish's belly with a big cleaver. After more slitting and cutting, she lifted the fish's skeleton, with the head still

13

attached. She pointed to its eyeballs. "Those are for you." She let it fall into the pot of bubbling water. It landed with a plop. Ching Ha clapped and leaned up to watch its eyes cloud white. Mrs. Wong placed the rest of the fish on paper towels.

A freshness filled the kitchen as Mrs. Wong washed and chopped the ginger, carrots, celery and a small chili pepper. Each crunch of the blade on the wooden board misted an herbal fragrance into the air. The vegetables tumbled over each other, as Mrs. Wong scraped them off the chopping board and into the pot. She bent down, so she was eye level with the stove, and turned a dial until the flame got smaller. Scooping up a cup of shiny white rice from a large tin, she placed it into another small pot, half-filled with water. Clouds appeared as she swirled the water with her hand. She placed her hand at the pot's edge and carefully poured the water out. She repeated the process until the water ran clear when she poured it out. Filling it for the last time, she stuck her index finger into the pot to measure the height of the water and covered the pot before setting it on the stove. A turn of a dial released a low hiss. Mrs. Wong lit a match and placed the flame under the pot until a large blue flame appeared with a whooshing sound.

"While we wait for the rice and fish soup, we will visit Tai Gung Gung," Mrs. Wong said, removing her apron. She cocked her head towards the three oranges arranged on a small plate on the table. She watched Ching Ha step purposefully into the living room as she held the oranges at eye-level. She bent her knees, lowering her whole body to set the plate gingerly on her great-grandfather's altar, next to the plate of oranges already there.

"Here are new oranges for you, Tai Gung Gung." Ching Ha clasped her hands together and bowed to the sepia print of a man. His dark hair and rectangular rimmed spectacles accented a twinkling in his eyes. "Ching Ha will eat your old oranges," she said with a broad grin and carried the plate of older oranges into the kitchen.

"Later," Mrs. Wong called after her. "Lunch is

almost ready." Ching Ha slumped her shoulders in mock frustration and stacked the oranges on top of one another. Mrs. Wong knelt in front of the altar and lit her incense sticks. She looked at the photo of her late husband and imagined his voice saying, "Lien Hua, you are not alone." The blur of the street, the buildings, and the people around her as she fell, obscured her thoughts again. If something happens to me, will Ching Ha be alone? She moved the sticks up and down in front of her, letting the smoke carry her prayers to the heavens. Show me what I should do. She placed the orange-tipped sticks upright in a small tin of rice and walked to the kitchen sink to wash her hands.

Ching Ha slid the plate of oranges aside and leaned her elbows on the kitchen table. "I'm ready for the cooking show."

Mrs. Wong lifted the fish fillets from the paper towels and laid them in a pan of hot oil seasoned with garlic and ginger. A concoction of vinegar, soy sauce and Shaoxing wine sizzled, as it splashed on the fish, and the skin crisped and turned brown. She flipped them over until the other sides were equally crinkly. She plated the fish and added more ginger and garlic into the fizzling oil, followed by a shower of slivered carrots and celery. "Carrots for your eyes," Mrs. Wong said as she pointed to her widened eyes. She put her right hand around her left elbow and scrunched up her face. "Celery is for my aching joints." Ching Ha copied her great-grandmother's expression of feigned pain and held her own elbow. "There's some ginger for your belly," she said, poking herself in the stomach. Ching Ha giggled.

"You are good girl, Ching Ha," Mrs. Wong said as she held the girl's chin. "Remember, Tai Poh Poh love you," she said in English.

"Love. You," Ching Ha repeated. She looked back and forth at her great-grandmother's eyes. "Tai Poh Poh, are you crying?" her small voice rising in pitch.

The woman wiped her eyes on her apron and forced out a chuckle. "No, Ching Ha. It's the onion. It makes me cry."

"I didn't see onions, Tai Poh Poh."

"The vegetables are bright and shiny." Mrs. Wong moved the vegetables around the pan and lifted the lid off the pot of fish soup, releasing a cloud of aromatic steam. She swirled her hand in the steam and inhaled.

Ching Ha mimicked the inhalation and clutched her belly. "I'm hungry."

"Listen." Mrs. Wong swirled a tall, slender bottle above the pan. There was a hissing as a light stream of black sauce fell onto the vegetables. She handed two spoons and two pairs of chopsticks to Ching Ha, and took three small ceramic bowls out of the cabinet and set them on the counter by the stove.

Ching Ha arranged the two spoons and one pair of chopsticks on the table. She held the other pair of chopsticks and swayed side to side, tapping them against the table's edge, like the drummer of a dragon boat. Ching Ha began a countdown.

"Ten, nine, eight . . ." A myriad of red, orange, and green vegetables decorated the steamy white rice. "Seven, six, five . . ."

Mrs. Wong scooped the steaming fish soup into the third bowl. She placed Ching Ha's dish of salted black beans on the table.

"Four, three . . ." Ching Ha sped up the beat of her tapping, as the food was set on the table. "Two . . ." the counting as Mrs. Wong sat down. "One!" Ching Ha clapped and the two of them leaned their foreheads together.

"Have a good lunch, my sweet child."

Mrs. Wong blew on the food, dispersing the steam and aromas through the kitchen. Ching Ha watched and did the same. The woman lifted her chopsticks and used them to select a couple of salted beans and place them on her rice. Ching Ha picked up the chopsticks and positioned them in her fingers. One she held like a pencil, and the other slid below it, and resting on the fourth finger. She picked up two black beans and put them straight into her mouth.

"Mmm. So tay-stee."

Mrs. Wong raised her eyebrows. "Your English so

good."

Ching Ha smiled and picked out carrots and ginger, which she put in a small heap at one edge of her bowl. She placed the bowl by her mouth and used her chopsticks to push a small heap of rice and vegetables into her mouth. She moaned as she chewed. Mrs. Wong laughed, admiring how much her great granddaughter loved food. After a couple of bites, the girl put down the chopsticks and picked up her spoon. She scooped up some fish soup, leaned forward, and slurped it into her mouth. She returned to her rice bowl and ate more salted black beans and stir-fried vegetables. Ching Ha picked up a chopstick and traced the pattern of the table's wood laminate.

"Eat until your belly is full," Mrs. Wong encouraged, nudging Ching Ha with her knee.

"Try this," she said, picking up a dab of chili paste and putting on the rice. "It will make your body strong." Ching Ha turned her face without taking her eyes off the new line she found to trace. She opened her mouth and allowed Mrs. Wong to feed her.

"Now for the special honor. It's tender and juicy. This is food that your brain loves. It will make you very clever." Mrs. Wong switched into English for the last words and tapped her head with the back of her chopsticks.

"I want to be very clever." Ching Ha leaned towards the cooked eyeball, which was no longer shiny and hard but soft and white like a sweet rice dumpling. She opened her mouth like a hungry bird. Her cheek swelled for a moment before she bit into it and began chewing. Mrs. Wong lifted the soup spoon towards Ching Ha, but the girl shook her head.

"Finished?"

Ching Ha nodded without making eye contact. She walked to the bedroom and returned with the old telephone book that she used for her drawings. A flutter, like hundreds of butterflies, filled Mrs. Wong's chest. The rising sensation of joy and love was quelled by a deluge of worry as her mind wandered again to the thought she had when she had fallen in the market, *What will happen to Ching Ha?*

Choices with No Options

Mrs. Wong picked up the phone receiver. "Wei." She looked towards the bedroom where Ching Ha was napping. "Yes, she is," she whispered. She hung up the phone and opened the door to the flat.

The lift dinged. Mei Hua stepped out, sunglasses on her head. She held her crocodile handbag in one hand and a sturdy department store shopping bag in her other.

"Hello, Ma," she said softly with a smile as she walked down the vestibule, her high heels tapping along the tile.

Mrs. Wong gave her daughter a hug and took the bag from her. "You don't need to buy from the fancy Japanese store," she said, looking at the Daimaru logo. "Our Chinese shops are better and much cheaper."

"I know," said Mei Hua. She put her glasses into her handbag, took off her shoes and followed her mother into the kitchen. "I was already there, and their produce is so fresh." She began emptying the bags. "How are you feeling? Why do I have to hear from your neighbour that you fell down?"

"I'm fine," Mrs. Wong said with a dismissive wave of her hand. "There was nothing for you to do. Anyway, I had Ching Ha with me, and you don't want anything to do with her."

"Well, you don't have to raise her," her daughter said, placing another can on the counter.

"Yes, I do. She is my great-granddaughter, my family," Mrs. Wong said. She examined the can of SPAM her daughter set on the counter.

19

"I know someone who would take good care of her," Mei Hua said. She placed a can of salty black beans on the second shelf of the cupboard.

"I'm happy looking after Ching Ha," Mrs. Wong said as she moved the can to the first shelf.

"Yes, I know, but this situation is getting very complicated." Mei Hua opened a cabinet by her knee and put a small bag of rice in it. "We can't keep sending Ling abroad to study and travel. What if Ling finds out that you have Ching Ha?"

Mrs. Wong said nothing as she moved the rice into the adjoining cabinet. She picked up the package of duck meat and dried shrimp and put them into the cabinet without looking at Mei Hua. Mrs. Wong rubbed her temples. She looked at the bedroom door and at her watch.

"If we tell Ling that Ching Ha is with me, we can fix everything," said Mrs. Wong. "No more secrets."

"No, Ma," Mei Hua said.

"I'm sure Ling would want her."

"It doesn't matter what she wants. Ling is a young, unmarried woman. A child would ruin her life."

"She should have thought of that before she was with that man," Mrs. Wong scolded.

"You should have thought about what keeping Ching Ha would do to us," Mei Hua said.

"The three of us aren't free to spend time together anymore and, you and I now have a secret from Ling."

Mrs. Wong glanced towards the bedroom again then looked at the ceiling, willing back the tears. She shook her head as she filled a kettle with water and placed it on the stove. Mei Hua was right. This situation was getting more complicated. How long before Ling realised Ching Ha was living in the home of her trusted grandmother? Mrs. Wong turned on the gas and lit the burner with a match. What would become of the child?

"Ching Ha is also my family."

"I know, Ma," Mei Hua said, "But, what about Ling? She would have no honor or opportunity to make a life for herself if people knew she had a baby and was not married."

Annoyance blanketed Mrs. Wong's sadness. Mei Hua was fooling herself if she thought no one knew about the girl. Six months after Ling left Hong Kong to study abroad and travel with her parents, Mrs. Wong began looking after a child. Her friends accepted the story that Ching Ha belonged to an ailing daughter of a deceased cousin. But Mrs. Wong was certain that they all suspected this was Ling's baby. No one spoke about it with her because it didn't matter to them. They were friends to the point of being family. Mrs. Wong turned off the stove and poured water into a teapot.

"If you have such a strong relationship with your husband and his family," she said, "why can't you tell them the truth?" Mrs. Wong asked and placed two teacups on the table.

"There would be too much shame and scandal if Benny's investors and clients knew."

"And what about the shame for Ching Ha with no family history, no family name, no mother to love her?" Steam rose from the cups, as the water poured in. "What opportunities will Ching Ha have?"

Mrs. Wong plopped onto the kitchen stool, rubbing her thumb across her wedding ring.

"We will always provide for her."

"Money? That's always your solution. What about family?" Mrs. Wong took a breath to slow her racing mind and tame her angry tongue. She lifted her cup to her lips, slurped and tried to calm down. She somehow needed to get Mei Hua aligned to her. "Do you remember how long it took for you to get pregnant?

"Yes, Ma." Mei Hua stood and looked in the cabinet. "It took me three years, and I almost gave up." She pulled out a tin of round almond cookies and set them on the table.

"Yes, and it took me *seven* years." Mrs. Wong pressed the tin against her chest. Wedging her fingers under the ridge of the lid, she pried it open and set the round tin in front of Mei Hua. "Seven years and no baby. Your father and I believed that the Gods had decided we were to be childless."

She laid a hand on Mei Hua's. "Then, they answered our prayers."

Mei Hua crunched on her cookie and nodded, her hand patting her mother's.

"The gods blessed Ling by giving her a child."

"Or maybe they cursed her by giving her a baby when she is still a baby — and an unmarried one." Mei Hua snatched her hand away from her mother's and pushed the lid back on the tin.

"Don't say that," Mrs. Wong said, pulling her own hand back. "A baby is a blessing." She pointed at Mei Hua's hair, handbag, and bold patterned dress, then waggled her finger in circles in front of her. "You call yourself a 'modern woman,' and you are afraid of what people think. So what if your daughter is not married? You have money. No man has to pay a bride dowry for a virgin."

"Ma . . . "

"Mei Hua. Please think about this. Your father and I refused arranged marriages to marry each other. We didn't like Benny or thought he was suitable, but we let you marry him because we knew he loves you. Sometimes rules do not make sense, so why do you follow them? Ling had a baby. We cannot change the past, only change how we respond to it. We are a family. We can all be a family." Mrs. Wong, eyes tearing, her voice hoarse from whispering loudly, put her hand on her daughter's once more.

"Ma, you know that's not possible." Mei Hua moved her hand and reached for her bag. "We can't be associated with this . . . situation." Mei Hua said the last word in English.

"Sit-u-a-tion?" Mrs. Wong mimicked, her jaw tightening. "You mean Ching Ha? What about her sit-u-a-tion?" Mrs. Wong asked, weaving sarcasm into her mix of English and Cantonese.

"I told you, we have an arrangement for her. She will be taken good care of. Someone else can raise her — anytime you want them to take over." Mei Hua unlatched the gold buckle of her black crocodile handbag and pulled out a large sunglass case.

"Take over? Take over what? Our morals and responsibility to a child that your daughter gave birth to?"

This time it was Mei Hua's sigh that silenced the dialogue. She looked towards Ching Ha's bedroom.

"I know. I know. You have to go before she wakes up and sees you."

"I worry about you, Ma. You work too hard." Mei Hua took out her sunglasses. "You should be enjoying life with us in a big house with whatever you need and servants to help you."

Mrs. Wong threw her hands up in the air and stood up. "I enjoy my life. Your father and I raised you living this, this . . ." She motioned around the small apartment. "This simple life."

Mei Hua snapped the sunglasses case closed. "Ma, when will we stop having this argument?"

"When we make things right," her mother replied, crossing her arms.

Another sigh escaped Mei Hua's perfectly-lipsticked mouth. She replaced the case in her handbag. "I'm trying to make things right, Ma. I don't want us to have secrets from Ling. I want you to be able to live with us, to spend more time with us."

"I do, too," replied Mrs. Wong.

Mei Hua stood next to her mother and motioned to the partially open door of the small room. "How is she?"

"Good," Mrs. Wong replied with a smile. "Would you like to see your granddaughter?" she added with eyebrows raised hopefully.

"No."

"She doesn't need to know who you are."

"No, Ma," Mei Hua said too quickly and sternly for her mother's liking.

Mrs. Wong gave a nod of understanding mingled with disappointment. "She is a good girl. I hope I do a better job raising her than I did with you. Or that you did with Ling."

Mei Hua raised a well-groomed eyebrow at her mother. "Time for me to go."

"Will you be going to my second cousin's wedding next month?" Mrs. Wong asked her daughter as they walked toward the door.

"No," Mei Hua replied nonchalantly, placing the sunglasses on her head.

Mrs. Wong nodded her head in understanding. "Oh, I forget. Your husband is too important for our low family connections."

"No, that's not it, Ma," Mei Hua replied. "Anyway, how can we go if you will be there with Ching Ha? You see what I mean about this is getting too complicated."

"If you don't go, Lam will be offended."

"We will send an expensive gift."

Mrs. Wong rolled her eyes "Again, money saves you."

"Money can make life easier sometimes."

"Money cannot save you from your demons. It's better to face the truth and learn to live with it — no matter how terrible it is."

Mei Hua's lips tensed, as though she were preventing herself from speaking. She slipped on her shoes and opened the door. "Ma, think about our choices," she said, giving her mother a hug. "It would also be better for Ching Ha. What if you had broken your leg, or worse?"

A mix of sadness and joy threatened to make Mrs. Wong cry, as her daughter's arms tightened around her. She wondered which was worse. Losing your great-granddaughter or losing both your daughter and granddaughter? She released her daughter from the hug. "Sometimes it feels like choices give you no options."

Lighting the Way

September 1970

A koi's translucent fins shimmered above Ching Ha's head. She tilted her head back and spun around, mouth open, arms up in the air. The glittering flaps of its tail caught the breeze and turned in slow motion. Next to it, animal-shaped lanterns began to dance as they dangled from tall bamboo poles. Ching Ha pointed to a round, pink lantern with swirling tassels.

"Are you sure that's the one you want?"

Ching Ha looked up at the lanterns hanging, and then at the chosen one. She squished her face and patted her cheeks in indecision before deciding. "Yes, please. I'll take this."

For three days, the lantern hung over Ching Ha and Tai Poh Poh's bed. It twirled and swayed when it caught a breeze from a fan or open window. On the afternoon of the fourth day, Tai Poh Poh placed her wicker basket on their table. She put in the silver thermos of warm water with lemon zest and grated ginger.

"Finally we're going to the Peak, Tai Poh Poh," Ching Ha said, examining the lantern that was now on the chair beside her.

"Tonight, we celebrate the moon festival," Tai Poh Poh replied. "We will light the lantern and walk up the mountain."

"Why?" Ching Ha asked. "What's on the mountain?"

Tai Poh Poh placed a small metal tin containing

25

small balls of rice with shrimp and pork and placed it in the basket. "We will eat our picnic and look for the goddess living in the moon."

"Waaah," said Ching Ha, her eyes growing wide with her smile.

Finally, Tai Poh Poh added a small orange, two large handkerchiefs and a ten-inch, thin bamboo stick.

"Please give me your lantern," Tai Poh Poh said, holding out her hands.

Ching Ha picked up her lantern and passed it to her great-grandmother. She looked at it from several angles. "Let's see if this can fold," she said and ran her fingers along the sides until the lantern gave way. Ching Ha gasped as the lantern flattened. "Don't worry. It's just folded so we don't damage it when we are on the bus,"

"Bus." Ching Ha clapped her hands.

The doors to Bus 15 opened with a clank. Tai Poh Poh's hand tightened around Ching Ha's, as the people pressed into a tight group, pushing to get on the bus. Tai Poh Poh boosted Ching Ha onto the bus with a lift of her knee.

"Upstairs," Tai Poh Poh said, throwing her change into the fare box.

Tai Poh Poh hustled the girl past an old man sitting on the aisle seat of a row of three, towards the window seat.

Ching Ha gazed out of the window of the big bus, her body swaying with the movement. This was so different from the street tram that was in the middle of the road. The bus moved side to side and stopped at the side of the street, close enough to reach out and touch the street signs and people's windows.

"Tai Poh Poh," Ching Ha said, as she tugged her great-grandmother's elbow. "Everything looks so different."

"It's good to see the same things from a new way."

Ching Ha nodded. Her eyes moved left to right like a frenzied typewriter carriage as the view whizzed past. The buildings dissipated as the bus wound up a steep hill. Ching Ha felt sleepy.

A child's voice yelled, "Mama." Ching Ha turned. A little boy smaller than herself tugged at his mother's bag. She watched his mother shake her head. But she finally rummaged in a bag and took out a small piece of yellow sweet bread and handed it to him. As the boy ate the bread, she wrapped her arms around him. The woman looked up at Ching Ha and smiled. Ching Ha smiled back and looked at Tai Poh Poh.

"Do I have a mama?"

Tai Poh Poh looked at Ching Ha. She turned and saw the mother holding her child. She tapped Ching Ha on the nose. "It's a long story for another day," Tai Poh Poh said as she put her arm around the little girl and kissed her forehead.

"A new story about my mama?" Ching Ha asked with a lilt in her voice.

"Yes and other things."

"What things?"

"It's for another day."

"What day?"

"One day, you will know your story." Tai Poh Poh pulled her great-granddaughter closer and pointed at the view of the city by dusk. Ching Ha looked at the building silhouettes, so different here than when in the belly of the city.

"Is that the Star Ferry?" she pointed to the boats that moved in the waterway between Kowloon and Hong Kong.

"Yes."

"The buildings here are short," Ching Ha said. She pointed to a cluster of eight storied buildings surrounded by grass.

"We're not in Wanchai anymore."

"Where are we?"

"San Deng," Tai Poh Poh replied pointing upwards, then added in English, "The Peak."

"The Peak!" Ching Ha repeated, and bounced up on her seat as she pointed in the air. She laughed, turning back to the scenery unfolding below her.

As the bus turned into its final stop, people stood

on the bus and lined up on the stairs. Ching Ha pushed against her great-grandmother, who sat, waiting for the people to move out of the aisle. She motioned to the window. Ching Ha watched the people leave the bus to join the crowds moving through the large parking lot.

Policemen blowing on whistles directed taxis, busses through the people traffic. Ching Ha sniffed the air, and searched for the food stands and carts. She could smell her favorite street food somewhere nearby: fish balls, tofu sticks, chestnuts, dragon beard candy and egg waffle cake. She saw children walking and holding their lanterns on sticks in front of them.

"My lantern." Ching Ha remembered and reached for the basket.

"Soon," Tai Poh Poh said, taking Ching Ha's hand as they stood up to leave the bus.

Tai Poh Poh guided Ching Ha to the bottom of a steep hill.

"The Peak," Ching Ha said, and again pointed to the sky.

"Yes, clever girl," Tai Poh Poh said with a nod. "But first, you must use the toilet."

She led Ching Ha through a doorway of a big building and down a dim flight of steps. They stopped in front of a door with an outline of a round female shape. Ching Ha's nose wrinkled at the humidity and stale-smelling odor. This was not one of the fancy city hotel toilets that Tai Poh Poh had taken her into before.

Ching Ha's mouth twisted at the sight of the oval-shaped hole porcelain toilet in the ground. Tai Poh Poh took tissue paper from her pocket, hung her basket on the hinge of the door and entered the stall with Ching Ha.

"It's so dirty," the girl said, allowing her great-grandmother to remove her underpants.

"It's cleaner than sitting on the other toilets," Tai Poh Poh said as she put Ching Ha's underpants in her pocket.

Ching Ha stepped around the narrowest part of the

toilet and stepped over the hole. Tai Poh Poh helped Ching Ha gather her dress in her armpits and held onto her body. "That's why we wear dresses when we go out."

Ching Ha squatted down, making sure her feet were not too close to the rim of the bowl.

"Good girl," Tai Poh Poh said and shook her head. "So much easier for men." She sighed.

"Why?" Ching Ha asked.

Tai Poh Poh laughed. "I'll tell you another time."

Ching Ha held onto her great-grandmother's shoulders and stepped back into her underpants, careful they didn't touch her shoes.

When they were back outside, dusk cast red and orange light over them. They stood under the streetlamp at the start of Mount Austin Road and lit their lantern.

"Waaah," Ching Ha as the candle inside the lantern glowed.

"Walk like a princess, Ching Ha," Tai Poh Poh said as she pointed from her nose to a space out in front of it. "Straight head, smooth steps." Ching Ha straightened. She looked straight ahead and pointed her toe as she stepped forward.

"Slow...ly," Tai Poh Poh said in English.

"Slow...ly," Ching Ha repeated as the two of them joined in the sea of lanterns bobbing up the steep hill.

The lantern swayed on the bamboo stick. Her eyes flitted from her lantern to those all around her. Her body close to her great-grandmother's, she sauntered up the hill within the swell of people. She licked her lips when she saw the small metal fryer and skewers of curried fish balls. She heard a clanking of a metal griddle and recognized the sweet smell of the egg-dough puffs. A vendor selling candles, matches, light sticks and flashlights — all in see-through pouches harnessed to his body, like a human vending machine.

In a cluster of buildings, people stood on verandahs, holding drinks. Ching Ha saw the orange glow of cigarette ends. She saw a flashbulb burst out a bright white light and heard laughter fluttering down through the trees. She wondered if they could see her moving up the hill like a slow, colourful firefly.

"We are stopping there," Tai Poh Poh said, pointing to the entrance of a park.

In the distant darkness, Ching Ha saw an oscillating line of lantern lights moving up the hill. She squeezed her great-grandmother's hand and motioned with her chin. "But where are they going?"

"To the top. This road goes all the way up the mountain."

Ching Ha looked towards the glimmering landscape of the mountainside. "What's up there?"

"Bigger gardens, bigger houses, prettier views."

"I want to go there, Tai Poh Poh," Ching Ha said tugging.

"Not tonight."

"Why?"

"Ching Ha," Tai Poh Poh said, crouching down so her face was level with her great-granddaughter's. "The road is long; the mountain is steep. This is your adventure for tonight. One day though, you will go to the very top."

"Promise?" Ching Ha asked with a scowl.

"Yes, my princess," her great-grandmother replied. "I promise."

An *Opportune Marriage*

4 October, 1970

Prismatic blue tints caught Svetlana Hoffman's eye. Three slender, young ladies tittered as they entered into the private banquet room of Maxim's Restaurant, bypassing the wedding line. Their form-fitting tops, combined with the soft bell shape of their knee length skirts, made them look more like ballerinas than bridesmaids. Svetlana ran her long fingernail along the edge of her mandarin collar and the top knot button of her black evening dress. She was pleased that her tailor had suggested adding these Chinese accents. Even though she and her husband, Dimitri Hoffman, were the only Westerners here, it made her feel like she was fitting in. She didn't mind going to Dima's business events. They were interesting enough, but she preferred to be puttering around at home with the dog and reading. If she could just get through this dinner, she'd be home soon enough for a quiet evening.

"We're next, Lana." Dima scowled at her cigarette and cocked his head to the end of the receiving line. As she took a final inhale, Lana watched him tug at his tie and surmised that she had tied it too tightly. She exhaled with a cough as she stamped her cigarette into a metal ashtray. He cocked his head toward the door.

"Okay, Dima. I'm coming." She put a hand to her brown-black, shoulder-length hair and touched a curl that was handmade and held in place by a layer of glossy Elnett hairspray. It bounced slightly, as she stepped into the banquet room filled with red wedding decor, including wall plaques of a dragon and phoenix. Dima nodded to the door attendant and handed him a red envelope containing the wedding gift to record the money. While he was signing the wedding scroll, Lana saw Dima's employee, Lam, the rosy-cheeked father of the bride hustled towards them.

"Mr. Hoffman," Lam said.

Dima shook Lam's hand and congratulated him. Dima placed his arm on Lana's back. "You know my wife."

She stretched her fingers for a handshake, and her thin painted lips parted into a wide smile, where it stayed until she and Dima were seated and had acknowledged the other guests at their table. A waiter brought two tall glasses of pale yellow beer and small shots of baijiu.

Lana opened her eel-skin handbag and took out a slender silver case the size of her hand. She pressed a small button, popping the case open to reveal an almost full line of cigarettes. She took one, put it into her mouth, and lit it with her silver lighter. She closed her handbag and listened to her husband conversing with the other guests in a mix of English and Mandarin.

One after another, platters of elaborately displayed food, accessorized by vegetables and fruits, carved into flora and fauna, were carried by waiters in a choreographed procession from the kitchen to the lazy Susan of each table. The jellyfish, seaweed and braised pork appetizers, the shark's fin soup and Peking duck had sated her appetite, and she wondered how many more courses were to follow.

She sat back for a rest between courses, her cigarette in hand; a little girl ran to the table and stood next to Dimitri. The child dodged her head this way and that, as she peered around dishes and glasses. Her eyes widened when they locked onto something on the table and she stood on her tiptoes. She stretched a thin arm towards the center of the table, walking her fingers forward. She frowned and grabbed a chopstick and reached out her arm again.

Lana leaned and saw that the desired object was a straw wrapped in paper. Dima picked it up and handed it to the girl, who plucked it from his fingers.

"Thank you, Gweilo," she said and began tearing an end of the paper wrapping. A mustached man called to the girl, but she remained focused on her task. He began to scold her, anyway, index finger wagging in the air as his words dissolved into the chatter and merriment of the banquet room.

"It's no problem." Dima waved his hand to dismiss the incident, then patted the girl on her shoulder.

She lifted her face to him momentarily and smiled.

Lana knew that while "white ghost" or "white devil" could be used as a pejorative term for a foreigner, this girl obviously meant no harm when she called Dimitri, "Gweilo." But, it was a moot point because the child had not heard a word of the scolding. Her head tilted up as she placed the straw, in its torn wrapper, to her lips. She blew, and the paper shot into the air above Dima's head. It spiraled down in front of him, and he caught it with a clap. His exaggerated look of surprise made the child laugh. He held the paper out to her, but she shook her head and pushed his hand away.

"See you, to mo low," the girl said to Dima with a wave. He smiled and waved back before turning to Svetlana. "Cute child," he said, pointing in the direction she had disappeared.

Lana took a sip of her beer, somewhat perplexed by Dima's interaction with this child. When had he become so good with children? She pressed her cigarette into the glass ashtray and watched the girl and her bright pink outfit weave through waiters and wedding guests until she reached a table at the opposite end of the room. The girl crawled onto the lap of a slender, older woman in an emerald green cheongsam. The old woman followed the girl's pointed finger, across the room, towards Lana who nodded self-consciously. But the old woman and the girl disappeared from view, as people stood to welcome the bride and groom.

There were loud cheers and the clinking of utensils against glasses. Lana looked towards the entrance of the room. The newlyweds were making their rounds again. This time the bride had changed out of her elegant red and gold cheongsam into a traditional, formal red gown with long, flowing sleeves adorned with golden embroidery of the phoenix and the dragon. Her phoenix headdress hid her face behind a veil of swaying tassels and beads. Lana blinked, as the white bursts of camera flashcubes exploded around the room.

The bride sipped from her small glass. Her groom didn't have it so easy. Heeding the goading chants, "Gumbai! Gumbai!" he slammed back the baijiu, only to have the glass refilled with rice wine every time he emptied it.

Lana grimaced, as the groom leaned on his bride for support, and the guests began to laugh. Some rituals and traditions had no boundaries when it came to individual's privacy. Her mind drifted to privacy about death, rules about grieving; life was so simple for some - rules.

A squealing sound made Lana look around her table. The girl had reappeared, squeaking her own return with a handmade noisemaker made from a piece of straw that was cut at the top. She blew into it as the bride and groom approached their table. Lana stood with the other guests, drinks in hand, and the cheering and rowdy provocations began once more.

As the toasts continued in the room, Lana watched Dima and the girl pointing and mimicking one another's actions, all the while laughing and smiling. It was nice to be around children, she thought. They could be so uplifting. Lana waved, as Lam approached the table. His cheeks were even redder now, and his eyes were glazed with happiness as well as an alcoholic delight. He stood by Dima and Svetlana, his hands on the back of their chairs.

"You need another drink, sir?" he asked, pointing to Dima's nearly empty glass.

"No, we're fine. Thank you," Lana said, as visions of having to stagger to the car with him filled her mind.

Dima motioned around the room. "This is a wonderful celebration." Lana nodded.

"I'm very proud," Lam replied, patting his chest as he bowed slightly several times.

Dima gestured for Lam to lean towards him. Keeping his hand low to the table, Dima pointed towards the girl. "Lam, who is this child?" He spoke in English, hoping to add some discretion to his questions.

"That is Ching Ha." Casting his gaze across the room toward the older woman in the emerald cheongsam, Lam added, "She is daughter of . . ." He paused and shook his head. "Mrs. Wong is Ching Ha's tai poh poh."

Dima cocked his head "Tai Poh Poh?" He looked at Svetlana. She shook her head. She didn't know what that meant.

Lam made a hmmm sound and tried to explain again. "Her granddaughter," he said as he glanced toward Mrs. Wong, "is Ching Ha's mother."

"Her granddaughter is Ching Ha's mother," Dima repeated slowly, as if solving an equation. "So, Mrs. Wong is this girl's great-grandmother." He looked at Lana and nodded his head. "Tai Poh Poh means great-grandmother."

"Ching Ha live with her Tai Poh Poh." Lam leaned closer. Lowering his volume, he added, "because no one want her."

Lana raised her eyebrows and looked at Dimitri. She had not expected this. Usually multiple generations lived together under one roof. But surprisingly, Dima's serious expression changed to a smile. He looked at Lam. "You're joking, right?" He pivoted slightly and placed his hand on Ching Ha's shoulder. "Because if no one wants her, I will take her," he said, as though delivering the punch line to a joke.

Lana let out a small gasp. This was no laughing matter.

Lam nodded without making eye contact with either Lana or his boss. "I understand," he said in a sober tone. He excused himself and walked away.

Dima Hoffman looked sheepishly at Svetlana, "I hope that I didn't offend him," he said.

"Boje moy," Lana said in Russian, although she didn't believe in God anymore. She crossed her arms tightly around her waist, hoping no one else at the table understood Russian, and turned away from Dima. Her teeth nibbled on her lower lip. He of all people should know better than to pry into the personal details of people's lives. She watched Lam walk across the room towards Mrs. Wong who leaned forward, as Lam put his face by her ear. Mrs. Wong looked up, and her body straightened.

Lana nudged her husband. "I think you might have offended the old woman," she said, reaching into her bag for her cigarettes.

"You still have one in the ashtray." Dima poked her arm and pointed to the Pall Mall with Lana's red lipstick signature on the filter tip. He looked towards Lam, seated beside Mrs. Wong. "I'll talk to him and straighten things out."

"More talk?" Lana groaned to herself and brought the cigarette to her mouth. *Just leave it alone.* She inhaled deeply as she watched the groom stagger towards another table.

Lana was completely full after the dishes that followed, but she was still closing her lips around a slice of chocolate cake when the girl arrived at the table. This time, she was not alone. Mrs. Wong approached the table and bowed her head.

"I am Mrs. Wong," she said in slow, clear English to the Hoffmans. Lana smiled and nodded, as she covered her mouth to hide her chewing. Dima stood and returned the bow.

"Hello. My name is Mr. Hoffman," he said in perfect Mandarin. "This is my wife." He swept his arm towards Svetlana. He motioned to the empty chair next to his. "Please, have a seat."

"You speak Mandarin," Mrs. Wong said, raising her eyebrows as she nodded her head, resorting to the same language.

"Yes, my parents are Russian, but I was born in Harbin," he replied in Mandarin.

Lana knew enough Mandarin, and had heard these sentences many times, to understand what he was saying. She knew he would resort to English soon enough if she needed to be included. "My wife does not speak Mandarin so well. Do you speak English, Mrs. Wong?" he asked, still in Mandarin.

"Yes, a little," she replied in English.

"She is a wonderful girl." He extended his hand to steady the girl, as she climbed onto Mrs. Wong's lap.

"Yes. Ching Ha is good girl."

"Chen Ha," Dima nodded towards the child, "how old is she?"

"*Ching* Ha," Mrs. Wong said, stressing the first part of the child's name, "is three-year-old."

Dima raised his eyebrows. "She is very clever for being so young."

Lana gave Dima a sideways glance. How he would know? It had been a while since he had been in the company of a three-year-old.

A wave of applause moved through the banquet hall, as everyone watched the bride and groom leave the banquet hall. No doubt for a costume change and to sober him up, Lana thought. It was going to be a long night for him. She sucked on her cigarette and watched the girl clamber off Mrs. Wong's lap and join the wave of children rushing past the table.

"You have children?" Mrs. Wong asked, her eyes moving between Lana and Dima.

Lana's body stiffened, and she stared down at the table, watching Dima from her peripherals. He looked at her, then answered.

"No."

Eyes frozen in a glare, Lana turned her head away from her husband, her breath held.

"We don't," he added, as Lana blinked once, very slowly like a possessed, mechanical doll in a horror movie.

There was a rage building inside her. But it extinguished in a cloud of sadness, as she let out a long breath that sent smoke dispersing in the air above her head. *How could he say that? Why did people think other people's lives were their business?*

As though Dima was trying to upset her further, he asked Mrs. Wong another question. "I'm sorry, but do you mind me asking what happened to Chen Hua's mother? Your granddaughter."

Lana stifled a scream as she glared at the black ashtray on the table and crushed her half-smoked cigarette into it. She crossed her arms and leaned on the table, staring into the banquet hall as she listened to Mrs. Wong's response.

"I am Ching Ha's family. Only me and Ching Ha."

"I see," Dima's voice faded, as though he was thinking of something else to say

Just stop talking.

"But, I too old. Not good for Ching Ha." Mrs. Wong's voice interrupted Lana willing Dima's silence. "Lam say you take Ching Ha."

Lana whirled her head around, her hand pressed against her collarbone as though she was choking. Dima's head was pulled back, his eyebrows lifted, like he couldn't focus on the old woman in front of him. Mrs. Wong pointed at them. "You, young. You have money."

Dima jerked his head back, his right hand in the air, as if to deflect a sudden blow. He put his hand on the table with a light slap and tilted his head in the wind as a "ha" escaped. "Not so young," he replied.

He was right, Lana thought. Fifty wasn't "old". She scanned Mrs. Wong's face and hands. It was difficult to tell the age of Asian women, especially when they used umbrellas, wore hats and long sleeves for protection from the sun, and steered clear of alcohol. However, judging from the translucence of her skin, the delicate nature of her skin, the fine wrinkles along her eyes, the frail-slenderness that comes with age, versus the strong-leanness of youth, Lana estimated that Mrs. Wong was in her seventies. Yes, she and Dima were younger than her, but not really young enough to raise a child of three. She hoped that Dima would convey this and end the conversation. Lana turned away and lifted her empty glass of beer, tipping it so the last drops rolled into her mouth.

"There was a misunderstanding," he said quickly in Mandarin.

"No," Mrs. Wong replied in English. "I understand."

Lana turned at the old woman's emphatic statement.

"This is op-por-tu-ni-ty," Mrs. Wong continued, drawing out each syllable of her last word.

"Opportunity?" Dima asked.

"Oh-pa-tu-ni-ty," repeated the child in a sing-song voice. She freed a glossy white candy from the wrapper and popped it into her mouth.

Lana freed a cigarette from its case and popped it into her own mouth. Her fingers probed her handbag in search of the lighter as the girl ran to the table and leaned against her great-grandmother's legs. Mrs. Wong gathered the hair from the child's face and pulled it back into a little ponytail that she bound with a pink elastic wrapped around her wrist.

"I don't know what to say," Dima said.

Don't say anything. Don't say anything. Lana squinted her eyes as she as puckered her lips gently on her cigarette, like mini kisses. She exhaled as she watched Mrs. Wong reach into the side of her dress and pull out a slip of paper. The slim dress had pockets, Lana marveled, noting this detail for her next tailored outfit — it would be the perfect spot for a cigarette and lighter. Mrs. Wong placed the paper near Dima's hand. He moved his hand away, but both he and Lana kept their eyes on the ragged scrawl of numbers for a moment. When had she written down these numbers? How did she know Lam? Ash fell from her cigarette and exploded onto the white tablecloth. Lana brushed it off the table, her cigarette precariously balanced between her lips. Her husband nudged her elbow, but she moved her arm away. She didn't know what to think. Was this a scam or a true cry for help? Even so, could they engage in such a . . . transaction?

Mrs. Wong tapped her finger against her head. "You think," she said. She looked at Dima and pointed to Svetlana. "You talk to wife about new baby." Lana raised an eyebrow at the indignity of it all. She didn't need or want a *new* baby. Mrs. Wong leaned forward and whispered into the girl's ear. Her round face looked up from the candy wrapper that she was folding.

"Hah-lo," she said through a smile forced wide to show her little, white teeth.

"You see?" the old woman said. "Ching Ha, good girl." Mrs. Wong pointed to her phone number on the chopstick wrapper. "You call me." She bent towards them as she stood and whispered, "Ching Ha wait you."

Starting Something

Lana and her husband left the banquet hall shortly after; they did not speak as they stood outside the restaurant watching for their car. Restaurant and bar signs high above them showered hues of red, green, yellow and white over them. Taxis drove past looking for their next fares in the people stepping out or stumbling from the restaurants and bars around them. The evening sky was clear, and the air had lost the mugginess of summer. It felt especially cool after the food, beer and baijiu that they had indulged in. Ordinarily, it was the perfect night to stop by the Star Ferry pier, watch the ferries bobbing across the water towards Kowloon, and chat as they gazed at the city lights twinkling along the harbour. But, tonight, there had been enough talking. Lana couldn't stop thinking about the interaction between Dimitri, Mrs. Wong and the girl. What was her name? Chen Ha? A sleek Chrysler pulled along the sidewalk and stopped. A tall, slim man got out of the car and walked around to open the door for Svetlana.

"Thank you, Benson," she said. When Dima presented his hand to help her, she leaned away from him and ducked in. Benson walked to the other side of the car and opened the door for Dimitri. Lana watched Dima get in the car without looking at her. He massaged a ripple of tension that danced in his jaw.

"Home, Master?" Benson asked as he turned the indicator away and pulled onto the road.

"Yes, please, Benson."

"Lana, why are you irritated?" Dima asked in a

hushed tone as the car headed towards Garden Road.

"I don't understand you, Dima." She turned her head towards Dimitri, but her eyes checked Benson's face through the rearview mirror quickly before she looked at her husband.

"What?"

"How could you . . . ?"

"How could I what?" His voice strained as it became a loud whisper.

"Why did you . . . ?" Lana put a cigarette in her mouth.

"What? For God's sake and mine, finish your sentence."

Lana glanced at Benson again, but his eyes did not waver from the road. She glared at her husband and lowered to reset the volume of the conversation. "We'll keep her?" she said, mimicking his jovial tone when he spoke to Lam. She flicked her thumb over the wheel of her lighter. She moved her head forward until the tip of the cigarette entered the edge of the flame.

"I was joking," her husband replied as he waved his hand in the air.

"Well," she said, "the punchline was lost in translation." She took her cigarette into her trembling hand.

"Only to the humorless."

Lana sighed, her tone now sad, rather than biting. "Dima. I thought we came here for a new start."

"Yes, two years ago." He looked at her profile as she stared out the window. He exhaled and looked downward. "You're right. We did." Dima reached across to touch her hand, but she placed her arm across her stomach.

"So what have you done?" She spoke like a ventriloquist, her jaw frozen, her lips still.

Dima made a groaning sound, like a kicked beast. "I didn't do anything, " he said with more volume, pulling his arm back.

"Yes, you did." Lana stared out the window, biting the corner of her lower lip.

"What did I do?" This time he shouted.

Benson glanced at the rearview mirror.

"I don't know," she said through gritted teeth. "But you started something."

*****

Mrs. Wong switched on the light as she entered her flat. Her friend, Man Yee stepped in, carrying the sleeping Ching Ha. He slipped off his shoes and followed Mrs. Wong to the bedroom. He glanced at the round-faced alarm clock on the bedside table.

"She had a big night," he said, and lay Ching Ha on the bed.

Mrs. Wong sighed as she led Man Yee out of the room and pulled the door almost completely closed. Yes, it had been a big night, for her, and Ching Ha. Mrs. Wong's conversation with the Hoffmans played like a fading sensation of a forgotten dream. "Would you like some tea?" she asked hopefully.

He lifted his hand and glanced at his watch. Mrs. Wong placed the kettle under running water. He put his arm back down and nodded.

"Thank you, Lien Hua. That would be nice." He seated himself on the stool at the kitchen table. He covered his mouth, as he yawned.

"I'm sorry, Man Yee," Mrs. Wong came out of her daze. "I have been talking since we left the wedding. You and your ears must be very tired of my voice."

"I'm never too tired for you." His cheeks reddened. "Please, finish telling me about the people you met at the wedding." Pinging sounds made music in the belly of the kettle. Man Yee turned off the stove and poured the water into the teapot Mrs. Wong had prepared.

She took two small porcelain teacups for the cupboards, set them on the table and sat down as Man Yee poured the tea. He placed the teapot on the table and sat across from her.

"Now, let's talk until your heart and mind are easy," he said.

Mrs. Wong pulled a torn piece of paper chopstick wrapper from her pocket. She continued her story about the night's events. She described Ching Ha's instant connection with Mr. Hoffman. It was an interaction that possessed Mrs. Wong to hatch a plan. She scrawled her phone number on the wrapper in a moment of inspiration or desperation. She recounted the way he sat back straight with a look of surprise or shock at her proposal. A proposal? Such a nice word to explain she was giving away a child. She placed her hands on her face to block the memories blurring her vision and mumbling through her mind.

A firm hand on her arm grounded her. "Drink your tea, Lien Hua," Man Yee said, "as you say, tea makes everything better."

Mrs. Wong looked up and caught sight of her reflection in the window. Her face was long, her sorrow welling in dark eye bags. Her throat burned, and her chest was hollow, unable to hold air. Her body filled with heaviness, drowning her in an emptiness looking frail. She had not felt this way since her husband died five years earlier. Was she feeling this because she was doing the wrong thing? Or was it because she was beginning to grieve losing another loved one?

"Thank you," Mrs. Wong said and patted her friend's hand. She inhaled to control her welling tears.

It seemed like a good idea, but I don't know what I started." She looked once again at the piece of paper in her hand, crumpled it and let it fall on the floor.

Discussions and Decisions

5 October, 1970

Lana and Dima sat at the round, glass-topped dining table, listening to anti-indigestion tablets fizzing in a tall glass of water. Dima's eyes were closed behind the elliptical lenses of his sunglasses. He opened an eye, saw that the tablets had dissolved and began to drink the gassy solution. He opened his hand and looked at the piece of paper in his hand. Ah Mui entered the room and set a saucer in front of Svetlana.

"Coffee, Miss."

"Thank you, Ah Mui." Lana waited until Ah Mui had gone back into the kitchen before she said, "Well, Dima?" She watched her husband's jaw ripple as he tapped the torn chopstick wrapper on the breakfast table. "Aren't you going to throw that away?"

"Lana, I told you I am going to think about it." He tipped a box of cereal and stared at the flakes falling into his bowl.

"What's to think about?" Lana slathered a slice of toast with marmalade.

"I will speak to Lam and find out who she is." Dima put the cereal box down on the table roughly.

"Tell me you aren't considering Mrs. Wong's proposition." Lana stared at her husband. Her knife scraped across the same path on the toast.

"If the child is destitute, don't you want to help her?" He poured the watery milk onto his cereal.

"That's ridiculous. There are hundreds of children in need. You want to help her? Write a cheque." Lana

45

bit into her crumbly toast.

"We would be giving her a life." The waves in his jaw appeared as the watery milk made from skim milk powder he had mixed the night before, cascaded onto his cereal. He noisily shoveled the cereal onto his spoon and snarfed it up.

If only they could give a child life, Lana thought. She raised the cup of coffee to her lips and blew across it mindlessly. She was looking at Dimitri, but her mind was in a faraway place. She was remembering her house in Ramat Gan, Israel. The one they left to come to Hong Kong. For Dima's job opportunity. To be closer to his parents. To quit her job as a chemist. To give her time for herself. So she could stop living in a house filled with reminders of how life used to be. She was here to recover from her breakdown, to begin anew. But, start over with what? A new family? She took a sip of her coffee. She could have stayed there rather than wait to visit the house, like it was an ailing relative. She could feel the house standing empty now, shuttered and dusty. It was waiting for her to return; to breathe life into it, into its memories.

"More coffee, Miss?" Ah Mui held out a china coffee pot.

Lana twitched. "No, thank you," she said, trying to mask her surprise. She put down her coffee and dabbed her mouth with the linen napkin.

Dima looked at his watch. "I have to get ready for the office. It's almost 8:00 a.m." He folded the newspaper unevenly. "My father should be here shortly."

"I don't understand. He's three floors down. Why you don't meet him on your way to the car?" Lana took another bite of her toast and marmalade. The doorbell rang, and Mack barked dutifully.

"Missy Hoffman, Mister Hoffman here," Ah Mui called, as she opened the front door.

"Your mother is here, too?" Lana dropped her toast onto her plate and took a quick sip of her coffee. She swallowed it as she ran her tongue across her teeth to clear off stray food particles.

Dima jerked up from his seat. He grabbed the

46

sunglasses off his face, squinting against the dazzle of the utensils and silver serving dishes reflecting the sunlight. He put the glasses into his shirt pocket and walked toward the door to greet his parents.

Lana put on a smile and followed her husband to the door.

"Good morning, Dimitri." Dima's father said in Russian. He nodded to Lana and extended his hand to his son.

"Good morning, son," Bertha said as she kissed him, leaving a dragon-red lipstick stain on his cheek. She turned to her daughter-in-law and kissed her. "Good morning, Svetlana," she said with a smile that revealed her front tooth jutting from her thin lips.

"Good morning, Bertha." Lana noticed her mother-in-law smooth her smart navy blue pinafore dress and glance around the room.

"Boris, you didn't tell me they had rearranged the furniture," Bertha said to her husband.

"I don't notice such things." Boris shrugged his wide shoulders. He looked at his son. "How was the wedding party?"

Dima began to loop his tie. He turned to Lana who looked at the dog who was scratching its ear at Bertha's feet.

"What happened?" both Dima's parents asked in unison.

Lana bent down to wipe slobber decorating the muzzle of her bull-mastiff-boxer mix.

"I'll tell you on the way." Dima grabbed his briefcases from the entryway chair and motioned his parents towards the door. He gave his wife a peck on her cheek. "We will talk this afternoon."

Lana nodded and opened the door for them. Although she had no idea what he was planning, she was quite sure that she would want no part of it.

The conversation at dinner that evening had been punctuated with chit-chat about the events at Dima's office and Mack's attempt to wallow in a small, muddy, ravine. Now that Dima had finished sucking on pork chop bones, Lana hoped that they could finally discuss the conversation from last night. She pulled her cigarette from the packet and tapped it as the table as she glanced at her husband.

He pulled out a small silver vessel that looked like a salt shaker, turned it upside down and shook it until a toothpick came out of one of the holes of its lid. His lips contorted, as he pushed the stick into the several gaps between his teeth. He ran his tongue over his teeth and dropped his toothpick onto the plate that Ah Mui was clearing from the table. "I spoke to Lam today."

"And?" Lana lit a cigarette to enjoy with her cup of tea.

"Mrs. Wong is legitimate."

Interesting choice of word, thought Svetlana, since the child probably wasn't.

"Lam told me that she is his . . ." Dima's voice trailed off. "Second cousin?" He looked at the ceiling, as though the answer was there. "Mrs. Wong's late husband was Lam's second cousin. Something like that. Anyway, she's his relative."

Lana hmph'd. She could have told Dimitri that. Chinese children called everyone "older brother," "younger sister," "auntie," or "uncle." Everyone was a relative in Chinese families. "What about the girl?" Lana asked. "What happened to her parents? Doesn't Mrs. Wong have any *real* family?" She smoothed the wrinkle forming between her eyes.

"Lam said that they abandoned the girl."

"What does that mean?"

"Lam didn't say anything else." Dima squeezed a balled fist until his knuckles cracked. "Just that it's only Mrs. Wong with the child."

"So why is Mrs. Wong giving her up?" Her suspicions still not placated; she only partially listened to Dima as he started a diatribe about the state of the world and their duty to help people. After all, they knew firsthand what it felt like to be Jewish refugees from Russia, and in Japanese internment camps in China. How fortunate they been because of help from strangers and friends. Lana was not enjoying her after-dinner cup of tea or smoke.

That was a waste of a good cigarette. She had no issues with helping people, but why did they have to get so enmeshed with this whole situation? Anyway, it seemed strange. Lana knew that babies were being adopted out from Asia to all parts of the world, but she imagined going through lawyers and bureaucracies, or visiting orphanages, where children had runny noses and phlegmy coughs, where you selected a child like you went to a dog pound and chose your pet. But, this? It was like placing an order for a child at a restaurant.

The vision of the girl's face faded from Lana's mind, and another face appeared. Maybe this would help her move on? Did she have to move on? That's what everyone kept telling her. Dima and his parents, at any means. She pressed her stomach, pushing away a sudden nausea. Yes, she could save this child, remove her from a loveless home with no chances and give her a life filled with whatever she could want, and a future.

A Teller of Fortunes

15 October, 1970

Ching Ha placed a metallic canister, two pencils, and some paper on the kitchen table. She was helping her great-grandmother get ready for work, and if she was patient, she might earn money, too. People called Tai Poh Poh, "The Lady of Letters and Fortunes." She read letters that her clients received. She also wrote replies for them or read from their book. But, people usually came to her so she could tell them their fortunes.

The doorbell rang. Ching Ha glanced at her great-grandmother and waved. "I'm going, Tai Poh Poh," she said as she skipped into her bedroom and closed the door, leaving the usual gap to peek through. Mr. Chen entered the flat and bowed to Tai Poh Poh. He removed his hat and shoes and sat at the kitchen table.

"How can I help you today, Mr. Chen?

Mr. Chen pointed to the round, red tin. The gold image on it had long ago faded, leaving behind thin metallic streaks. "I want guidance about my health and my finances." He crossed his arms and waited.

Ching Ha sat on a small stool by the door, watching as her great-grandmother closed her eyes and began rocking her head back and forth while she shook the canister at an angle. Dozens of thin wooden sticks shifted until several stuck up. Tai Poh Poh once told Ching Ha that she wanted to buy a bird and train it to pick the sticks for a more mystical experience. But, she did not like the idea of something trapped in a cage. Tai Poh Poh pulled each of the three sticks and placed them on the table. She examined the characters and the numbers and began to decipher Mr. Chen's fortune. As she pointed to each stick, she drew shapes in the air with her hands. He watched her, nodding as he listened in anticipation.

Tai Poh Poh had told her that the sticks told a different story for each person. The pictures and her feelings usually answered her clients' questions and worries. Ching Ha pretended to understand everything her great-grandmother said. She even imagined she could hear the things that weren't said. She felt like she could touch the oceans inside people's hearts and feel their laughter or tears getting ready to spill out, even before they heard the reading.

When Ching Ha grew bored with watching her great-grandmother and her clients, she pressed her face against the cool, black window rails and stared at the windows of the next building. She saw a child slouched, cross-legged on the floor, in front of a television. An old woman squatted next to him and spooned food into his mouth, then hers. Why couldn't the building be closer, so she could watch the television, too? A man in a sleeveless white undershirt sat at a table reading the newspaper. A woman in a flowery sleeveless shirt stared out the window. She rested her left arm on her head while she fanned her unshaven armpit with her right hand. She switched arms as she moved away from the window and disappeared from view. An old woman clipped a peg onto a pillowcase on the makeshift clothesline outside her window. There was so much to see that Ching Ha decided she didn't need a television.

When her great-grandmother finally closed the door after her last client, Ching Ha stepped out of the room and sat at the table. She traced her finger along the tin's edges.

"How do you tell a fortune?" Tai Poh Poh sat down opposite Ching Ha and picked three sticks. She examined the characters on them.

"These are numbers, words. They are the beginnings

of feelings and movies that begin to play here." She tapped Ching Ha's head. "And here," she said, pointing to Ching Ha's sternum. "And here," she said, poking the girl's belly. "The real magic is in you. The secrets come to you," she whispered with a lilting voice. She winked at Ching Ha.

"But, what's my fortune?"

Her great-grandmother looked at her with no expression, although Ching Ha felt a sadness.

"Why can you tell everyone's fortune, but not mine?" Ching Ha asked.

"Sometimes we can't see things because there is nothing there. Other times, it is because we are afraid to see them."

The girl smiled and shrugged. Her great-grandmother often said strange things that didn't make any sense to her.

Tai Poh Poh reached into her pants pocket and pulled out a coin. "This is for you."

Ching Ha let the coin fall into her palm. "Fifty cents," she said, turning it, so it caught the light from the window. "So shiny," she said, practicing her English.

"Because you were so patient and quiet," Mrs. Wong said.

"Thank you," Ching Ha said, as she rushed into her bedroom. Behind the door, there were two jars with coins. She dropped the coin into the half-filled jar, lifted the jar to her face and examined the uneven pile the way she examined the rhinoceros beetles that she sometimes found in their bag of rice. Another good day at work. As she skipped towards the kitchen, where Tai Poh Poh was washing her hands, the telephone rang.

Preparations

25 October, 1970

Lana sat on her closed toilet, listening to the tub draining, her coffee-stained bridge book on her lap dog-eared at the latest game. She wore a batik gown from her last trip to Indonesia over her control top underwear. She just needed to remove her curlers, spray her hair and get dressed, and she would be ready for her bridge luncheon at 11 o'clock. But before then, she had to get things ready for the social worker's visit tomorrow. A few days after that, the girl would be here. "Just one more," Lana thought to herself and lit a cigarette.

It had been a long time since there was a child in the house. What was she doing? Would she be able to have time to herself?

"Svetlana?" Dima's voice grumbled from the bedroom. He knocked loudly on the door. "Are you almost done? Ah Kain has questions for you about preparing the bedroom."

Lana looked at her freshly lit cigarette and sighed. She already had to hide in here from her husband. What would she have to do when there was a child in the house?

"I'll be right there." She flushed the toilet for effect, put her bridge book under the laundry basket, and opened the door. "I'll get my curlers out." She looked at Dima's scowl and changed her mind. She stepped out of the bathroom and towards the bedroom door. "What does Ah Kain need to know? I've been over this several times."

"I don't know." Dima opened his closet and reached for a tie.

Lana walked down the hallway towards the living room. What else did they need to prepare? The guest bed had fresh sheets; there were new clothes, toys and shoes. She stopped at the guest room, where their servant of three years was folding a pair of silk pajama pants.

"Hello, Missy," Ah Kain said in her usual cheerful manner. She smiled and the mole above the left side of her mouth moved towards the middle of her face. Lana noticed that her hair was loose, hanging around her ears.

"New hair cut?" she asked, touching her own hair.

Ah Kain put her hand to her head. "No," she said, "same."

"Oh," Lana said. "Did you have a question for me about getting the room ready?"

Ah Kain held up the pajama pants. "Big girl," she said. "How old she?"

Lana looked back to her bedroom door to see if Dima was coming out. "Three. They might be too big. I can take her shopping when she gets here."

"What her name?" Ah Kain asked.

Lana wanted to say, "Chen Ha," but she didn't want to introduce the girl with a Chinese name, in case the servants started calling her that. It would be too confusing. The girl needed a Russian name that would make it easier for her to assimilate into the new culture, and so she wouldn't stand out. However, Lana had not yet discussed this rather crucial detail with Dima. She looked to the bedroom for her husband. Now it could be her turn to storm into the room and rush him out of there. She left Ah Kain's question unanswered and walked towards the bedroom in her black, silk embroidered slippers.

"I'll see you tonight." Dima hurried past her in the hallway. "Don't forget we are having dinner at my parents."

"I'm playing bridge at the Jewish Club," Lana called, "so I'll need Benson off and on."

"Okay," he called back. He kissed the air twice and turned out of the hallway, into the living room.

A blanket of calm settled over Svetlana. She clucked lovingly at Mack as she entered the room. Usually, the seven-year-old boxer followed her everywhere, but the move from Israel last summer had weakened him. Actually, it was not so much the flight from Israel, as the six month quarantine in Hong Kong's beastly animal control facility. She had visited him everyday with fresh water and homemade food, medicine and toys to keep his spirits up and pull off ticks and clean his goopy eyes from the dust and dirt of the indoor/outdoor kennel. His health and the brutal quarantine were more reasons she had not been eager to move to Hong Kong. Lana rubbed a stockinged foot on his belly. He rolled to his side and closed his eyes with a groan.

Curls escaped, as Lana unlocked her rollers. She combed her fingers through them gently and reached for a tall, gold can from the mirror's cabinet. Squinting, she held her breath and pressed the button, releasing shiny stickiness across her hair and around the back of her head. She replaced the can and closed the cabinet door, revealing the face she had just been looking at for the past ten minutes. She stared at her face, long and drawn. She turned sideways, took off her robe and flung it onto the laundry basket. She stood on her toes, looking down into the mirror at her backside. When did her bottom get so round? She unrolled the top of her control top panties, and her belly rolled out. She rolled it back up. What had happened to her body in the last year? She knew.

She padded toward her bedroom dresser, picked up an ornate 8 x 10 inch gold-rimmed frame housing a varnished photograph of her mother wearing a mink coat. She picked it up, flipped it over and lifted the backing. Another photograph, this one with frilly edges, slid out. Lana turned it over. Her chest trembled, as she sighed. She bit her lip, although she wasn't sure if it was to bite back the tears or smile that wanted to escape each time she saw the eyes of this young man she had known for twenty-four years. His long face and dark eyes and hair were just like hers, although his nose and mouth were Dimitri's. She slid the photograph back in its secret place, behind the photograph of his grandmother. Both of her beloved family members were gone, one natural, another so unnatural and untimely. But the pain of losing them, especially him, still was so fresh, and often so unbearable. She set the frame in its place, so she could see it from her side of the bed.

Mack groaned. She looked at him and felt the too-familiar crushing on her heart. He would be next. She touched him again with a stockinged foot, rubbing his haunches until he flopped onto his side, his large mouth opening to a yawn. Lana took a navy v-neck dress from the closet and slipped it on. She pulled out her matching shoes. Her life would change in a few days. It had already been changing. She wasn't sure what she would do with the girl. Did she have enough love for another child? And what would happen to her social life? She had come here with a plan to start over, but not like this, with the girl. They would have a party to usher in this transition, to introduce the girl to everyone. Lana's spirits lifted a little, as she began planning the dinner party. She put on her gold watch and haphazardly sprayed Guerlain Eau de Toilette around her body. Most importantly, she thought, they would need a name and stop calling her "the girl."

Transforming Life

4 November, 1970
Han Lok Seung Legal Office

Mrs. Wong's attention waned, as her lawyer read aloud the details of what he called the "transaction." She was listening to her great-granddaughter chattering, playing and singing with the official's secretaries. Ching Ha's voice was an upbeat melody of morning bird songs that signaled the beginning of a new day.

"A social worker will make routine checks for a period of . . ."

The official read the whole paragraph in Cantonese before pausing for the British lawyer to translate his words to the Hoffmans. Mrs. Wong watched them sitting across from her: allies for Ching Ha's future, but sitting as opponents. He sat with elbows pressed on the table; his left fist balled in his right; his chin planted on both. Although his eyes were on his lawyer, his smile and the almost imperceptible movements of his head suggested he was listening to Ching Ha's song. His wife leaned against the tall back of her chair, her arms crossed over her body with hands-on each elbow. Twice, she looked at Mrs. Wong and twisted her mouth upwards, as though trying to smile. But, her eyes were large and dark. She looked sad. Mrs. Wong wondered if it was pity, resentment or something else. Empathy?

* * *

" . . . There will be no payment for either party involved. . ."

Of course not, Mrs. Wong thought to herself. Ching Ha is not a bag of rice. Still, the Hoffmans had paid for all the transactional fees; and Mei Hua had provided her lawyer to assure that her family would remain anonymous.

"There will be no visitation rights . . ."

Mrs. Wong's breath caught. What had she expected? To continue being Ching Ha's Tai Poh Poh? To see her regularly and be part of her life? Of course not. Ching Ha was being adopted. Mrs. Wong was giving her away with all the experiences of raising this child, this wonderful girl.

"Date of transference will be 18th November, 1969 . . ."

Her breath lurched again. Yes, an auspicious date. But so soon? Better to let Ching Ha become part of the new family as quickly as possible, so she doesn't get too attached. Too attached to what? Her family? Mrs. Wong felt a rush of heat surge through her body. What was she thinking? All Ching Ha knew was a life with her. This would be a cruel shock. This was a mistake. What was she doing giving away this little child?

Mrs. Wong wanted to shout, "Stop." She wanted to push the papers away, to knock the cup of tea onto the words, to wash them away. She wanted to end this evil deed and leave the room. She wanted to grab the child and go. But go where? To their cozy home, where Ching Ha could continue to grow up hidden in shame? Where both of them could go on keeping secrets? Mrs. Wong hiding Ching Ha from Ling? Ching Ha growing up knowing her mother did not want her?
    She put on her glasses, though she wasn't sure she wanted things to be clearer. She read the Chinese characters dancing down the paper in columns. She

looked at the rows of English words. Some were recognizable. Others were heavy and mystifying, like her heart. Stamps, signatures and numbers in red and black ink scattered her attention. A sob escaped before Mrs. Wong could squelch it. She cleared her throat to mask the emotion. She refocused her teary vision on the papers. Her fingers numb, she managed to pick up the pen. With Ching Ha's song blurring in her brain and her hand shaking, she wrote her name on the document. Writing on paper. This is how she had started the whole thing.

Facing Demons

9 November, 1970

Mrs. Wong sat at her kitchen table, staring at a large brown envelope. She took out the papers and set them down. A teardrop fell, then another, and, another. The wetness landed onto papers spread on Mrs. Wong's kitchen table. She had not expected the procedure to be finalized so soon after it started. Only the powerful white man could have gotten these expedited through the bureaucracy. This influence would be a good thing for Ching Ha's future; Mrs. Wong tried to persuade herself.

Now, the great-grandmother wished her tears could wash these pages. She wished they could transform them into pure, white paper on which Ching Ha could draw. She reached for her glasses but stopped. She did not need to read anything. She remembered every detail of this ongoing nightmare.

She looked up and gasped when she heard faint, fast knocks at the door. The grieving woman covered the document with the envelope and stood up. She sniffed back a tear and padded around her eyes with a handkerchief. She looked through the peephole. It was her daughter. She stepped back from the door and paused for a moment. It was strange, not to first have received the customary call to make sure Ching Ha was napping. She shook her hands three times to rid herself of bad chi, took a breath and straightened her shoulders. She opened the door but said nothing.

"Hi, Ma."

"Hello, Mei Hua."

"I see the papers arrived." She reached into her shiny black bag and pulled out an embroidered handkerchief. She handed it to her mother through the space in the doorway.

"How did you know?" Mrs. Wong looked at the almost-invisible pins in her daughter's hairpiece. Several curly strands embellished the tight beehive.

"My lawyer told me he was delivering them this morning." She shifted her weight, as if starting to move forward.

"Yes, of course." Mrs. Wong continued to look at her daughter, but did not move.

"Are you going to let me in?"

"What are you doing here?"

"I came to bring you this." Mei Hua handed her mother a white and orange striped paper bag with the name Maxims across it. Mrs. Wong looked into the bag. An expression flickered across her face. Happiness turned to sorrow. Through the clear panel of the cake box, she saw two egg custard tarts and a small sponge cake topped with fluffy whipped cream.

"Ching Ha's favorite. Thank you." She stepped back, her hand ready to close the door, "Goodbye."

Mei Hua put her hand against the door. "Ma, I also came to be with you."

"If you did not come to see Ching Ha, or to say goodbye to her, let me cherish my last days with her."

"I thought we could have some tea." She paused. "I know this is very hard for you."

"Sometimes doing the right thing hurts, but this . . ." Mrs. Wong struggled to maintain her composure. "This is anguish. What I am doing fills me not only with sorrow but with shame."

"You're doing the right thing, Ma." Mei Hua leaned against the door, her head close to her mother's.

"Yes. I know."

"So, why are you so sad?"

"Because, now I am a monster - like you."

Reparations

11 November, 1970

Mrs. Wong held onto Ching Ha, as the mini bus wound too quickly around the mountainous roads from Central to Repulse Bay Beach. Today, she had promised to take Ching Ha there so they could eat ice cream and walk on the sand, their feet free of shoes and socks. As they dismounted the bus at the foot of the Repulse Bay hotel, Mrs. Wong pointed to a procession of gleaming cars with sleek lines and curves lined up to drop off their passengers.

"We are going this way," she told Ching Ha, who held a red, plastic bucket containing a small, yellow shovel. They stood at the top of the sandy concrete steps leading to the beach decorated with beach umbrellas, and groups of people who were playing frisbee, walking, swimming or just lounging on bold, primary-coloured, striped towels. Mrs. Wong felt a breeze across her face and inhaled deeply. "Smell the fresh air of the sea. It's so good for you."

Ching Ha's chest and shoulders lifted, as she took a deep breath and lifted her nose to sky. "It's like smelling vegetables."

Mrs. Wong pointed back at the white hotel on the hill with the view of the bay. "People pay a lot of money to come here and enjoy this air to heal themselves from sickness."

"Why, Tai Poh Poh? Is sea air magical?"

"Yes. The sea has a special power."

Mrs. Wong squatted at the bottom of the steps and

unbuckled their shoes. She wrapped them in a plastic bag and placed them in her wicker basket before they walked towards the beach. Mrs. Wong set their things out of the sea's extending reach. Ching Ha took her dress off and admired her white swimsuit with pink and silver stripes before putting the dress in the basket. Mrs. Wong hiked her dress up past her knees, tucking fabric into her waistband to secure it into place. She held Ching Ha's hand as they stood at the water's edge. The summer sun had worked hard to warm the deep green sea that sent its white, foaming waves to drag sand from under their feet. Mrs. Wong wished that she knew how to swim, so Ching Ha could be immersed in the purifying, cleansing calm of the water. This was enough, she told herself, to stay cool and enjoy the beach.

They stepped out of the water's edge and Mrs. Wong laid out their towels, sat on hers and took out a bag containing ice cubes, two long strips of fabric and a face cloth. She tied the strip of fabric around her neck to keep her cool. She opened her umbrella and sat cross-legged on the beach while Ching Ha plonked herself in the wet sand and began to build moats around her feet and legs.

Seagulls cawed as they drifted across the blue above them. Ching Ha sang and laughed as the rushing water pushed against her feet, sometimes spraying up to soak her face. Mrs. Wong could feel the water on her face - not from the sea, but the occasional tear. Repeatedly, she told herself to focus on the joy of the moment, not on the sadness.

In their last two weeks together, Mrs. Wong planned to do all the things that Ching Ha loved to do. Last week, just before dusk, they had taken the ferry and a bus through Kowloon to the night market. They sat at a food stall near a makeshift stage where actors wearing dramatic costumes and painted masks performed Cantonese opera. Ching Ha and Mrs. Wong slurped noodle soup and chili paste-covered fish balls as the intense, high-pitched falsetto of male singers and the canorous music of the erhus and violins swelled and receded into the darkening sky.

Although there were markets closer to home, Ching

Ha had asked to go to Temple Street to see the neon lights whizz past the windows of the double decker bus and the glow of the city reflecting in the water as the ferry bobbed towards Hong Kong. There were still more things to do: a street tram ride all the way to Shaukiwan and back towards Western market, and a stop for dim sum at a new restaurant. A chuckle broke through Mrs. Wong's sombre contemplation. Ching Ha always had food planned in her adventures.

*****

Mrs. Wong looked at her watch. Almost an hour and a half had passed since they had arrived. She looked towards the Southeast end of the beach, where the tall statues of the goddesses of mercy and compassion, Kwun Yam and Tin Hau, stood monitoring the sea. Mrs. Wong wanted to still visit the temple before the sunshine and humidity exhausted her.

"We must go soon."

"We just arrived, Tai Poh Poh," Ching Ha said without turning. She sat in the hole she dug, shoveling sand into the bucket between her legs.

"You have ten minutes more, then we are going." Mrs. Wong chastised herself for not staying for as long as Ching Ha wanted. This could be the child's last time on this beach. But she was tired from the heat, even though she had put a new, cold strip of fabric around her neck. She walked into the water and cooled her feet. She returned to their things and yawned as she put away the picnic of fruit and vegetable dumplings that they had been snacking on. She watched Ching Ha dump a bucketful of sand and began to refill it. Mrs. Wong felt a wave of regret and sorrow envelop her, as she remembered the words Mei Hua had said many times. "There is no choice." She was beginning to believe it *now*. *Now* that she had been sitting under her hat, under the warm sun, not swimming or playing with Ching Ha because she had to conserve energy for the rest of the day. *Now*, she couldn't see Mei Hua or Ling whenever she wanted because Ching Ha was the secret keeping them apart. *Now*, that she had signed the papers. *Now*, Ching Ha would be gone in a week. She wiped her hands across her eyes and took a deep breath. She exhaled and in a lilting voice, said,"Your ten minutes is over. It's time to go now."

"We just arrived, Tai Poh Poh." Ching Ha said for the second time in ten minutes.

"I know you want to stay, but it's time to go."

Ching Ha turned around and smacked her shovel on the sand, sending up a spray of sand that made her flinch. "I don't want to go, yet." She scrunched up her face. "Please, Tai Poh Poh, let's stay longer."

"I already gave you an extra ten minutes," Mrs. Wong said with an even tone.

"Why does my good time always have to end?"

"If we had only good times, would we know they were good?"

"What?" Ching Ha said, her head cocked to its side.

"It's time to go on the next part of the adventure." Mrs. Wong pointed towards the beach.

"Another adventure?" Ching Ha craned her neck as she got onto her knees and looked down the beach. She stood up and brushed the sand off her legs and bottom. She handed her bucket and shovel to her great-grandmother, all the while asking for details about the adventure. The questions continued as they walked towards the two statues. Ching Ha ran ahead and stood by the base of the statue that towered over her like two shiny, mosaic high-rise buildings.

"We must get dressed before we go into the temple," Mrs. Wong said. She took the towel and brushed the sand off her great-granddaughter's almost dry body. She dropped the pink, cotton dress over Ching Ha's shoulders and slid the damp swimsuit off before adjusting the dress through Ching Ha's arms and putting on the girl's underwear. They kneeled on the sand and put on their shoes. Mrs. Wong packed the damp items into her basket, and they walked towards the temple, so she could ask for mercy for the deed she would soon commit.

★★★★★

Mrs. Wong and Ching Ha sat on the living room sofa in their pajamas, hair damp from their evening bath. Mrs. Wong was especially happy to have her feet up, sipping a cup of tea.

"I can't get all the tangles out," Ching Ha said, holding up a wooden comb. Mrs. Wong put her tea cup on the side table and sat up, a knee on either side of her thin great-granddaughter's waist. She slid the teeth through Ching Ha's wet ebony strands, gathering beads of water that dropped onto a towel draped around the child's shoulders. Mrs. Wong leaned forward, resting her lips on the back of the jasmine-scented hair.

"Tai Poh Poh love you." She wrapped her arms around the girl and pressed quivering lips onto her temple.

Wiggling thin fingers and a roaring rising from behind her tiny teeth, Ching Ha turned, ready to tickle her great-grandmother. But, the light in her eyes faded. Her arms fell to her side. "What's wrong?" She lifted a gentle hand to the serious face.

"You are growing up so quickly," she said. "And Tai Poh Poh is getting old so quickly," she said. "Sometimes, it makes me sad."

"Don't be sad, Tai Poh Poh." Ching Ha took the comb and pulled it through a few loose strands of hair around her great-grandmother's face. "I'm not getting old," Ching Ha said. "I'm still little." She placed her hand on the top of her head.

Mrs. Wong let out a laugh. Ching Ha giggled as the towel was removed from her shoulders and used to squeeze the remaining water from the end of her hair. Mrs. Wong dabbed the bunched up towel on the girl's nose — those little nostrils that occasionally became home to a wiggling finger or left gooey streaks on jacket sleeves in winter. Mrs. Wong noticed the little mouth that was usually either eating, talking or releasing a made-up song every waking hour. Ching Ha took several strands of hair and put them into the corner of her mouth. Mrs. Wong took them out and wiped them with the towel. Although she felt the heaving of a sob, Mrs. Wong smiled, not wanting to worry the child. Those little brown eyes, framed by a long frill of dark lashes, that watched her. They shone like a diamond, when she asked her thousands of questions each day,

"Where does the water from the toilet go?"

"How are there so many pictures inside the television?"

"Why is the moon so high?"

Mrs. Wong wondered if she would drown in the quiet absence of this child.

Goodbye, Ching Ha

18 November, 1970

The afternoon sun provided a warm hug on the fall day. Mrs. Wong stood in front of her building, the mechanical sounds of vehicles and voices of people around her muffling in her ears. In one hand, she held Ching Ha's small hand. In the other, she held a white suitcase decorated with small plum blossoms. Today was the day to say, "Goodbye." It was taking all her strength not to cry, to kneel down and hold her great-granddaughter and never let her go.

A thin, muscular man in a straw hat jogged by, pulling a red rickshaw. His passenger, a woman in a long-sleeved dress, peered from beneath the green awning roof and motioned towards the curb. He turned towards the curb, stopped and bent down, placing the handles on the ground so that the rickshaw tipped forward. His fare handed him some coins. She straightened her form-fitting dress as she stepped out of the rickshaw and onto the pavement. She waved and winked as she passed Ching Ha and slipped cat-eye-shaped sunglasses onto her nose. Honk. A taxi turned away from the curb. A long, blue four-door Chrysler took its place. Mrs. Wong stiffened.

"Ngo oiy lay." She kneeled and kissed Ching Ha on the cheek. "Never forget that."

Ching Ha gave her great-grandmother a robotic hug, her attention on the car. Dima stepped out, his white hair slicked back, glasses on his face. He waved and smiled broadly as he strode toward them.

"Gweilo," Ching Ha shouted and waved.

Mrs. Wong wanted to correct her, but wasn't sure how Ching Ha would address her new father. "Say, 'hello,'" she said, standing and nodding.

He extended his hand. Mrs. Wong shook it limply, as though she were too weak to grasp it or the reality of what was happening.

"Hello," Ching Ha squealed.

"Hello," Dima said. He released Mrs. Wong's hand and bent down to shake Ching Ha's. She gripped it enthusiastically with one hand and then two. She jumped to shake it more vigorously. He motioned to the man standing by the car, who approached and took the case from Mrs. Wong. A wave of nausea churned through her as she watched the suitcase disappear into the car.

"My wife is in the car waiting. She is not feeling so well today." Dima motioned to the car.

"Let's go, Tai Poh Poh."

Mrs. Wong caught Mr. Hoffman's eye, then glanced away. "You take good care of Ching Ha." Her whisper warbled in the air, as she staggered towards the car. Her body felt cold. She looked back where her friend Man Yee, and his sister stood, waiting to pick up the pieces if she shattered. She stopped and kneeled, pulling Ching Ha towards her. She made a soft clucking sound, as she drew her precious great-granddaughter into her chest for the final time. She put her face against the girl's smooth forehead. She pressed her nose into her floral-scented hair and inhaled her smell.

"Let's go," Ching Ha said, wriggling out of the hug. She pointed to the car.

"No. I am going there." Mrs. Wong pointed in the opposite direction.

Ching Ha's smile drooped. Stabbing pains seared through Mrs. Wong's bosom. Her mouth was wet and dry at the same time. Her body felt dense and heavy, yet ready to break. She noticed Mr. Hoffman take off his sunglasses, exposing an expression of worry, sadness and doubt.

"This car will take you to your new adventure," Mrs. Wong said in forced high tones, freeing herself of the arm wrapped around her leg.

"What adventure?" Ching Ha asked.

"Do you want to go for a ride in this pretty car to see a big house?" Mrs. Wong asked with a smile and lilt in her voice that she didn't know she would ever conjure again.

Ching Ha raised her shoulders and held them there before plopping them down in uncertainty.

Mrs. Wong placed her hands on Ching Ha's shoulders. "If you want to have big adventures in life, you must be brave and want to learn new things." Her voice was steady and firm, although her emotions were wobbling and weak.

Ching Ha looked at the driver who reached for the back door and opened it. The refreshing blast of cool, pine-scented air drifted out. Ching Ha sniffed the air and waved. Mrs. Wong bent forward and peered inside. Two elegantly crossed, stockinged legs led towards a blue dress that matched the car. Mrs. Hoffman nodded. She removed a cigarette from her mouth and curved her lips upward, but her eyes looked melancholy as she patted the seat beside her.

"See you to-mo-low," Ching Ha said as she slid an arm around her great-grandmother in a half embrace.

Mrs. Wong felt Ching Ha slip through her fingers like a melting ice cube on a hot day.

She forced a playful lilt into her voice. "Fai dee lah," she said, as she ushered the child into the car. Hurry, she thought, before the tears come. Fai dee lah, before I change my mind about handing you over, my sweet angel. Hurry, before you understand what is happening. Fai dee lah, before our hearts break open.

"Chi di geen, Tai Poh Poh," Ching Ha said as she stepped into the car.

No, I won't see you soon. "I. Love. You." The English words flooded with emotions drowned quietly in Mrs. Wong's throat, unable to free themselves and float from Mrs. Wong's lips into the sunshine of the November day. She watched Mrs. Hoffman pull a reptile-skinned bag onto her lap and motion for Ching Ha to scoot closer to her.

Mr. Hoffman shook Mrs. Wong's hand. He held it a moment as he looked at her. She averted her darkening pools of sorrow. She didn't know what to say. It was not about her lack of fluency in Mandarin, English, or whatever languages he spoke. No. Even in her native language, she didn't know what words to use. There were none to express what was happening and how she was feeling. Worthless words.

"Don't worry." He stopped speaking and blushed. "We will take good care of her." More words stumbled out of his mouth, but she was not listening.

"Yes." Mrs. Wong could think of nothing to say. Could think of nothing and could do nothing, as though in a space between dream and wakefulness. Mr. Hoffman released her hand and placed a hand on his heart before he stepped into the car. The driver closed the door.

Mrs. Wong had made no effort to reply to his last words. There was nothing to say. The deed was done. In those few seconds that Ching Ha had clambered into the car, images flashed through Mrs. Wong's mind. She remembered when her granddaughter had announced the unplanned pregnancy. She could never forget the look on Mei Hua's face when Ling had asked if she could keep the child, innocently saying that she had even picked out her name. Mrs. Wong remembered the moment at the nursery, when she saw the round-eyed baby girl with her black hair and jerky arms reaching for the heavens and knew she was going to keep Ching Ha.

"See you to-mo-loh," Ching Ha's voice floated through the air like the scent of flowers as the car window rolled closed and the car began to pull into traffic.

Mrs. Wong felt arms around her, holding her up, as Man Yee and his sister stood on each side. She wanted to run after the car, pound on the windows and claim her Ching Ha. But she was immobilized by shock, sadness and shame. Instead, she waved. The white tissue in her hand unraveled and flapped weakly in a final surrender. Mrs. Wong squashed it and pressed it under her nose to calm her quivering lips. She turned away even though she knew Ching Ha might still be watching. The girl would either know that her great-grandmother was crying or think that she had turned her back on her. Once again, Mrs. Wong was left with no options. "Forgive me, Ching Ha," Mrs. Wong whispered into the busy street. "Joi geen. Goodbye . . ." Her sentence faded away with her farewell.

Goodbye, Tai Poh Poh

Ching Ha stared at the window as it slid closed and the car began to move. Confusion increased as she replayed what just happened as she left her great-grandmother. Whenever she said, "See you tomorrow," Tai Poh Poh would tap her nose and reply, "See you tomorrow."

But this time, Tai Poh Poh had said nothing. Or had Ching Ha not heard? Had she been too distracted by the shiny big car? A tightness formed in her chest and throat. She stood, leaning against the seat back as she stared out of the rear window.

Ching Ha watched her Tai Poh Poh leaning on her friends, then free an arm and wave. Ching Ha's eyes and mouth opened wide. She waved, shouting, "Bye-bye, Tai Poh Poh. See you tomorrow."

But, Mrs. Wong turned away; the girl's joy plummeted and a sudden worry gripped her. She leaned her face towards the rear window. "Tai Poh Poh." Was something wrong? Why were her friends leaning so close to her? Were they looking at something? Did she find a pretty bird? Ching Ha lifted her leg, so she could squeeze right up to the rear window, tap on it, so her Tai Poh Poh would turn around. Her foot bumped the cigarette smoking woman's coiffed hairdo.

"Sit," she told Ching Ha and pointed to the seat. The woman's red lips moved some more before stopping in a pout.

Ching Ha turned again to look for Tai Poh Poh but was poked in the ribs. This time, when Ching Ha looked at the woman, she made a clucking sound and shook her head. She tapped a fingernail on the seat again. Ching Ha looked up but could not see Tai Poh Poh. She plopped herself on the seat in a mix of annoyance and anger. She waited for the next instruction from the cigarette lady, but none came.

She studied the driver's head and face in the rearview mirror. His hair and eyes were like hers. He was Chinese. "Hello. What's your name?" she asked him. He glanced into the rearview but said nothing. She looked up at the man that she had referred to as "Gweilo" after she had seen him at the wedding and in the big office. Tai Poh Poh had told her not to call him that, but had not told Ching Ha his name, so she would just have to call him, "Gweilo," for now. She'd whisper it, so it wouldn't be so rude.

His face turned toward her, and she waved at her reflection in his sunglasses. He smiled and pointed to chest. "Dima," he said.

Ching Ha pointed to her chest. "Dima."

The car filled with a hearty laugh, and he shook his head. He pointed to himself again. "Dima." He pointed to the woman, whose lips had softened and lifted into an awkward smile. "Lana." He pointed to the driver and said, "Benson." He repeated this circle of pointing and naming once more before Ching Ha joined in, naming everyone around her.

"Ching Ha." She pointed to herself to show she understood the game, but the soft humming inside the car died away. Dima looked at Lana, who looked back at him. Ching Ha looked back and forth between them. "Hello," she said.

Dima chuckled, smiled at her, and pointed at her. "Bella."

"Bella?" she said. She poked herself in the chest. "Ching Ha."

Dima pointed to her. "Bella," and proceeded to name everyone once more. When he pointed at her, Ching Ha opened her mouth, waiting for the sound from his mouth to guide her response. "Bella," she said with him. He cheered and looked at Lana with a nod of his head and put his hand, palm up, for a high five. Ching Ha smacked her hand, palm down, onto it with a loud clap. "Ow," He let out a quiet and dramatic sound as he shook his hand in feigned pain. Ching Ha laughed and repeated the high fives until they stopped at a traffic signal.

Ching Ha leaned forward to stare at the waves of people outside the quiet, air-conditioned car. They bumped about in buses or street trams; some snacked; others smoked as they stared out the window. A young man moved his head up and down, as he pressed a transistor radio against his ear. A woman ran past the car and around bamboo scaffolding, her arms laden with bouquets of white and red flowers wrapped in paper and a wide ribbon. Ching Ha thought of Wanchai Market and sniffed the air. There was no floral fragrance, nor the aroma of roasting chestnuts or sweet dough balls. The smell of the car fumes and people's sweaty bodies were also gone. Ching Ha's little nose only detected cigarette smoke and spicy perfume. She leaned towards Dima and sniffed his arm. She leaned towards Lana and sniffed. Ching Ha nodded. *That* was the smoky smell of stale herbs and matches. Dima laughed and smelled his jacket sleeve. He stroked Ching Ha's head. She took his hand and held it as she continued to look out of the window.

Ching Ha listened to the car's rumblings and to Lana and Dima murmuring in Russian. She wondered when she was going to see her great-grandmother. But how would she ask in the new language they used?

The car moved out of crowded roads of Wanchai and Central, up the winding mountain roads, past Mid-Levels, towards The Peak. The density of buildings gave way to trees and forests of ficus and bamboo. Sometimes, the branches even reached far enough to tickle the car's windows. The sunshine danced through the leaves and landed on Ching Ha's face. Her belly was full of sausage and duck-egg congee. She rolled her eyes closed and opened, closed and opened. A red double-decker-bus ahead of them sparked the memory of her lantern-lighting excursion. Ching Ha smiled, comforted by her belief that she recognized the roads and knew where she was going.

* * *

Ching Ha's neck relaxed, and her head dropped forward, jolting her awake. She looked up as a trickle of saliva dribbled onto her chin. She slurped it and wiped her mouth with the palm of her hand, then transferred the slime onto her dress. She turned towards Dima.

"We are almost home." He bounced her hand in his, clapping them together. He sang: "You are going to be home soon."

Ching Ha didn't understand what he was saying, but she liked the rhythm of his song. She swayed her body from side to side. The chanting faded into humming. Ching Ha's body leaned back into the seat as the car moved up the mountain's steep gradient. Ching Ha looked at her fingers poking out of Dima's big hand. The bright pink nail polish on her bitten nails was chipping. Ching Ha heard a phlegmy noise erupting from the woman's throat, turned and squinted. The woman was backlit by the sunlight, and her bold silhouette was nodding its head to the beat with each cough. When she stopped coughing, she placed the cigarette back into her mouth. Her silhouette blurred into a cloud of smoke that danced around her for a moment before it disappeared.

Ching Ha scooted to the edge of her seat and stood up, so she could get a better view through the window. She saw children climbing a big tree that leaned against a shiny railing of a building complex. In a deep curve off the road, a pagoda-style hut angled to provide a view of downtown Hong Kong and Kowloon. A vendor in front of the pagoda pulled a bottle of water and a vanilla ice cream cone out of the ice chest attached to his bicycle and handed them to a woman wearing a wide-brimmed hat and a short dress.

The car stopped in front of a wide wrought-iron gate of a four-storied structure. An old man went to the gate. His smooth baldness gleamed in the sun, like the car that he had been polishing. He held onto the iron bars and leaned back, using his body weight to pull open the gate. He wiped his forehead as he waved the car through. Ching Ha smiled and waved back.

A set of stone statues guarded the stairs leading into the building. Ching Ha saw sacred guard dogs like these at the Buddhist temple that Tai Poh Poh visited. At the temple, though, the dogs did not look as imposing as they did here, at the entrance of this small building. Ching Ha did not follow Dima out of the car. The openness of this space, the absence of noise, cars, and people, was strange. She took a small breath and held it, a cry brewing. Dima held his hand out to the doe-eyed little girl who moved away from the door. He leaned into the car and scooped Ching Ha into his arms. She began to tremble.

"Do you know what that is?" Dima stood next to the statue of the large stone lion.

"Fu gow."

Uncertain what she said, Dima put his hand out and patted the statue's head. "Lion."

"Ly . . . ?" The girl stretched out her hand and imitated his actions.

He repeated the word. "Lion."

"Lion."

"Yes, li-on." He set Ching Ha down.

She patted the statue roughly. "Lion."

Dima motioned to the entrance of the building. He held out his hand. She hopped up the steps counting.

"Yut. Yee. Sahm." She let out a squeal on three.

Dima grabbed both her hands and swung her through the doorway to the shiny and mirrored lobby. There was a chime and two of the large mirrors separated, revealing a lift. Ching Ha looked around, as though she had entered a magical world. It reminded her of the Mandarin Hotel. She and Tai Poh Poh walked through the fancy lobby whenever they were in Central, and it was hot or rainy. Ching Ha stepped in and watched her reflection appear, as the mirrored doors closed. She bared her teeth in a smile, twisting and turning in exaggerated motions. She stopped when the elevator bounced and stopped moving. It beeped and the doors opened with a swooshing sound. Dima pointed to the door on the right. Ching Ha ran towards it and examined the bright, cloth flowers that poked out of a vase that was almost as tall as her. A dog barked a deep, loud sound. She heard voices speaking Cantonese. A mix of excitement and relief danced in her heart. A woman opened the door. She was Chinese. But nobody that Ching Ha recognized. Another Chinese woman appeared. She was shorter and older than the first, but she was also no one that Ching Ha knew.

A large brown and black dog bounded out the door and placed its face in front of Ching Ha's frozen body. The dog's head was twice the size of Ching Ha's, and his dark eyes were level with hers. She scrunched her nose and put up her hands to shield herself from the slobber wobbling and glistening around his muzzle.

"No, Mack." Dima grabbed Mack's collar to keep him from knocking her over, while she fanned the beast's fishy breath away from her face with her hands.

The woman stepped forward. "Good, Mack." She made oohing sounds at Mack, who sat in front of her, still panting. His bobbed tail moving side to side, as she caressed his wide jowls and patted his head.

Ching Ha watched the interaction between the woman and Mack, and Tai Poh Poh's words about being brave on her adventure drifted into her mind. Enlightened, Ching Ha strode towards the dog. "Lion," she said as she patted his big head. "Lion."

A Place to Call Home

Ching Ha trotted after the dog into the flat but stopped just inside the doors. She wanted to know what this place was and where exactly she and Tai Poh Poh would be spending their time. She gazed down the long hallway of the kitchen that had a large white refrigerator, a silver stove and oven and sink on one side. She let out a sound, something between a gasp and a sigh, as her eyes travelled the length of a wall of white countertops and from the ground to the ceiling, studying the white cabinets. At the end of the hallway was another large space, a small table and two brown stools, just like the ones she and Tai Poh Poh had at their house. Two women dressed in black flowing pants and white tops moved around the kitchen, filling trays with cups and saucers, dishes filled with cream-filled cakes, and baskets with bread rolls and cheese that they carried farther into the house.

As she bent down to take off her shoes, Ching Ha noticed that everyone was still wearing their shoes. Lana had her shoes on when she disappeared into the back of this place, so perhaps this was not someone's home. Ching Ha looked through another door and saw a table and chair; a wide bed decorated with a thick, cream and brown bedspread and a plush pillow; a bed with a table and lamp next to it and a door into a pink and black-tiled room with a pink bathtub. She stood, the buckles of her shiny, back shoes still fastened, and took Dima's hand as they walked past walls of windows and large rooms with a yellow L-shaped sofa and brown, high-backed

79

armchairs underneath huge paintings of city lights and lacquer artwork.

He led her to a room and placed her small suitcase on the bed's yellow embroidered covering. She sat on the bed gingerly. Surprised at its bounciness, she placed her hands by her side and bounced up and down as she looked around the room. Just like the other room, it had a bed, chair, desk and a door to another room. There were also four high doors with long, wooden handles. When Dima opened them to hang up his suit jacket, she saw they were full of men's clothes. Ching Ha walked towards the window, and clambered onto the arm of a large orange sofa. The green and white capsule-shaped Peak Trams glided through a vertical landscape. She did not yet know it, but she had made it to the top of the mountain she had climbed months before, led by her glowing lantern.

Ching Ha walked to the partially closed door at the end of the room, and pushed the door to reveal a grey toilet, sink and tub in a black and white-tiled bathroom. She entered the room and stepped into the tub. Leaning back against the cool porcelain, she exhaled a loud, "Ahhhh." Ching Ha if one of these rooms would be for her and Tai Poh Poh.

Lana's voice drifted into the room, speaking the unfamiliar language she spoke with Dima. He answered in the same language before motioning to Ching Ha. "Come on, let's see the rest of the house," this time in English. She looked at him. He extended his hand and pointed to the door with his head. She nodded, took his hand and followed. A telephone's ring detoured them back through the main part of the house. Dima picked up the receiver of the ivory telephone.

"Hello?"

Her hand still in his free hand, Ching Ha looked up at him and said, "Hello," though it was to no one in particular.

Above the sounds of Dima speaking Russian, Ching Ha heard her own language. She let go of Dima's hand and walked toward the kitchen. The two women she saw earlier were there. The older, shorter one was

standing at the counter pouring water from the shiny
kettle into a glass bottle, while the younger, heavy
one with a raised brown bump on her face was washing
dishes. When they saw Ching Ha, they stopped what
they were doing and quickly approached Ching Ha,
their voices high and happy as they kneeled beside
her.

"I am Ah Kain." The younger one smiled as she
smoothed down her uniform."That is Ah Mui." She
pointed to the other amah.

"There is food on the table for you. Are you
hungry?" Ah Mui asked.

Ching Ha opened her mouth to launch into
questions, but found herself suddenly very wiggly
and crossing her legs.

"Oh. You need to use the toilet," Ah Kain said,
quickly picking Ching Ha up and carrying her into
the closest bathroom. She sat on the toilet and
stared at the lines that the pink and black squares
made all the way from the floor to the ceiling.

Dima appeared at the door as Ching Ha was drying
her hands.

"Thank you, Ah Kain," he said in English. "My
mother and father will be coming for tea at half-
past five. Please make sure Bella has a bath and is
dressed nicely. Also, please put the food away."

"Yes, Master," Ah Kain answered in English.

Ching Ha cocked her head. Who spoke to whom in
what language?

"First, let us see the house," Dima said, taking
Ching Ha's hand. "And let's find Lana and Mack."

She looked back at Ah Kain as they walked out of
the room. "When will I see you?" she asked.

"I'll see you soon," Ah Kain responded in
Cantonese, following them until she reached the
round dining room table. Ching Ha watched longingly
as she and Ah Mui carried the plates of food back
into the kitchen.

Ching Ha walked past the room where her suitcase
lay open on the bed. She sniffed the air as she and
Dima followed a trail of smoke towards another door.
When she stepped into the room, Ching Ha spun around
with her arms outstretched, marveling at the bright

light and the hugeness of the space that was even bigger than the other rooms. Lana was standing between open closet doors. In one hand, her long fingers wrapped around a cigarette that created a curling trail of smoke. She pushed the door closed with her foot, took the turquoise dress she held and lay it onto the bed. Dima looked at her dress. He let go of Ching Ha's hand and disappeared out of the room.

Ching Ha studied the bed. It was two pillows wide, instead of one like the other beds. She and Tai Poh Poh could sleep on this bed and never even touch one another. Ching Ha pressed on the thin, hard mattress. She lay her head on the pillow. It smelled like the streets of Hong Kong, the bus to Stanley Market, the small dim sum restaurant in Happy Valley. It also smelled like the ashtray beside the bed, filled with cigarettes and long noodles of black and grey ash. At the foot of the bed, by the windows, stood another bright yellow armchair, like the one in the main room. She climbed onto it, and stood. She leaned forward, pressing her nose against the window at the grand view of the city below. Seeing the green and white Star Ferry pushing along the waters below, she remembered her own rides to see Tai Poh Poh's herbalist in Kowloon and how the wind and occasional sea spray blew into their faces.

"Lana," Dima said as he walked into the bedroom and rushed towards Ching Ha. He pushed her gently away from the window until she was leaning against the back of the chair.

"Be careful," he said, moving his finger in front of her like a windscreen wiper. "Never lean so close to the window. You could fall."

Ching Ha didn't know his words, but she knew when someone was afraid and angry and shook their finger at her. Tai Poh Poh had done this before when they tried to hurry across a street. She nodded, a small smile appearing on her lips.

It worked. Dima smiled back and lifted her off the chair. He carried her around the room, pointing to a low square stool and the short table that had an oval mirror attached to it. She got down and peered

at the little glass cylinders and plastic tubes, the
shiny silver containers and curvy, glass bottles.
She ran her index finger lightly over the items.
There were so many little treasures around her. She
wondered how much time she would have to explore
them all.

Ching Ha woke from her daydream when the dog
bumped against the bedroom door. Mack's face was wet
from drinking water. He wandered into the room, and
stood next to Ching Ha. His large, square head
nudged her body as he sniffed her hand. She giggled
when his cool, damp nose tickled up her arm, but
scrunched her face and made a sound of disapproval
when she saw the trail of slime Mack had left
behind. "No, Lion." She wiped the drool across his
back. Ching Ha followed Mack, as he wandered out of
the room. He clambered onto a low armchair that was
covered in a chocolate suede fabric and leaned his
head across the arm. She touched his face, then
walked towards the large, high windows of the
enclosed patio. She clambered onto the yellow, high-
backed armchair, taking care not to lean towards the
window. She looked at an almost identical view of
the city that she had at the bedroom, with the
silvery trail of cargo ships, junks and ferry boats
moving to and from the heart of the city. She
wondered if somewhere in the buildings at the bottom
of the great mountain, Tai Poh Poh was getting ready
to come get her to explore their new home.

*****

Mrs. Wong waved goodbye to Man Yee and his sister
as they stepped into the lift. She closed the door
to her flat. She pressed her forehead against the
door, mentally quelling a surge of dread about
turning around and seeing her home — now quiet,
empty. She turned, each degree bringing her closer
to the monster that waited to attack her with
loneliness. Guilt. Shame.

She walked into the kitchen, picked up the teapot
and cups, and placed them in the sink. She forced
her attention to flit from one song to another song,
but she could not remember the words or the melody.
Her memories of Ching Ha's presence in their home

poured from the tap, frothing the dish soap, covering her hands, penetrating her skin. She turned off the water and dried her hands, leaving the teapot and cups in the soapy suds. Mrs. Wong looked out of the window. The windows of the other buildings surrounded her, watched her in her misery, looking for Ching Ha who used to watch what she called the "window television."

Brriing brriing, brring briing. The ringing telephone startled Mrs. Wong. She walked towards it mechanically, hand extended to lift the receiver. Her heart hoped that the Hoffmans were calling. They were unable to go through with this. She stopped as her brain told her that it was probably Mei Hua checking on her. It was ironic that Mrs. Wong had given up Ching Ha to solidify her relationship with Mei Hua and Ling. But now the idea of seeing them roiled in her belly. Would she think only of saying goodbye to Ching Ha whenever she would see her daughter and granddaughter? She slumped onto the sofa that felt hard and uncomfortable without her great-granddaughter on it.

The phone continued to ring, its shrilling now a muffled buzz, as Mrs Wong lifted the old phone book from the end table. She flipped through it. She stopped at a page with a big, round circle containing four smaller circles. Another circle contained three circles. A third large circle contained three triangles. A fourth circle had small lines in it. Mrs. Wong examined the shapes, the flecks and dots, her frown of confusion lifting, shifting into an expression of delight, as her brain reinterpreted the lines, shapes and patterns into dim sum baskets. She let out a stifled laugh. The Hoffmans will be surprised to see how much Ching Ha eats, she thought. Her small release of joy brought tears to her eyes, but these quickly blurred her vision as they flowed freely, no longer tinged with joy, only melancholy.

Finding Family

The child's face floated in airy bubbles and warm water. She stretched out her body in the bathtub and angled her body to the left and right, like a giant fish, to release white suds from her shoulder-length black hair. She watched the water spiral away down the drain as she stepped out of the tub.

Ah Kain engulfed the girl's body in a fluffy towel. "Fai dee lah."

The memory of Tai Poh Poh hurrying her into the car earlier that afternoon popped into Ching Ha's mind and she wondered again if Tai Poh Poh was coming to get her from this place filled with big furniture, a dog named Mack, people who smoked, spoke different languages and wore their shoes inside the house. Ah Kain wrapped a smaller, pink towel around Ching Ha's shiny and dripping tentacles of hair. The girl contorted her face dramatically, squishing and stretching her eyes and wiggling her nose into different expressions as she stood on a stool and watched in the mirror. Ah Kain combed her hair and sang to her in Cantonese.

"Tai Poh Poh hai been doh ah?" Ching Ha asked, hoping that her great-grandmother was on her way here. Ah Kain stopped singing, and the hair combing slowed down until Ah Kain stopped and looked at the child in the mirror . The expression that crossed the woman's face was gone almost as soon as it appeared, too quickly for Ching Ha to know what it had meant.

"Someone is coming to see you, so you must get dressed nicely," Ah Kain said as they stepped out of the bathroom, back into the child's bedroom.

Ching Ha brightened, ran to the bed and examined her pajama pants and shirt. Her finger outlined one of the bright pink flowers on the white fabric. Tai Poh Poh would be happy to see her in this outfit. She giggled, remembering the vegetables at the market, and lifted the shirt to her nose to smell a flower.

Ching Ha paraded into the living room in her new pajamas. Dima and Lana sat on the long, mustard-yellow settee, talking in quiet tones. Lana swirled a clear drink in one hand, clinking the ice around her tall glass before she brought the drink to her lips. Her other arm formed a large, elegant "V" as did the fingers holding her cigarette to her mouth. Mack lounged in his favorite spot at Lana's feet.

"Sit next to me, Bella," Dima said, patting the space next to him. "You like your pajamas?" he asked, pulling gently at her sleeve.

Ching Ha rolled the fabric between her fingers and sat in the silence between them, watching Lana and Dima communicate via chin nods and eye movements. Lana pulled a rectangular package, wrapped in polka dotted paper, from behind her back and handed it to Dima.

"This is for you," he said and placed the gift on the child's lap.

She looked at him, pointed at the present, then at herself, her mouth open and eyes bright. When Dima nodded, Ching Ha put her finger in a space between the clear tape and pulled, tearing the paper until she saw the book cover. She lifted the book out of the paper and placed it back on her lap. She turned the pages, examining the pictures, letters, words and sentences. "A. Appol," she said, pointing at the drawing of the apple, and the letter beside it. Tai Poh Poh had given her a book that had this same letter and a picture of an apple in it. Some of the other pictures were of the similar things. Ching Ha couldn't remember the English words for those objects, but she anticipated that Tai Poh Poh would remind her of them as soon as she arrived.

Mack rolled on his back and let out a snort, followed by a sloppy sneeze. Ching Ha laughed, closed the book and joined him on the thickly woven yellow rug.

The doorbell rang. Mack barked and moved towards the door with slow, hobbled steps, Ching Ha in tow. She looked out of the window and noticed the darkness seeping into the sky and knew it was time for Tai Poh Poh to take her home. She swiped the hair off her face and smoothed her hands across her pajamas as Dima and Lana stood behind her, watching as Ah Kain opened the door. Ching Ha ran towards the door, but Tai Poh Poh was not standing there. Instead, there stood a short woman with porcelain-white skin and dark hair wrapped in a tight bun. Beside her a tall man, with wide, boxy shoulders smiled down at her, exposing a shiny gold front tooth.

Ching Ha stared at them, craned her neck to look behind them. No one was there. Tai Poh Poh wasn't there.

"What a doll. Really, she's a doll." The old woman opened her arms as she stepped into the flat, ready to embrace her new granddaughter.

Ching Ha opened her mouth, and her chest began to quiver. No sound came at first, but then a low wail climbed out of her belly, like a drowning beast's final cry.

"Wait, Mother," Dima said as he took Ching Ha into his arms.

She wrapped her arms around his neck and buried her face into the crook of her arm, wailing over his coos and cuddles.

"This is your Baba and Deda," Dima said, gesturing towards his parents.

Ching Ha shot Dima's parents a sharp look and pouted, as anger slowly melted into her disappointment.

"Tai Poh Poh. I want my Tai Poh Poh," Ching Ha repeated, quivering and crying. "Where is Tai Poh Poh?" she demanded, her legs kicking.

"Ah Kain," Dima called towards the kitchen. "What is she saying?" he asked.

"She want her Tai Poh Poh," Ah Kain answered as she approached. She rubbed Ching Ha's back.

Dima's mother tried again to hold Ching Ha, but the girl screeched and kicked her legs, tightening her arms around Dima's neck.

"See if you can calm her down." He handed her to Ah Kain.

Ching Ha turned and flopped her shaking body into Ah Kain's embrace, and they walked into Ching Ha's bedroom.

"Where is Tai Poh Poh?" the child asked again, her voice threatening to become a shout, as she began to cry again.

Ah Kain dried Ching Ha's eyes. "MaybeTai Poh Poh won't come tonight, but you can meet your Poh Poh and Gung Gung. I think Tai Poh Poh would want you to meet your new family and be happy."

A Poh Poh and a Gung Gung? Ching Ha didn't have a grandma and a grandfather. The child cocked her head, like a little puppy learning new instructions. Ah Kain's words didn't answer her question about her great-grandmother, but her voice was soft, serious and calmed her. Ah Kain sounded so much like Tai Poh Poh.

Ching Ha, eyes red and breaths still broken, trailed behind Ah Kain as they returned to the living room. Dima held out his hand, and Ching Ha reached for it, not letting go of Ah Kain's hand until she was settled on Dima's lap.

"Baba," he said, looking at Ching Ha, then pointing to his mother. "Deda," he said, pointing to his father. Ching Ha looked at him blankly.

"Son, forget the introductions," Bertha said, waving a dismissive hand. She elbowed her husband and pointed to the leather tote at his feet. Boris pulled out a package wrapped in brightly colored paper and handed it to his wife. She, in turn, held out the package to Ching Ha, who looked at it, crossed her arms and leaned back onto Dima's chest, pouting. Dima nudged Ching Ha with his shoulder. She shook her head then picked up Dima's hand and pushed it toward the package. Everyone chuckled. Dima took the package from his mother.

"Thank you," he said to his mother and handed the gift to Ching Ha.

Once again, she dug her fingers into the seam of the paper and noisily ripped it until she saw enough of the gift to make her gasp. She pulled the last pieces of paper off and placed her fingers softly on the face of the doll. Its short, light brown hair wasn't painted on like other dolls she had owned. It was real, soft and moved. The blue eyes weren't just stickers, but looked like marbles that gleamed and disappeared behind eyelids and long, black lashes when the doll lay flat. The doll's hands weren't hard but smooth and squeezable; the fingers were long, with pink fingernails. The doll wore a dress of white and pink and blue, and it wore white socks with little frills and little black shoes that could be taken on and off.

Ching Ha scooted off Dima and stood next to Baba. She moved the doll's legs back and forth, and her fingers gently touched the moving eyelashes as she opened and closed her own eyes. Bertha laughed and without thinking or waiting for an invitation hugged Ching Ha. The girl froze, but the smell of Baba's floral perfume in the silky cool scarf around Baba's neck distracted her, and Ching Ha relaxed, wondering if Tai Poh Poh would like Baba.

Dinner with Destiny

Red embers dissolved into grey as Lana crushed her cigarette into the iron ashtray. "It's time for dinner," she said.

Ching Ha looked from Lana to Dima. He brought an empty hand to his mouth and repeated Lana's words. Nodding, Ching Ha brought her hand to her mouth, as though she was going to eat her fingers. Aromas she had never smelled before had been drifting out of the kitchen, and her belly was ready to be filled. "I'm so hungry," she said in Cantonese, pointing to her stomach. She placed her doll on the sofa and ran into the kitchen and stood by the sink, hands in the air.

"Good girl. You know to wash your hands before eating." Ah Kain boosted her up with a raised leg and placed their hands under the running water. When her hands were washed, Ching Ha clambered onto the stool at the servant's table.

"What are you doing?"

"Dinner," Ching Ha said.

"Not here." Ah Mui spooned rice into a glass bowl and handed it to Ah Kain. "At the other table."

Hopping off the stool, the child followed the younger servant into the dining room, where Dima, Lana, Baba, and Deda were seated around the table. Ah Kain put the rice on the lazy Susan and lifted Ching Ha onto the high chair and returned to the kitchen.

Ching Ha looked at the small round plate, and the small, silver fork, knife and spoon laid on the red, rectangular placemat in front of her. She made fists around the ends of the fork and knife and gently hit her fists on the table as she counted. "Yut, yee, sahm . . . "

"No, Bella," Lana said, picking up her own fork and knife and setting them down firmly. Ching Ha looked at her small fork and knife and pressed them down on the table with matched severity.

"Molodetz," Baba said, clapping. "She's clever."

Lana spooned food onto the plates, and Ching Ha felt saliva pooling in her mouth. She swallowed it, only to feel more return as she sniffed the hot rice and sweet milkiness of the sauce in front of her. She looked at the rice and chicken piled on her plate and watched everyone pushing the food onto their forks which they lifted to their mouths. She picked up her fork, laid it flat and shoveled it across the plate, so the rice and saucy chicken piled up. She opened her mouth, like the hungry, little terrapins in the tanks at Wanchai Market, eager to catch a bloodworm. But as she lifted the fork the goopy mix fell back on the plate with a splatter. Ching Ha tried again; this time, she held her knife blade at the edge of the plate to stop the rice and sauce from falling off the plate as she tried to pile the food onto her fork. This time she lowered her face close to her plate to meet the fork as it lifted from the plate. Her lips closed quickly around the food, and she sat back in her high chair, shoulders relaxed as she chomped on the tender chicken. She bent her face until it hovered just above her plate and scooped the food into her mouth.

"No, Bella."

Ching Ha looked up, still noisily smacking on her food.

"Like this." Lana sat up straight and leaned forward slightly. She lifted a forkful of food to her lips and closed them gently around the fork. Her chewed with her mouth closed, without making a sound.

"Use your spoon." Baba held up a spoon and ladled up some food.

Ching Ha took her small spoon and put it into the rice, fishing up half a spoonful of food. She ate it and scooped again and again, faster and faster, speed making up for the small portion she was gaining. She looked up, her face red with a scowl on her face. This food was difficult to eat.

Ah Kain, who had been watching from the doorway, placed a blue rice bowl and a pair of long wooden chopsticks in front of Ching Ha. The child's tight lips relaxed into a smile, and she sat up with renewed interest. Lifting and lining the edge of the plate to the bowl, Ah Kain scraped the food into the child's bowl before winking and returning to the kitchen. Ching Ha picked up the chopsticks with the expertise of a master of his craft and wove them into position between the fingers of her right hand. She lifted the bowl with her left hand, placed it to her lips and proceeded to scoop the food into her mouth. The bowl came away from her face only when she was chewing or making a moan of resounding approval. When the last grains of rice had been slurped up, Ching Ha set the bowl down in front of her, and a barrrrrrp crawled out of her throat. Dima let out a chortle. He hit his palm on his belly, then raised the same hand in a closed fist, thumb extended.

"Chi bao le. You ate your full."

"Chi bao le," she repeated. The food here was different than Tai Poh Poh's, but it was also delicious. Her full belly made her smile, but the joy dimmed a little when Ching Ha looked through the dining windows and saw only darkness.

First Night

A furry blanket with hues of pink, yellow and blues lay across Ching Ha's body. Her belly was full of chicken stroganoff and chocolate ice cream. She closed the pages of the Cat in the Hat dictionary that Dima had left on her bed. She opened her mouth to release a slow, mewling yawn. Tai Poh Poh is so late, she thought, as she glanced out the window at the darkening sky.

"Where's Tai Poh Poh?" She placed her book under her pillow.

Ah Kain tucked the silky top sheet around Ching Ha's little body. "You go to sleep. She will be in your dreams." She unfolded a light pink and blue blanket and placed it over the sheet.

"Will Tai Poh Poh come tomorrow?"

Ah Kain bent down so her face was directly in front of Ching Ha's. "Your tai poh poh loves you so much. But we do, too. I am going home now, but I will come back early in the morning.

The child sucked in several short breaths, as though gasping for air, a prelude to a flood of tears. "I want Tai Poh Poh."

"I know." Ah Kain hugged her. "Be a brave girl. Don't cry. It makes everyone sad." She looked at Ching Ha. "You don't want to make your new mama and daddy sad, do you?"

Ching Ha stopped her panting sob. She wiped her fingers across her eyes. "I have a mama and a daddy?" She had never asked Tai Poh Poh about a daddy, only a mama. Now, she understood why she was here. Tai Poh Poh had found her a mama. She would give Tai Poh Poh the biggest hug when she saw her.

Dima kneeled on the floor and placed his elbows on the bed. He leaned in, so Ching Ha could rest her arm on his shoulder. "Good night, Bella." He kissed her nose.

"Good night, Bella." She smiled and kissed Dima on the nose.

He pointed at her, "Bella." He pointed at himself, "Dima." He repeated the "Good night," pointing to each of them. Ching Ha imitated Dima's words and actions. Dima clapped. Lana walked into the room, followed by Mack.

"Good night, Lana." Ching Ha said, pointing to Svetlana. "Good night, Lion."

This time Dima let out a small cheer as he clapped. Lana leaned down and pecked Ching Ha on the forehead. The kiss was so quick that the child didn't have time to put her arms around her new mother. Ching Ha reached to grab Mack around the neck, but he turned and followed Lana out of the room. Dima blew her a final kiss and flicked off the light. He and Lana walked down the hallway and closed the door to their room.

As her eyes adjusted to the darkness of the big, quiet room, Ching Ha touched her forehead. She smiled. Moonlight snuck in through a gap in the curtains and danced on the walls and ceiling. Ching Ha climbed out of bed and ran towards the light switch. She stretched up her hand, but couldn't reach. She watched the frightening shadows, real and imagined, surround her. She dove back into her bed. She heard small voices deep down the hallway darkness, then quiet. No rumblings of traffic or colourful, twinkling city lights shining through the window. Darkness wrapped around a house. The big rooms and tall ceilings weren't fun to be in anymore. Now, they were scary. She missed hearing the sounds of her home: the murmur of street traffic below, punctuated by honking bus and car horns; the scraping and clanking of the elevator doors; the neighbours talking in the hallway; the tiny squeaks as Tai Poh Poh wound the small, noisy alarm clock and the swooshing of Tai Poh Poh brushing her hair.

"Tai Poh Poh." Ching Ha whispered to the room. She could only hear her own breath in the room. Tai Poh Poh's words about a new adventure, and Ah Kain's words about being brave, and not calling for Tai Poh Poh repeated in her head. But they made her sad, not strong. She began to cry.

"Tai Poh Poh." She sat up in bed and shouted this time, but still no one came. Running to the other end of the hallway, she banged on Dima's door, her fists hitting harder and harder as she wailed louder. The door opened, and she fell against his pajama'd legs. He picked her up and rocked her little body. She trembled, trying to catch her breath. Lana looked up from her low vanity. Dima placed Ching Ha on the bed and left the room. A door in the hallway creaked open. The scent of mothballs wafted into the room. Ching Ha scrunched her face, as Lana, a thin layer of white cream covering her neck and face, pushed out her bottom lip and and wiped away her tears with a greasy hand.

When Dima returned to the room, he had a metal frame. He unfolded it and squeezed it between his side of the bed and a small dresser that doubled as a television stand. Ching Ha crawled onto the cot. Tai Poh Poh had found her a mama, a daddy and a television. She squinted at the brightness of the black and white Sanyo. Two men with angry faces and deep voices shouted. The short man pushed the tall man against the wall. Bang and a flash of light sparks. The tall man fell on his back and lay there. Ching Ha's fists closed on her blanket, and she gasped. Dima pushed a button. It made a pop sound. The brightness drained into the center of the screen and disappeared.

Ching Ha blinked towards Dima. He was a blurry, dark figure. She rubbed her eyes and looked again. He was holding her pillow, blanket, doll and book. Placing her book under her pillow, she lay down and snuggled with her doll, and blanket. Dima sidled alongside the bed, sat and placed his legs under the blankets with a grunt. His hands slid to one side of his face. He closed his eyes, and opened his mouth into an O shape. A strange sound came out. Ching Ha laughed and imitated his snoring.

She closed her eyes as he sang, "Ssh. Ssh. Bellachka," over Lana's dry, grating cough. A click made Ching Ha open her eyes. The steady, neon green light of the radio on Dima's bedside table now gleamed. Wordless music came out of the little holes. It reminded Ching Ha of the sounds of the street musicians at the night markets. She closed her eyes again, and everything faded into Dima's song, filled with words she could not understand.

A New Day

November 1970

A toddler kneels on a cold floor. Her belly protrudes from her short, pink shirt. One arm stretches through the black door railings. She is crying, nearly screaming, to a pair of thin, stockinged legs in shiny, black high-heel shoes. Tap, tap, tap. They move away from her. Over small black and white square tiles. A swoosh as doors close. The legs and shoes are gone. Someone lifts and bounces her in a tight embrace.

"Ching Ha, nay m'hai dak yat goh yun." The smooth voice repeats, "You're not alone," until it is drowned out by the sound, imagined or real, of a phlegmy scream beseeching,

"Mama. Mama."

Ching Ha's arms stretched towards the ceiling and grasped at nothing. A low moan struggled out as she kicked her leg and released a shriek and started crying. A big hand pressed against her shoulder and rocked it back and forth.

"By-u by-u shki by-u . . ." A male voice sang a Russian lullaby. The singing paused and resumed after a snort roused the singer awake. The words trailed off again, this time becoming a low mumbling, interlaced with humming. Ching Ha opened her eyes. She wiggled in the bed; the dream, vague in details but emotionally vivid, made it too hard to get back to sleep.

She pulled at the soft, pink blanket on her cot.

Where am I? As she surveyed her surroundings, her heart beat rapidly at the top of her throat. Classical music played in the background as she listened to Dima snoring and watched his belly moving up and down. She unclenched the blanket, remembering that she had run into this room at night. The room was dark except for a sharp outline of sunlight around the heavy, deep green, velvet curtains. Ching Ha repositioned her head on the small, pink pillow decorated with kittens and heard two short tones, followed by a long, steady tone coming from the black box next to the bed.

"This is the BBC World Service," a voice announced.

"BeeBeeCee Whirser." She mimicked the dramatic modulations. Ching Ha listened to the words whispering from the radio, waiting for ones she could understand, but the person spoke too quickly.

The cot squeaked, as she crawled off it, causing the dog's ear to twitch and Lana to mutter in her sleep. Ching Ha pulled on the partially open door. Her heart lightened when she heard the clink of dishes, and she ran toward the sound, her warm, bare feet slowly cooling on the hardwood floors. Instead of Tai Poh Poh preparing breakfast, the two Chinese women from yesterday were there. They set platters of fruit and cakes on the table.

"Jo sun, Ching Ha." Ah Kain was high and bright.

"Bella," Ah Mui reminded the younger maid, before adding her own morning greeting.

Ching Ha nodded and said, "Jo sun," as she approached the two servants.

"Where is Tai Poh Poh?" Ching Ha asked.

"Did you go to the bathroom and brush your teeth already?" Ah Kain asked.

The girl shook her head and took Ah Kain's hand as they walked to Ching Ha's bathroom.

Ah Kain's face was a happy one, with the black dot that danced around her face when she talked, and big cheeks that made wrinkles around her eyes whenever she smiled. Her gentle voice reminded Ching Ha of Tai Poh Poh, as did the way her fingers fit around Ching Ha's hand. Even the things that Ah Kain said sounded like Tai Poh Poh. The words made sense, but when they were in a sentence, they created a meaning that she did not understand, like: "Sometimes nighttime is frightening because we see things more clearly."

"Where's Tai Poh Poh?" Ching Ha asked again as Ah Kain handed her a small toothbrush topped with a swirl of white toothpaste.

"Your mama is in the bedroom with your father."

Another answer that sounded like Tai Poh Poh's, Ching Ha thought. The answer that was to a different question, not the one she was asking.

"I do?" Ching Ha said, frothy toothpaste slobber dribbling out of her mouth. *I wanted a mother, but I didn't know I could have a father, too.* She spat the toothpaste into the sink, sipped the glass of water, and let the water dribble out of her mouth.

"Who are you and Ah Mui?" Ching Ha asked, pointing to Ah Kain who dabbed the child's mouth with a facecloth.

"Ah Mui and I are the Amahs. We clean the house and we cook."

Ching Ha stepped off the stool and followed her into the bedroom. Ah Kain took an outfit out of the closet and held it up to Ching Ha's body. "I also help take care of you." She kneeled and let the child hold her shoulders as she stepped out of her pajamas and into her matching pants and top.

"And, Tai Poh Poh?" Ching Ha asked. "When will she come?"

Ah Kain was silent and did not look at the child.

"Did she forget about me?" Ching Ha's voice rose, as her breaths became shallower.

Ah Kain put her arms around Ching Ha, hugged her then picked her up. They sat on the bed as Ah Kain did her best to explain what she understood to be true.

Cantonese words danced around Ching Ha's head, soothing, comforting words: "You will be happy here. Everything will be good." She understood the words, but their meaning was still unclear. "This is your new home. You will live here with your new mother and father. Ah Mui lives here, and I will come nearly everyday to see you."

"Where is Tai Poh Poh?" This time Ching Ha whispered, the energy draining. "I want my old home. My own home."

Ah Kain squeezed Ching Ha once more and put her on the ground. "It's going to be okay. You're a big girl. A brave girl." She nudged Ching Ha towards the hallway with a tenderness that only made the child want to stay with her. "Go see if your mother and father are ready to get up for breakfast." Ah Kain motioned her on her way. "Go."

As the girl walked to the room where her new family lay, a cloudy coma engulfed her, as the words she had heard in her dream played in her mind. *Am I still dreaming? Where is Tai Poh Poh? Is this a new adventure?* Ching Ha's stomach grumbled, and distracted her, just for a moment, from her worries and the new family she wasn't sure she wanted. *Is Tai Poh Poh going to be in my new family, too?* Her eyes felt dry, dusty, as though she had been walking in the city on a windy day, but she felt tears coming. *How can this be my new family? I don't know what they are saying. They don't even speak Cantonese.* Her body shook with an emotion that was somewhere between fear and despair.

As the questions exploded in her mind, the feelings became a flurry of distress in her belly and with each stamping footstep towards the bedroom, developed into a fury. I want to go home. I want to see my Tai Poh Poh. Now.

Ching Ha ran the last steps toward the room and pushed on the door. The darkness and quiet extinguished her fire. She always had to be quiet when it was nap time for Tai Poh Poh. The grumbling of Ching Ha's stomach and visions of the fruit and bread on the dining table swallowed the girl's questions, and she gingerly crawled onto her new parents' bed. She didn't know how to wake the large bumps under the covers.

She bounced gently on the mattress. The man groaned. Ching Ha froze mid-grimace, waiting for another sound from the stirring giant. There was none, so she turned her attention to Mack. The boxer lay on its left side, legs completely outstretched, its back as long as Ching Ha was tall. His big black and brown muzzle and pink jowls billowed with the half-yelping breaths that accompanied twitching paws. Ching Ha smiled and tickled his paw. He twitched again. She laughed out loud. Mack lifted his head, revealing droopy eyes, a shiny pink layer of the inner eye and the ooze running out the side. He looked at Ching Ha, then flopped back down.

The movement of Mack's head awakened Svetlana. A gurgling erupted in her throat, and she coughed, a wet, messy sound. She threw off the white and yellow floral sheets, decorated with holes from cigarette ash, and slipped her feet into yellow slippers. She opened the bedside drawer and shuffled objects about before pulling out a tin from where she took a green object out and popped it into her mouth. Replacing the tin in the drawer, she let out a husky grunt and shuffled into the bathroom.

Ching Ha crawled to the woman's side of the bed and examined the items on the cluttered bedside table. A book, pieces of a newspaper, an overflowing ashtray and tissues. Ching Ha turned to face Dima as a deep snore turned into a deep exhale; and the smooth voice of the radio announcer lulled him back to sleep once again. Ching Ha returned to her investigations of the woman's bedside table. She ran her finger along the curved edge of the wrought iron ashtray. A cigarette stuck in the notch, suspending a quarter-inch long ash over the ashtray. Ching Ha poked at the cigarette. It disintegrated into a fine powder. She looked at the grey soot on her fingers and sniffed. A smell, reminding her of the mothballs, stung the inside of her nostrils, so she moved it away and wiped her fingers on the bedsheets. She picked up the gold tin and twisted the lid. Helping herself to a green jelly dot covered in sugar granules, she sniffed its minty herbal smell before putting it into her mouth. She sucked on it, then twirled her tongue around to melt the sugar granules. She bit into the pastille. A coolness trickled down her throat as she inhaled. Ching Ha bit down again to get another hit of the minty flavor, but the cool sensation turned so cold, it burned her mouth. She spat the mangle pastille into the ashtray. Eager to rinse her mouth out, she swung her legs over the side of the bed to jump off and let out a scream of pain as she grabbed the back of her legs.

The man startled out of sleep and rolled over. Mack jumped off the bed and the bathroom door swung open. Ching Ha lay on her back, whimpering. A triple stripe band of purple, blue and black appeared on the back of her thighs. A plank of plywood that was placed between the mattress and the bed frame had pinched her flesh. The woman turned Ching Ha onto her belly and applied a wet facecloth to her skin. The man rubbed the child's back as she moaned into the mattress.

Ching Ha turned her head, straining her neck to get a better view of the site of the pain. When she saw the widening, darkening shape, she let out a shriek of horror and cried. Dima, half singing a lament for the girl, walked around the bed to pick up Ching Ha, but stopped. Lana was leaning over the child and pulling her into an embrace, rubbing the fast approaching bruise. Dima lifted his hand to pat the woman's shoulder, but put it down.

"I'm sorry. I'm sorry."

Ching Ha gave into Lana's gentle words and leaned in, allowing herself to be held and rocked. Lana stroked the girl's hair. She leaned back into her pillows, pulling Ching Ha next to her. She slid the covers over the two of them. Ching Ha rested her head on the woman's pillow. It smelled like cigarettes, not Tai Poh Poh's herbal ointment, but Ching Ha didn't care. *I'm not alone.* She nuzzled against Lana. This is my new mother, she thought, feeling her warm, soft skin, that smelled like lemon cream. Dima sat on her other side and put his big hand around hers. *This is my new father.*

"Bella, Bella, Bellach-ka," the voices crooned.

That's my name here, she told herself and closed her eyes. Bella took a jagged breath and let the sound of Lana's heartbeat drown out the burning in her leg and her longing for Tai Poh Poh.

Far from Routine

There are wonderful paradoxes in children. They are at once simple and complex, naïve and wise, delicate and resilient. In the next months, Bella adjusted to her new life with an innate understanding that there was no good option except to fit in and find her place here, until she was reunited with Tai Poh Poh. In the meantime, she decided that Ah Kain would be her guide.

The child realized that although each day had variations, she could depend on the routine of her new life. The glow of dawn streaming through her windows woke her early, and she spent the early mornings with Ah Mui, who lived in the servant's quarters in the rear of the kitchen. She listened to the tinkling of teacups against saucers, the plonk, plonk of water flowing from the tap into the metal kettle for tea and drinking water.

"Tai Poh Poh drank tea every day, too," Bella told Ah Mui.

"Tea is good for your body," was all that Ah Mui said.

When Ah Kain arrived, the kitchen was often filled with the aroma of fresh fruit and vegetables that she bought at the market. When Bella and Lana purchased the produce at the Dairy Farm Supermarket, it had no smell and lay on polystyrene trays that were covered in plastic wrap.

"I used to buy choy sum with Tai Poh Poh in Wanchai," Bella once said to Ah Kain, submerging the leaves in the plastic tub, as she washed them. Ah Kain mumbled a soft *hmmm*, but nothing more.

Each weekday morning, Bella performed her self-appointed duties to the hum of conversation, dotted with trills of laughter between her, Ah Kain and Ah Mui. Ah Mui filled old vodka bottles with boiled water and prepared the tea and coffee tray. Bella rolled slices of swiss cheese and pale, pink ham, keeping them tightly formed with a wooden toothpick in the center. Ah Kain washed, cut and plated the fruit tray. Each of them brought an offering to the breakfast table that was adorned with grey and white plates and silver utensils.

"In my home with Tai Poh Poh, we usually only used bowls and chopsticks," Bella said as her finger touched the "H" engraved on the knife.

Ah Mui nodded.

After Dima guzzled down breakfast, talking through mouthfuls of food to save time, he left for the office, and it was Bella's time to be with Lana and the dog. They strode along the picturesque paths of the park at the top of the hill. Bella's short legs skip-walked to keep up with Lana as they wound through the trees, hydrangea and hibiscus bushes of the landscaped park. Bella wanted to mention that there were big flowers at the market where she went with Tai Poh Poh, but remembered Ah Kain's words from the first night, so said nothing.

Upon their return home, Lana once again demanded time to herself and disappeared into her bathroom for daily ablutions. She emerged over an hour later, hair washed, face red, bridge book damp and the room as steamy as a Roman bath. She then began the task of selecting her non-dog walking attire for the day. This part of her day took two or three times longer if she was heading out to play bridge.

Bella wanted to say that Tai Poh Poh had long black hair when she was younger, and now it was short and white. But she didn't.

* * *

While Ah Mui took charge of the kitchen, Bella and Ah Kain tackled the house cleaning. They flapped the bedsheets in the air, scrubbed toilets, rolled the fat canister of the Hoover around the house as it sucked up a never-ending amount of dust from the hardwood floors and carpets.

"My house with Tai Poh Poh was easier to clean."

"It feels good to be in a clean house,"Ah Kain said.

By the time they were done with the cleaning, Bella was ready for lunch, after which she was expected to practice her mother's favourite motto: "Entertain yourself."

"I was never bored in my old home," Bella said.

Ah Mui nodded, silent.

Lana returned to her bedroom, changed back into her nightdress to lay in bed, read and nap. Bella played with her Legos and Barbie dolls, built towers with cards and blocks and flipped through books. She tried to remember what toys she had when she lived in the other house.

She moved into the living room, rummaged through the drawers stuffed with cassette tapes, bags of coins that didn't look like coins they used, letters covered in writing she couldn't read because of the squiggles.

"I'm a reader of letters," she told Mack.

There were days that she pulled out the typewriter in the blue metal case. It wasn't as fancy as the one Dima's secretary used, but it worked. Bella lined the paper on the edge of the roller and turned the dial until the paper was directly across the hammer of the letters. She tapped out sentences from her dictionary, each word a process that became less tedious as she began to recognize where the corresponding letters to the words were on the keyboard.

"I'm a writer of letters," she said to the room.

Her last source of entertainment, in what seemed to be the longest part of the day, was the kitchen, where she sat in Ah Mui's room. She listened to the Cantonese songs on the radio, occasionally thinking that she knew a song.

Bella went into the spare servant's room and leaned on the bed. She watched Ah Kain write letters to her family in China. She listened to the scraping of the pen against the thin paper and laminate tabletop and remembered her own phone book with drawings in it that must still be in her Tai Poh Poh home.

Before Ah Kain left each night, she gave Bella a bath and played games that recollected their day. "How much money did we find in the big armchair?" "How many carrots slices did you eat for lunch?" "What color socks was Ah Mui wearing today?" The child made loud sighing sounds when she didn't have an answer.

"You must pay attention to details around you," Ah Kain said, as she let water fall from her fingertips onto Bella's head.

"To-moh-low." Bella would reply, the word somehow reassuring.

For many nights, as she put on her pajamas, Bella asked Ah Kain "Where is Tai Poh Poh?" It was becoming more of a ritual than an expectation of seeing the woman who was fading from her reality each day, like a shadow disappearing as dawn broke.

When Bella asked this question, Ah Kain said, "I don't know where she is, but I know she doesn't want you to wait for her. She wants you to be happy."

Each time Bella heard the answer, she understood it more, in an obscure sort of way. She knew that Tai Poh Poh had to stay in her head, in her dreams. And as she held on to her secret time to visit Tai Poh Poh, the nights were less frightening and her longings started to hurt less and less.

Something Wicked This Way Comes

January 1971

Bella had a strange feeling when she sat at the table. Dima was sitting there, too. Why was he home? It wasn't Sunday. He grumbled and loosened his belt, which was almost at the last hole. This morning, instead of his usual bread with ham on toast, he ate spoonfuls of his goopy oats and apples concoction, forcing each swallow with a snarl of disgust. He checked his watch, leaned back in his chair every few minutes, craning his neck to look out of the window, then returned to his breakfast, only to repeat the whole process several more times.

"Enough," Lana snapped. She tapped a pack of cigarettes on her placemat until the head of a cigarette poked out. She grabbed it with a speed used for moving objects, put it in her mouth with equal rapidity, then reached for the heavy glass lighter next to her coffee cup. "You're making me nervous." Her marmalade toast untouched, she sucked the cigarette with a long, intense inhale, relaxing her shoulders as she breathed a grey cloud across the table towards Bella.

"Office today?" the girl asked Dimitri, as she bit into her buttered challah bread.

Lana flinched. "Don't talk with your mouth full, Bella."

"Not today," Dima said.

"Why?" Bella asked as she chewed her food.

"We have a visitor."

"Who?"

Dima glanced towards Lana who shrugged her shoulders and looked into her cup of coffee.

"Someone for work," he replied.

Bella looked from Dima to Lana suspiciously. Her bread was losing its flavour, and her stomach was starting to hurt. "What's wrong?" she asked.

"Finish your breakfast and go play," Lana said. "Ah Kain," she called towards the kitchen. "Please take Bella."

Bella smiled and dropped her bread, reaching her arms out to Ah Kain who helped her out of her high chair.

"Who is coming?" Bella asked Ah Kain as they walked towards the girl's bedroom.

"I don't know, but you help me clean and we can play."

Bella nodded contentedly. She liked her time with Ah Kain, even though today the girl felt a tightness in her chest, and her brain tingled.

"You okay?" Ah Kain asked Bella, who kept staring into space.

"Why are they angry?" the girl asked half in English and Cantonese.

"You be good girl and everything going to be okay," Ah Kain replied, also in a mixture of English and Cantonese.

Bella nodded. But, yet again, although she understood the definition of each of the words that Ah Kain was saying, she didn't understand what it all meant. She turned the pages of her Cat in the Hat dictionary, looking at the pictures and trying to figure out what the words said when she heard Dima calling out.

"Lana, she's coming."

Bella ran to her window and saw a thin woman walking up the hill, dressed in a black dress. An odd thing, considering the air felt warm and muggy. Something about the woman's militant, quick steps and tiny body made Bella's belly squeeze. As the woman got closer, Bella remembered she had been here before and asked many questions. Why did she have to come back? To eat the cream cake that Lana had bought? To put everyone in a bad mood again?

* * *

Miss Winnie Leung, a social worker for the Hong Kong Children's Society, ate a slice of vanilla roll, took the cloth napkin, dabbed the corners of her mouth, opened the dark green notebook and began her questions.

"Please remind me, how old is Ching. . ." Miss Leung paused as she checked her book. "Bella?"

"Bella is three," Dima said.

"And, how is she?" she asked.

"We think Bella is doing very well," Dima said proudly, lightly patting the girl's back.

"As I said last time, I think it's not good for a child to leave her own culture. She can be confused, so we must be certain she is adjusting," Miss. Leung said slowly in English, her Chinese accent crisply decorating each word.

"What does she eat?"

"Everything," Dima laughed. "She has a terrific appetite."

"Chinese food?"

"Sometimes.".

The woman marked her papers with a sound of discontent. "Does she appear confused with the new cultures?"

"I don't think so," Dima said, his sentence faltering. "As we explained last time, my wife and my family are from Russia originally, but we lived in Shanghai for many years. I speak Mandarin fluently. We speak English with Bella."

"Well, Mandarin is not the same dialect as Cantonese," Miss Leung pointed out condescendingly. "Does Bella still speak Cantonese, or does she speak English?"

"Both," Dima stammered. "People around her speak both English and Cantonese."

"I see," Miss Leung said. She turned to Bella. "Do you speak English?" she asked Bella in English. Bella folded her arms tightly across her chest and stared silently and sternly at the woman.

"Oh. She doesn't speak?" Miss Leung said, after repeating the question in Cantonese.

Lana and Dima looked at one another. "She's a

child," Dima said, trying to hide his exasperation. "She doesn't know you, and she is shy."

"Can you show the lady how well you speak English?" Lana asked.

Bella looked at Miss Leung, then hid half her face in Dima's chest. He put his arm around her protectively, and the stern woman marked her book. Although she had one cigarette still balancing on the edge of the porcelain ashtray, Lana lit another one in the silence.

Ah Kain walked towards the master bedroom carrying a vacuum cleaner.

"I want to vacuum," Bella said, She towards Ah Kain.

Miss Leung let out a small sound of surprise at the young girl's declaration that was in a mix of Cantonese and English.

"Later," Ah Kain replied in English. "You go to mama and daddy."

"No. I want to vacuum, now."

"Not now," Ah Kain said to her firmly in Cantonese.

Miss Leung made a note of this, creating a flurry of glances from person to person.

"We vacuum later. OK?" Ah Kain added in English before walking away.

Bella stomped back toward the group and plopped herself on the sofa next to Dima. She let out a long and exaggerated sigh. She crossed her arms and frowned at the woman who was interfering with her day.

"Do you like to help clean the house?" Miss Leung asked in English.

Bella nodded.

"I see she understands English," Miss Leung said to Dima and Lana. "Does she usually want to clean the house with your amah?

Dima sat upright. "She is a child and likes to play and do many things in the house," he said, clenching and releasing his fist.

"I think maybe she thinks she is the child of your amah," Miss Leung said as she reached for another piece of Bella's favorite cake.

Dima raised an eyebrow. Lana let out a breath through twisted lips, revealing a moment of irritation and scorn. Miss Leung's outspokenness was a far cry from the British diplomacy or the Chinese deference they were accustomed to. Lana ground her cigarette into the ashtray. Dima's jaw tensed, but he let out a laugh and took a large slice of the vanilla cake.

Dima stood at the window, watching Miss Leung walk down the hill. "That bitch."

Lana stood beside her husband and squeegeed her lips. "She's right. Bella *is* very fond of Ah Kain. It might be making it harder for her to adjust to life with us."

From her bedroom door, Bella watched Lana whispering to Dima, who stood with hands clasped behind his back, his shoulders rising and falling with his loud exhalations. Although she had not heard the words, Bella felt a rush in her chest, like tiny, glass marbles whirling around, and still did not know what it meant.

*****

Three weeks later, Bella woke up with a spinning feeling in her chest and stomach. There was something frighteningly familiar about this feeling, but her brain couldn't remember what her heart was "remembering".

"I will come back to visit you," Ah Kain said as she softly brushed the girl's cheek.

"Where are you going?" Bella asked, reaching for the woman's face.

"I must go away."

"Why?" Bella asked, her voice getting louder, as Lana took her hand and pulled her away.

Ah Kain took a deep breath.

"No," Bella snatched her hand from Lana and clung to Ah Kain's legs, crying. "Don't go."

Dima pulled the almost-screeching girl off Ah Kain and rocked her in his arms, as though she were a baby.

Lana shook Ah Kain's hand. "Thank you," she said, and handed her a white envelope before walking her to the door.

Ah Kain forced a smile and glanced towards Bella without making eye contact. "Bye, Bella. I see you again," she said in a high-pitched voice that sounded like she was going to cry.

A sickening flutter rose from Bella's belly to her chest when she saw tears in Ah Kain's eyes. She threw her body forward with arms outstretched, almost falling out of Dima's arms. "Ah Kain."

As the door closed, Bella screamed. "Please. Don't. Go. I be a good girl." She kicked her legs so wildly that Dima put her down. She ran to the door and tugged at the doorknob before crouching against it, sobbing. Lana walked away, sniffling away tears and patting her pockets for cigarettes, with Mack following obediently. Dima stood, head lowered, his hands held behind his back, watching as Ah Mui crouched down next to the girl trying to console her.

Bella bolted up and pushed past Ah Mui and Dimitri. She ran to the dining room windows where she stood on her tip-toes, waiting to see if she could see Ah Kain walking away. But, all she saw was the peacock blue car moving out of the gate and down the hill.

"Good bye, Ah Kain," she whispered through the quick breaths that jolted through her body. And, with an unrecognized familiarity of a phrase, she added, "See you . . . tomorrow."

Taking Care of Business

February 1971

Dima's black suitcase lay open on the bedcover as he decided what to pack for his week-long business trip to Europe. Lana sat on the bedroom armchair watching him, a wispy nebula of cigarette smoke above her head, Mack breathing heavily at her stockinged feet.

"Why can't I go with you to Rome?" Lana asked. "I always travel there with you en route to Israel."

"Because Bella needs you here," Dima replied dismissively.

"Why don't we take her with us?"

"We can't leave the country with her. We don't have her passport yet." Dima looked at Lana, a frown digging into his forehead. "Anyway, do you want to leave Mack when he is so frail?"

This time Lana frowned. She didn't want to feel as though the new child was affecting her freedom. Dima knew how important it was for her to go to Israel. But, he was right. She needed to be home for Mack.

"What will I do with Bella?"

"What do you mean?" Dima grimaced and shook his head as if rattling around the words she just said. "Take care of her."

Lana stood up with a huff. She walked to her bedside table and stuffed her cigarette butt into the ashtray. Yes, of course she would take care of the child. But she wanted to know what specifically he thought they could do. She wondered if his excitement had already worn off, like it did with the new car or the television set? He worked in the office. He didn't have to deal with this child all day. Lana tapped her cigarette on the ashtray as she tried to grasp the reality of what she and her husband had done. Had they really thought this through? Had it been sane to adopt a child? Especially so soon after . . . Lana shook the rush of memories from her mind and refocused on the child they had now.

"You have Ah Mui to help you." He put a pair of shoes that Bella had polished unevenly that morning, in a plastic bag and put them in his suitcase. "And my parents asked if they can take her to the Jewish Club with them on Saturdays and enroll her in Sunday school."

Lana's lips stiffened. "Does she really need to go to Sunday school?" She turned her head, so Dima wouldn't see her roll her eyes. "It's not enough that I converted so that I was good enough for the family?"

"Boje moy," Dima yelled.

"Boje moy," came Bella's voice from the hallway, imitating Dima and taking God's name in vain in Russian.

"It's not just learning Hebrew; it's about Bella being entertained and us having a relaxing weekend, even when Ah Mui has her days off." Dimitri dropped three ties on top of his undershirts. "Plus my parents would be thrilled to spend time with her — probably for as long as you need."

"I don't want to ask them to help me with her because that will look like I can't take care of her myself." Lana lifted the wad of cashmere-silk blend ties and laid each one flat in the suitcase.

Dimitri looked at her and raised an eyebrow before opening another drawer.

Lana clenched her teeth, and she felt her eyebrow twitch. She knew that look, as though she was mad and useless. Had he forgotten that she was the one who learned Hebrew when they moved from Shanghai to Israel? That she worked long hours as a chemist in the labs of Osem food factory to support them while he worked odd jobs translating documents and trying his hand at being a writer for anyone who wanted to publish his stories and opinionated essays? She was entitled to some time off now that they had been completely uprooted for his new job.

"Don't worry. We will stay busy."

He looked back at her. "Bella should have her passport by the time I get back, and we can all go to Israel."

"No," Lana swirled a finger inside a pack of cigarettes laying on her dresser but came up empty. "I prefer to go alone — for at least part of the time." She flattened the empty pack and handed it to Dima. "Please see if there are any of these at Duty Free."

"Well, I was going to swing through Jakarta and Singapore on my way out," he said, as he took the packet from Lana. "Don't you want to go?" He slipped it into a small pocket of his alligator briefcase then snapped the case closed.

"I'll go another time." Lana stepped towards her side of the bed and opened her drawer of her bedside table. "I really need some time to myself."

"Who will watch her while I'm in meetings?" Dima asked, as he watched Lana pick up an empty-looking pack of Pall Malls and fish through it.

"There are servants in both those places. Have them do it," Lana said, turning to see Bella skipping into the room.

Bella stopped and pointed to Dima's clothes stacked in the suitcase. Lana watched Bella set the doll she was carrying onto his grey pullover and run out of the room. She returned a few minutes later with an armful of clothing and dropped it into the suitcase, then scoop the doll into her arms again before leaning against the bed.

Dima laughed and placed her things beside her.

"No, Bella. This is my suitcase." He pointed to the suitcase, then his chest. But she simply dropped her things back into the suitcase, shook her head, pointed to the suitcase and then her chest. Her persistence was both annoying and admirable. Again, Dima took out her clothes and placed them on the bed. There was a patter of feet as she ran out of the room, returning moments later with her small, flowered suitcase which was kept on the floor of her closet. She pulled at the latches several times before they opened. She lifted her clothes off the bed and placed them in the suitcase.

"This my soot case." Her finger touched the rim of the little suitcase, then her chest.

Lana smiled, as she watched Dima and the child communicate in a language made of words and mime. Somehow, they had always managed to understand one another, and at very least, enjoyed the challenge of trying. Now that Ah Kain was gone and the child was speaking more English, Lana imagined it wouldn't be long before the girl could turn into someone Lana could also relate to. She lit a cigarette and watched Dima lift the hues out of the pink out of suitcase, close the suitcase and set the clothes on top.

"You stay here." He pointed to her and pointed to the floor. "Dima is going," he said, pointing to his chest and then spreading his arms and making a whooshing sound for his impersonation of an airplane.

Tears fell as the girl's light tones and grin having turned into wide eyes and a downturned mouth as she pointed to the floor and spoke in low, long tones. "You stay here."

"No," he said with a wag of his finger. "I go."

"No. No." She stamped her feet and thrashed her arms at her sides. "You no go."

Lana jerked her shoulders back and blinked. Despite being surprised and a little afraid of the tantrum, she admired the child's chutzpah to be demanding and raise her voice to Dima. But tears came to Lana's eyes as she watched sorrow surge, and the little creature's thin shoulders shake and her arms latch around his legs.

"Bella, Bella, Bellachka," Dima sang as he picked her up and rocked her gently. "Don't cry. I'm coming back soon." He kissed her forehead and placed her on the bed. He took his black leather planner from his briefcase and kneeled in front of her shuddering body and flipped through the pages until he reached the monthly calendar. "Today is Tuesday." He pointed to the square and his finger followed his words as he explained, "I leave tomorrow and come back seven days later."

They sat side by side, the body of the girl, possessed by ragged breaths, so dwarfed by Dima's broad shoulders and comfortable living. Her barely audible voice was monotone as he moved her finger across the calendar, and they counted together. Lana wondered if the child was thinking about the people who had left her. Was she longing for the people she had already lost in her short life? At that moment Lana felt a glimmer of hope that she finally had a connection with the child.

A Woman's Best Friend

February 1971

Lana sat on the floor next to Mack as he strained noisily with each breath. Her cries were intentionally quiet, so the child wouldn't hear her, wouldn't wake and come in with all her questions. Lana just wanted to be alone with Mack in his final days, hours, whatever moments he had left; to give him whatever energy she had left.

She ran her finger around the left wrist of her cashmere cardigan and pulled out a white silk square bordered with lace. She looked at it, remembering the village shop in the south of France where she had bought it, before blowing her nose and replacing the handkerchief up her sleeve. *Thank God, I didn't go to Europe with Dima.* Who would have expected that Mack's health would deteriorate so rapidly?

Lana leaned over, placing her face against Mack's. His breath was hot and foul; his paws twitched whenever he released a drawn-out whine, like he was in pain. She thought back to the last few weeks, his walking turning to hobbling, his lack of appetite, the skin on his once-sturdy frame now hanging, the shine of his eyes becoming barely a glimmer of life or joy. This state had not been sudden, she realised. She just hadn't wanted to see it. She put her face on his head and let her tears anoint his head with her love and sorrow. He tried to sit up.

"Sssh, my darling." Lana stroked his head, swallowing her sobs. *Don't upset him. Be strong.* "You are my good boy," she said to him, as the face

118

of another good boy appeared in her mind. She reached for a bowl of fish broth with rice and ground chicken she had made for him and held the spoon to his lips. He moved his tongue and swallowed, though most of the food ran onto the towels on his padded bed. She spooned up more food and let it trickle into his mouth. He panted, and moved his head away from the spoon.

Lana slouched against the wall, her hand on Mack, feeling the rise and fall of his chest. She would not take him to the vet, so they could dump his body in a landfill or whatever they did. Instead, he would be buried along one of the mountain trails, where they took their long walks. *How will I dig a hole? How will I carry him along the trail if I can barely move his head now?* If they were in Israel, she would have buried him under the mango tree. Death. Burial plans. Israel. Lana pressed her twisted face into her palms, but her son's face still appeared in her mind. She hadn't had time with him like this before he died, time to remember the good times, to say goodbye, and that she loved him. But would she have spent those moments wisely or would be sitting as she had done with her mother, and was now doing with Mack in a state of uncontrollable grief that engulfed all logic and reason? Would time together have been better than the Israeli Army Officer showing up at the doorstep to say that her son had been killed? Lana massaged her chest. It was getting so tight that she struggled for air. She felt dizzy. She wanted to throw up. Was she having a heart attack?

"Lana, I can't sleep." The door opened, and the girl walked in. Air escaped Lana's throat. She released a startled shriek as small, cold hands moved across her face, brushing the hair from her eyes, and the girl looked into them, searching them in that invasive way she always did. She was always looking for secrets."What's wrong?" she asked.

Lana almost said, "Nothing," but she was tired of being "good" or "fine" for everyone, tired of being on everyone's schedule but her own for getting better and moving on. She had lost her son two years ago. Who can be normal after that? Lana remained silent. Tired. The bathroom light lit the girl's face and the endless tiny circles within circles in the dark pools of her brown eyes. Lana could fall in and never surface again. But, Bella broke the spell as her deep, brown eyes blinked and moved off Lana.

The girl kneeled at the edge of Mack's bed and stroked from the tip of his nose to the top of his head. "Are you sleeping?" she asked him in a haunting voice that didn't seem to make a sound; as though she was communicating psychically. Bella looked at the still dog and tilted her head. She leaned downed, nestled her face against his still mouth, and whispered. "Lana, Mack is with Tai Gung Gung."

Help Wanted

March 1971

Lana lined up the edges of Mack's blanket and folded it. Restraining a sob, she held it to her chest before placing them gingerly on the top shelf of her wardrobe next to her prized eel-skin handbags. The last month without Ah Kain had been difficult. But this last week since Mack's death had been especially difficult for Lana. She wondered how she would pass the time she had spent with her devoted companion. She straightened her shoulders when she realized she was being watched.

"Why don't you go play?" Lana pressed her lips against her teeth. She could barely manage her own grief, let alone the child's growing desire for attention and increasing tantrums.

"What should I do?" she whined.

What indeed? Lana felt around the piles of mail on her dresser for a pack of cigarettes. "Why don't you read?"

"What else can I do?" Bella swung her legs against the bed, each bump like a drop of water against Lana's throbbing forehead.

"Well, you have to learn to entertain yourself." Lana fished out a cigarette. "People are busy and can't play with you all the time."

"What are you doing?"

"I'm busy." She put a cigarette into her mouth.

"Doing what?"

"I'm going to rest." She searched for a lighter.

"Before lunch?"

121

"Yes. I'm tired." She took the cigarette out of her mouth.

"But what about our walk?"

"Mack isn't here anymore, so we don't need to walk." Lana inserted a photo of Mack in the corner of the gold frame housing her mother's photo. There was no response from Bella, so Lana turned so see her looking back at her with arms crossed and nose scrunched up, as though ready to fire another question.

"What can we do?"

"Please ask Ah Mui to make tea for me," Lana said, pulling a lighter out of her handbag. The girl-with-a-mission hopped off the bed and skipped towards the kitchen yelling, "Ah Mui, Ah Mui, please make tea for Lana."

Lana put the cigarette back into her mouth and watched Bella skip down the hallway. She could be adorable, but had they had made the right decision by adopting a child? If you could call it adoption, given the uniqueness of how it all came about. Yes, they had taken strays off the street, but this was different. Dogs were predictable, easy to love and always ready to obey. A walk, a nap, a bone, a pat on the head and kind words easily resolved their issues. Dogs were loyal, patient, obedient. This child was not. She had a mind of her own. You could give her food, chocolates, toys; and she would busy herself for a short while, but then, she wanted attention. And there was her constant questioning and chattering, mostly in English now, but occasionally in Cantonese or maybe another language. The most disconcerting thing about that child was her brown-almost-black eyes that could invade your space just by looking at you. No, she didn't look at you; she looked through you. She watched everything with a quiet eeriness; her shiny eyes wide, examining you with a scrutiny that felt like she could read your heart and mind. A shiver shimmied through Lana's arms and torso. She lit her cigarette and inhaled.

Lana sat at the dining table, a cup of Lipton tea in

front of her. Bella sat across the table from her, flipping through her big dictionary.

"Listen to me read, Lana. Family. Fan. Far. Fast."

"Very good," Lana replied, although she wasn't sure if Bella was reading or deciphering the illustrations with each word. There was a crinkling, as Lana reached into her pocket and pulled out a flimsy packet of cigarettes and an amber, glass dropper bottle. She placed both on the table and twisted open the bottle. She squeezed and released the rubber top and lifted the dropper out of the bottle. She held it over her tea cup and gingerly pressed the dropper, releasing several drops of see-through liquid. She sealed the bottle.

"Why do you always put that into your tea?"

"It helps me."

"What is that?"

"Something to help me."

"Help you what?"

"It just helps me relax."

"Maybe that's why you always have to rest."

Lana didn't respond. She sipped her tea, listening to Bella resume her reading in concerto with the sound of Ah Mui pounding chicken breasts for the schnitzel dinner. It was becoming clear that Ah Mui didn't have the time to do the housework, cook and look after Bella. Lana wasn't keen on the girl spending most of her time with her grandparents. Firstly, Lana was sure that their increased involvement reflected badly on her parenting. Secondly, she did not want Bertha and Boris to take control of Bella's life, the way they had forced their opinions and rules on her and Dima when they were younger. Religion or not, Lana wanted Bella to be well-rounded, not just consumed with the Jewish Club activities. So Lana had to be responsible for the child's entertainment during the day. As she sat watching her studying her book, Lana was blessed with an epiphany.

"Hurry." Lana took a final sip of her tea. "We are going out."

"What about lunch?" The girl closed her book and ran to the door.

Although the girl's preoccupation with food was exasperating, her eagerness to go for a walk and the way she ran to the door was endearing, reminding Lana of her dearly departed Mack. They left the house, hand-in-hand, Bella skip-running to keep up with Lana's purposeful stride up Mount Austin Road, on the same route they usually walked with Mack. But they turned right, behind they reached the park.

"Where are we going, Lana?"

"We are going to visit someone"

"Who?"

"You'll see," Lana answered happily. Moments later, her manicured finger was pressing the doorbell at Flat G3. A young woman wearing a colorful hairband opened the door, and a waterfall of children's laughter and chatter poured out from behind her.

"Hello," Lana said, placing her hands on the girl's shoulders. "I would like to enroll my child into your preschool."

*****

Lana unfolded Mack's blanket and carried it into the living room. A young, lean, cognac-coloured boxer trotted after her. Lana marveled at the perfect timing. About a month after enrolling the child into the daily four-hour Montessori program, Lana had happened upon this newest family member.

"Dima, don't you think she is beautiful?" She sat the dog on the blanket and began to brush her. "I think she's pure boxer."

"You just found it on the street?" Dima watched Lana from the dining room table, where he was having afternoon tea with Bella.

"Yes, I saw her on the way home from dropping you off at work," Lana replied. "It was just past Cat Street." She chuckled at the irony. "Some man was shooing the dog away from the bins." Lana pet the freshly groomed dog that she had found earlier that day. "Isn't she a beauty?"

"Yes, she is." Dima said as he crunched on a tea biscuit. "And you already got her examined and vaccinated?"

"Yes. I stopped at the vet on the way home."

"What name did you decide on?" Dima asked.

"Chocolate?" asked Bella.

"Hmm," Lana considered. "Yes, you are a sweetie," she said as she held its face in her hands."Candy," she said. "You are my sweet Candy." She made a cooing sound at the dog. It wagged its tail. "What are the odds of finding a dog like this on the streets of Hong Kong, especially, only a couple of months after Mack's death?" Not usually a fatalist, Lana was certain this was a sign.

"I don't know," her husband said with a shrug. "I just hope she doesn't belong to anyone."

Lana glared at Dima. Still petting the dog, she glanced at Bella who was dipping her tea biscuits in a glass of purple Ribena, and replied, "If someone wanted her, she wouldn't be here with us." She stood up and marched out of the dining room with the dog following, leaving behind a wake of silent drama.

"Bye, Candy," Bella said, slurping a wet biscuit into her mouth.

Lana sat on her bed and patted her lap. Candy set its paw down gently on her leg. She leaned forward, placing her head against Candy's and whispered, "I get to keep you. You are going to be my stray."

Pass the Matzoh

April 1971

Bella put her hands over her growling stomach, sure that everyone at the Seder table could hear it over her grandfather's incantations. She looked around the table, but no one was looking at her. There were more people here at the Goldstein's Seder than at her Baba and Deda's the night before. Her friend David had told her that the seder at his house would be bigger, but Bella didn't expect twenty-five people. Hopefully, it didn't mean that it would take longer before the food came because, as much as she liked vegetable sticks, the karpas dipped in salty water had not squelched her appetite.

She flipped through her Haggadah, counting down the dog-eared pages, marking the highlights of this long dinner. She and David had already hidden the Afikomen. The Four Questions were asked, although David had taken over for her because she forgot the lines — even though she had practiced for what felt like a million times that day. Now, all that kept her from gefilte fish and the rest of the dinner was the Maggid. Once the story of the ten plagues and the slaves following Moses out of Egypt was read, they would sing, eat the little matzoh bites and she could finally feed her grumbling belly before the final part of the seder. Bella's body swayed as she began to hum the uplifting tune of Dayenu.

Her grandmother elbowed her gently, turned the pages of Bella's Haggadah back and began moving her finger across the page, in time with Mr. Steinham's narration: "And Moses told Pharaoh that if he did not free the Israelites, that God would bring plagues upon Egypt."

Bella dropped her gaze to the book, following her grandmother's finger until she took her hand away, at which point Bella resumed her page turning, past the pictures of the ten plagues and Moses crossing the Red Sea, past the song, to the page with the double dog-ears and a heading that read: "We eat the festive meal."

"Six pages, eleven sides," she said to herself.

By the time the sixth page was done and a trio of servants in bright white tops and black pants began weaving in and out of the kitchen doors with shallow dishes, Bella wanted to clap. She picked up her spoon in anticipation. "Thank you," she said as the dish was placed in front of her. She stared at the peeled egg in a clear liquid, wondering if it was a version of the Matzoh ball soup she ate the night before. She chased the smooth white oval around the bowl, trying to break it. She looked around the table, wondering how everyone was able to drive their spoons through the bright yellow yolk and break off a segment to eat. Bella decided to start with the soup. She sipped a little and quickly scraped her tongue across her teeth several times to rid herself of the taste as she scrunched up her face. The soup was cold and salty.

"My soup has too much salt, Dima," she said, leaning towards her father, wiping her tongue on the palm of her hand.

"It's supposed to be salty," Dima replied, wiping her hand with his napkin. "That's the sweat and tears of the Israelites."

Bella looked at her soup and crinkled her face. "What?"

"Not real sweat and tears. Didn't you listen to the story? It's so we remember our ancestors' suffering and sacrifice." He scooped a piece of egg into his mouth.

"Why don't we just remember good things?"

"We also remember good things. But remembering bad things that happened can remind us not to do the things that created the suffering."

"Can't we remember bad things but eat good food like barbecue pork buns?"

Dima made a sound with his mouth, like he was sucking food out of his teeth and tilted his head indicating that the conversation was over. He returned his attention to the egg. Bella, tired of chasing her egg around the bowl, stuck her finger nail into the glossy white egg and used her spoon to break the egg into pieces, releasing bursts of bright orange clouds in the water. She scooped a serving of the egg and water into her mouth, and chewed, deciding that it didn't taste too bad.

The gefilte fish, decorated with three little circles of carrot slices, was warm, and definitely tastier than egg. It was so good, she wanted to ask Dima for his portion, but knew he was probably hungrier than her. He had not eaten all day while she had eaten a whole roll of chocolate smarties before they left the house. She looked at the large fork and knife still on the table and realised more food was coming, so she nibbled on matzoh and swung her legs impatiently.

While Dima sliced the chicken on her plate, Bella looked through her Haggadah again, tapping the last of the pages with the bent corners. Two more things to do before the end of the dinner. First, she and David would have to bargain with her grandfather if he wanted the special matzoh returned to him. She wondered how much he would offer for the Afikomen. Her father's secretaries had each given her two dollars in red lai see envelopes for Chinese New Year. Surely, the Afikomen was worth more, because the Seder could not be finished without it. She wished that when she and David were hiding it in the bookcase, she had asked how much to ask for its return. He would know stuff like that. He was almost seven.

Bella didn't look up when her father put a fork full of chicken into her mouth before settling in and eating his own meal. She was looking at the picture of the wine glass for Elijah on the final page she had folded. That would be when she and David would open the front door and invite Elijah inside to drink the wine. Bella did not see him the night before, and her grandfather had ended up drinking his wine. She wondered if he would make it to Seder tonight.

By the time dinner was over and everyone closed their Haggadah, their voices were tired from reading, singing, talking and wishing one another Chag Pesach Sameach. Bella placed her hands on her full belly, excited to go home, where she would feed the crispy five-dollar bill that her grandfather had given to her for the Afikomen to her hungry piggy bank.

Peace of Mind

Lana stepped into her friend Lyudmilla's flat. Grace, the ten-year-old black toy poodle, ran towards her, tail wagging. Jun, the twenty-something amah, took Lana's tweed coat, hung it in the closet by the door and disappeared into the kitchen. Lana noted Jun's jet black hair that draped down her back and the young woman's peaceful stride. She wondered if Jun would be this calm in the Hoffman house.

Lana followed Grace down the hallway into Lyudmilla's bedroom.

"Drasti, Mila." Lana approached the bed where the elegant Lyudmila sat cross-legged in an embroidered pale grey gown that cascaded around her slender body. They exchanged air kisses on both cheeks.

"You're early." Mila pointed to the art books on the bedside chair and patted the bed.

Lana picked up the books and placed them on the bed. "I dropped Bella off at ballet early so we could relax."

"I thought you were picking her up late, so we wouldn't be rushed." Mila lowered her glasses and raised a drastically-plucked eyebrow.

"Well, now we can really relax." Lana dropped into the armchair.

"If I relax anymore, I'll be dead," Mila said.

Jun sauntered into the room, holding a tray with two teacups and a plate of tea biscuits. She placed the tray on the waist-high table beside the two women and handed a teacup to each of them.

"Anything else, Mila?" Jun asked.

"No, thank you."

Lana admired Jun's graceful silence as she drifted out of the room. In fact, Lana loved the serene energy of Mila's home. How did she do it? "I need more drops," Lana said, taking a bite of her biscuit and setting it down on the saucer.

Mila sipped her tea, then set it down on the tray. She moved at half of Lana's speed giving her an air of great poise. Her slowness was partially because of her fibrositis and a heart condition that led to a sedentary life managing pain. Mostly, her leisurely pace was due to her placid nature. Lana suspected that the drops didn't hurt Mila's inner tranquility. Although, truth be told, those same concoctions had not been completely effective in Lana's household.

"Maybe something even stronger," Lana added, "she's still having tantrums."

"The drops might help Bella calm down, but they aren't going to change her personality," Mila said, taking a pack of cards out of her bedside table. "Anyway, the drops are for you, not your daughter."

"But, they won't hurt her."

"They shouldn't, but the doses are for you. To help *you* be calm." Mila shuffled the cards and began to deal. "How is Dima?"

"You know. Dima is Dima." Lana put her teacup back on the tray.

Mila gave Lana a knowing look. The two school friends picked up their cards and started their game of gin rummy.

The plate with the tea biscuits was empty, as were the teacups. The ashtray had three cigarettes, Mila stealing puffs of Lana's cigarette for a taste of the habit she had given up for her health. The page of the score pad was covered with numbers.

Mila looked at the slim silver band on her wrist. "What time does Bella's ballet lesson end?"

"3:30 P.M." Lana drew a card and rearranged the cards in her hand.

"Well, Lana-chka, you should be going. It's almost 4:00 P.M."

"Oh. I have such a good hand." Lana put her cards

down with a *tsk*. She paused. "Let's just finish this game. Bella is used to me being late," she said and picked up her cards.

*****

Lana had dropped Bella off at ballet class early again. This time Bella was so early that none of her friends and their mothers were there. Tired of watching the earlier class, Bella decided to find out where the carpeted stairs from the ballet hall led.

A tall woman who had been sitting in the garden area entered the hall and made her way towards the stairs. Bella hurried to catch up with her. She pattered several steps behind the woman. They walked up the stairs and under the sign that read "Residents only." They moved behind the arrangement of leather sofas and cloth arm chairs and past wooden stands holding racks of newspapers that hung like freshly washed laundry. When the woman reached a glass door and windows, she opened it and disappeared inside.

Bella peered in. A short, red-haired lady sat in a very high-back, black chair, behind a desk that was on a raised platform. Books were piled on her desk. The lady stamped a piece of paper and put it into a book. Bella pressed her nose against the glass. Along every wall of the room there were bookcases; each of them filled with books. She noticed the sign in the window.

"Helena May Library." She grinned and clasped her hands together. She had seen libraries this big in her books and on television, but never in real life. They made the bookshelves at home, filled with volumes of *Encyclopedia Brittanica*, look tiny. Bella frowned. The women who lived in this private residence for unmarried women were lucky to have their own library. Her eyebrows relaxed as she surmised that they probably needed the books, because without children or dogs, they probably had nothing to else to do.

Bella stepped aside as the tall woman walked towards the door. She stepped out of the library and left the door open for Bella, who peeked in.

The red-haired lady looked up and waved. "Come in, come in," she said.

Bella entered the library, eyes roaming the shelves, and walked towards the desk.

"How can I help you, dear?"

"Am I allowed to borrow books from here?"

"If your mother lives here, or is a member of the library you can. If she's not, you can always come in and read. It's so nice to see young people reading."

"My mother doesn't live here, and she's not a member. . ."

"Let's just check the accounts. What's your name?"

"Isabella Hoffman. My mother is Svetlana Hoffman."

"Hoffman?"

"She's not Chinese," Bella said.

The red-haired lady smiled, which made her front teeth jut out of her little mouth. "Oh. But, I think we have a Hoffman." The lady looked through the cards in a large file box at the edge of her desk. "So, you take ballet classes downstairs." she said.

Bella put her hands on her pink leotard, "Yes. . . Mrs Stan-lay."

Mrs. Stanley looked up from the cards, cocked her head to the left and opened her mouth. Bella pointed at the gold and black nameplate on the desk.

"Ah," she said, looking at the nameplate and nodding her head, "you're a good reader."

"I go to a Monster Story School," Bella said nonchalantly.

"I see," Mrs. Stanley said, resuming her card search.

"I'm sure my mother isn't a member, or she would have brought me here," Bella said. "She knows I love books. And she says I'm always bored."

Mrs. Stanley put her index finger in front of a card, stopped, and peered over her glasses at Bella. "Svetlana Hoffman on Mt. Austin Road?"

"Yes?" Bella said with a lilt of confusion.

"Yes, she's a member," Mrs. Stanley replied cheerily. "So, as soon as I have her permission, you can borrow books."

A weight strangled Bella's excitement about having

accessibility to these books. Bella wasn't sure if she was more disappointed that she had not discovered this place first, or that Lana had not shared this place with her.

"Is there a book that you were looking for?" Mrs. Stanley's high voice roused Bella from her contemplations.

"I have the *Cat in the Hat Dictionary* and *Treasury of Grimm's Fairytales*. I don't know any other big books, just Golden Books from my school library. Bella pinched her fingers together to represent the thin books.

"Do you like stories about animals and real things, or Fairy Tales?"

"Well, sometimes fairies can be real," Bella said.

"Oh. Yes, so they can," Mrs. Stanley said happily. She got off the chair and disappeared as she walked around her desk. When she reappeared and stepped off the podium, Bella saw that she and Mrs. Stanley were about the same height but her arms were longer. Mrs. Stanley also stood lopsided, her chest rounded like a robin fluffing itself up before song.

"I know the perfect books for you," Mrs. Stanley said, leading the way towards the back of the room. She walked crookedly, her right left lifting her up slightly more than her left leg, making her sway with each step.

Bella followed Mrs. Stanley. She wanted to copy the way Mrs. Stanley walked by stepping on her tip toes with her right leg, then stepping flat with her left leg, to see what it felt like. But, that would be rude. And, it might hurt her feelings.

"Enid Blyton wrote many books about fairies and children." Mrs. Stanley motioned towards a section of books. "Stay here as long as you like," she said with a wink, and began her undulating walk back to her desk.

"Thank you," Bella called after her and positioned a wooden step stool in front of the bookshelf. She pulled out a book with gold letters pressed into the green leather. She opened it and read the title, "Mer-ry Mis-ter Med-dle. Merry Mister Meddle." A low chattering followed by piano music drifted up from the floor vents. Bella drew in a quick breath and covered her open mouth. Her ballet lesson was starting. She closed the book and leaned forward to replace the book on the shelf. She felt another stab of disappointment rise. She considered for a moment, reopened the book, and started an adventure with Mister Meddle. This was going to be her little secret.

Giving up on Chinese

Bella sat at the table in the kitchen. She often sat here under the flowing bedsheets and laundry that hung on bamboo poles strung to the high ceiling. Ah Mui and her friend Ah Heng, the next door neighbor's amah, prepared tea for themselves. There was something comforting about listening to their chatter in Cantonese - the long drawn "ahs" and "wahs"' mixed with the faster chattering that made Bella think of chopsticks clicking. A tiny beetle crawled across the kitchen table.

"Where is your lady-boss?" Ah Heng asked. "Asleep?"

"No. Today she is playing bridge."

"Again?"

"At least once a week."

"Why get another child if you are too busy to be with them?"

Ah Mui glanced at Bella, then looked at Ah Heng. "What do you mean 'another?'"

"Oh, you don't know?"

Bella turned to look at the women. She wanted to know, too.

"Know what?" Ah Mui said in hushed tones. She smiled at Bella, then leaned in towards Ah Heng.

Bella looked back at the beetle on the table top, still straining to hear the secret.

"She had a child," Ah Heng said.

Ah Mui scooped three cups of rice into the rice pot and added water. "Really?"

"Yes." Ah Heng leaned forward, eyes widening. "A boy."

Ah Mui turned off the water and motioned to Ah Heng to lower her voice and lean closer.

"She still speaks Cantonese? I thought she is only supposed to speak English now," Ah Heng said, her volume unchanged.

Ah Mui put her hand into the rice pot with a splosh and her voice became almost inaudible over the swishing water. "She doesn't have to speak to understand." She poured out the water and added water to the pot once more.

The sound of talking turned to murmuring over the rice washing. Bella gingerly placed a finger down to keep the glossy, horned bug from crawling off the laminated table.

"What else do you know?" Ah Mui poured out the water, replaced the rice pot into the rice cooker and turned it on.

"The boy died two years ago."

"How old was he?"

Ah Heng paused as she tried to remember. "Twenty-three or four, maybe."

"Where? When?"

"Christmas time. When they lived in Israel."

"How do you know this?" Ah Mui dried her hands and moved towards the child.

Bella was staring at the tiny, slow-moving black dot, even though her nose was feeling ticklish and her vision was blurring with tears. Stroking Bella's head gently, Ah Mui's hands moved over her ears. Bella wiggled her head free.

"Miss Nellie told me," Ah Heng said, as she examined her nails and picked out dark matter from underneath them. "She is friends with Miss Lana."

Bella's beetle-friend was almost at the makeshift finish line, the toothpick at the edge of the table, when Ah Heng looked down at the table and gasped at the insect. Before Bella's little hands reach up, Ah Heng's fast-descending thumb crushed her friend, daydream, and her heart.

Answering Questions

May 1971

Bella was at her rug focused on bead transferring using tweezers. She loved going to Mrs. Dobry's every morning to sit in circle time, do the "work", sing songs and play with her friends. It made Bella feel like she was living on Sesame Street.

"I see your grandma outside with the dog,"

Bella looked up, expecting to see Baba with Candy. But it was Lana.

"That's not my grandma. That's my mum."She looked at her friend, Sophie.

"It is?" Sophie looked outside the window again. "Sorry, I always thought she was your grandma because she looks so old."

"No, she doesn't," Bella said, glancing away. She placed the last bead into the small, glass dish. She wanted to tell Sophie off for being rude, but she knew she wasn't trying to be mean. This wasn't the first time Lana had been mistaken for being her grandmother. But now Bella knew that people thought Lana was her grandmother because Lana looked old, not because they didn't look the same. She peeked up at Sophie, waiting for the usual follow-up questions like, "Where's your real mum?" "Why don't you call your parents 'mummy' and 'daddy'?" "What's your real name?" But Sophie was picking up her tray and carrying it back to the shelf to get ready for circle time. Bella stood with her tray and looked out the window. Lana, cigarette in one hand, dog leash in the other, was standing away from the other mothers, patting Candy.

Bella had answers to questions that people asked her. Lana was her real mum. She didn't have another. Her imaginary mum was from a bedtime story she had heard. She was someone who had left her under a tree with pretty pink and white flowers. Bella called her parents, "Lana" and "Dima," because those were their names. And that's how they introduced themselves to her. She knew these were answers. She also knew they were very good ones. And neither did other people because these answers often led to more questions about the same thing.

"Is your real mum dead?"

"Why aren't you with her?"

"Do you miss her?"

"Do you wish you were back with your real family?"

"Why don't you speak Chinese?"

"You don't look Jewish?"

Bella didn't have the answers because when she asked Lana and Dima questions like that, Lana would get a fresh cigarette and squirm in her seat, crossing her legs one way and then the other like she had to go pee. Dima would look out the window and shrug or stare at his dinner plate and say something like, "So many questions for a little girl."

She knew what it felt like to worry that someone was going to ask you to talk about something you didn't want to talk about, something that you hid away in your brain and heart, so you wouldn't see, feel or think about it. Bella didn't want Lana and Dima to have that same fear that someone would discover those secrets and rip them out of their hiding places. Also, when Bella had once asked where she had been living before she moved to Mount Austin Road, Lana and Dima had glanced at one another with angled eyebrows before turning their glares to her and bombarding *her* with questions.

"Who is asking?"

"Did something happen?"

"Is something wrong?"

The conversation had ended because when Dima asked Bella, "Why do you want to know?" She had answered,

"Because," which Dima said was not a proper answer. Lesson learned: don't ask questions. If only Bella could get other people to learn that lesson.

A cheery tune perked the children's attention and energy as Mrs. Dobry's fingers trotted across the piano keys. Bella placed her tray on the shelf and clapped in time with every nod of her teacher's head. As she sat in the circle, Bella looked around the room and wondered how many other children suspected that Lana and Dima weren't her real parents. What was 'real', anyway?

Pictures of small flowers falling off trees to shower a baby that slept in blankets on a snow-covered field and skipping through building-lined streets full of people, cars, and food stalls drifted through her mind as she tried to remember where she had seen those pictures of busy and happy places.

Though the feelings and dreamy scenes felt like they were at her fingertips, she couldn't grasp them. They were like drops of soya sauce in a bowl of shchi, the black droplets disappearing into the translucent cabbage and broth.

The thought of soup made Bella hungry, and her wonderings about what she would have for lunch meandered into ponderings about her life before she became a Hoffman.

Fish for Dinner

A long, deep chant rose up from the street through the open windows of the dining room. Bella lifted her head from the washes of blue and green soaking into textured paper of her art book.

"Youuuuuu." The call sounded again, ringing through the air like a warrior from the past, summoning her engagement. She set her brush down on the small tray of paints, hopped off her chair and hurried to the window. Standing on her tiptoes, she could see a man trudging up the steep hill. Body leaned forward, his head tilted to the left, a large wicker basket on his right shoulder.

Ah Mui rushed into the room.

"Who is that howling?" Bella asked.

"It's the Fish Man," Ah Mui said, picking up a white envelope from the sideboard. "Come with me."

"Fish?" She had been asking for fish for several weeks. The crunchy kind that Lana bought from Dairy Farm and put in the oven didn't taste like fish. And there were never eyeballs in the package.

"Quickly, so we get first choice." Ah Mui held out her hand for Bella, and they hurried through the kitchen, where Ah Mui picked up a plastic tub before heading out the back door. The back door led to a narrow landing, painted a stark white, and shared with the back door of the other flat. The ceiling was low, decorated with fossilized insect carcasses. Bella stooped instinctively, as she followed Ah Mui down the narrow winding steps, past doors where servants had placed folding stools and old tea tins filled with sand that held ends of burnt out

141

incense. Some had small folding stools in the middle of the landings.

The back entrance exited to the open stairwell at the side of the building. As she descended the final steps to ground level, Bella saw the man standing by the gate, where he had hung his coat. A cigarette hung from his lips. With a flick of the wrists, he pulled up his pants ever so slightly right at the top of the leg and bent his knees. Squatting by his wicker basket, he took out a thick, wooden cutting board and a pile of newspapers and laid it front of him. Ah Mui pulled at the top of her cotton slacks, then squatted by the Fish Man. Bella pushed her dress between her legs to hide her panties and crouched down beside Ah Mui, watching as the Fish Man slowly unwrapped a bundle from his basket. It was a shimmering fish, just like the ones Bella remembered seeing at a market long ago with the woman whose name she wasn't supposed to say out loud - the name she sometimes could not remember. "All the fish are freshly caught this morning." He pointed to the scales, glittery and pink.

Bella looked into its eyes. They were so sad and strangely familiar. They stirred up a glimmer of something in her mind and chest. It was a picture of something, but it was too blurry to see the details — like seeing the shape of something in waves by the beach and not being able to grasp it.

"I need a bigger fish." Ah Mui pointed to Bella. "She is a small girl, but she eats like a man."

The Fish Man hmm'ed. He re-wrapped the fish tightly and replaced it in his basket. He pulled out another package. "You like fish?" The cigarette held between the teeth at the side of his mouth released a block of ash that shattered and disappeared on the concrete.

Bella nodded slowly, her shoulders rising to cover her cheeks. She didn't like talking to strangers because they always asked questions about her.

Ah Mui looked at her. "She is learning English," she said to the Fish Man, nodding at the fat, silver fish that he held out to her.

"Is she your daughter?" He took out his cigarette

142

and crushed it under a brown shoe with splatter marks on it.

"No. My employer's girl." She placed the plastic container on the ground, opened the envelope, took out some paper bills and handed them to the Fish Man. He reached into a zippered bag around his waist and gave her back some coins, which clinked as they fell into the envelope.

"Does she speak Chinese?" He placed the fish on the chopping board.

Bella let out a low, reverberating sound like Dima did when he was waiting to leave for a business dinner, and Lana was still in the bedroom getting dressed. Why did everyone ask her who she belonged to and what languages she spoke?

"Yes, of course." Ah Mui nudged Bella. "Right?"

"Hai," she said in a whisper, although she wasn't sure she did. She could say words in English and Cantonese, and she understood both languages, but she didn't know how to speak either one properly anymore.

Sparkling scales made a lustrous frame around the chopping board, as a cleaver scraped up and down along the fish. Wham. Silver on silver, metal on fish, the cleaver cleanly severed the fish's head from its body.

Bella scrunched her face when the fish body flinched when the head came off. Bella looked at the eyes and thought of soft, white dumplings in soup. More twisting of his wrist, like an artist with a paint brush, the Fish Man moved his cleaver in and around the fish until Ah Mui's plastic tub had two thick, opaque filets atop a pile of tubes and bones and skin.

The Fish Man handed the container to Ah Mui as she stood and wiped his hands on a fishy-smelling cloth draped over his basket. He took out a red and black lined notebook from his bag and started writing.

"Shrimp," Ah Mui said. "If not, bring me another fish - same size."

He nodded and waved as they walked toward the side entrance of the building and pulled out the fish Ah Mui had rejected for the Filipina maid who were next in line.

Bella sat at the dining table, eyes on Baba breaking off a piece of dinner roll, slathering it with butter, then popping it into her small mouth with its lips outlined with her usual orange-red lipstick. Lana's eyes were mostly downcast, as she also performed this ritual with the bread. The conversation was a concert of voices with Dima and his father as the lead singers. The song started and stopped, started and stopped. Deda, as usual, spoke in low, constant tones while Dima's words rose and fell in volume through buttered bread while occasionally, the high squeaks of Baba talking to Bella broke the monotony of the men's voices. The chit chat had stopped when Ah Mui brought in a tray of soup bowls.

Bella leaned over her bowl sniffing up the scent of fish and ginger, as the rising steam warmed her face. She made a slurping noise as she wagged her tongue in and out of her mouth, like Candy did when she lapped water from his bowl. Baba chuckled. Lana looked up from her bread, eyes staring at Bella as her brows dipped almost imperceptibly, and she turned her head from side to side. Baba looked at Lana, then looked back at Bella and winked. The child blinked-winked back at her and picked up her soup spoon. She scooped up the soup and let it slowly drip back into the bowl, cooling it, as she had been taught. Sipping the soup out of the spoon, Bella let out an "ahh" with each taste. She watched Lana, who silently poured the soup from the spoon into her own dainty mouth.

"Is it delicious?" Baba asked in Russian and English.

Bella slurped louder, prompting more laughter and another dipped brow response from Lana, who glanced at Dima.

"That's enough," he said, sipping more quietly from his spoon.

Tired of the spoon, Bella put it down and picked up the bowl. Bringing it to her lips, she tipped it gently, tilting her head back farther and farther until the soup was gone. She set the bowl down. A long burp rumbled from the depths of her belly. Her eyes widened, as did Lana's, although Lana's pursed lips revealed that she was not amused. Deda smiled, and Baba winked in approval.

"Chi bao le?" Dima patted his stomach and raised his thumb into the air.

Bella shook her head. "Where are the eyes?" She tapped the edge of her eyes.

"Whose eyes?" Dima asked.

"Fish eyes." Bella turned the empty bowl towards him. "Now, I eat the fish eyes."

"She wants to eat the fish eyes?" Baba said, her mouth opened in surprise.

Dima shrugged. "Well, it's very common." He looked at Lana. "Where are they?"

Lana's eyebrows relaxed as her lips twisted upwards. "I fed them to Candy."

Bella leaned forward, hands on hips, a scowl on her face. "Why?"

"She loves them," Lana said evenly. She broke off a piece of bread and dipped it into her soup.

Bella folded her arms across her chest and glared at Candy, who lay peacefully on the armchair, drool running out the side of her mouth and wondered why a dog needed to be clever.

Pushing the Limit

May 1971

Lana was reconsidering the benefits of preschool. Having provided her eager-to-know-everything daughter with the gift of a rich vocabulary, her demands were being articulated with intensity and perseverance.

She lay on her bed, holding her bridge book in front of her, imagining the quiet, cool walls of her house in Israel, with stone floors and high ceilings. The long, lazy days spent listening to the rustling of the eucalyptus trees outside her window and the occasional voices of passersby. She half-listened to the girl's endless chattering and twittering in the background like a noisy bird testing her patience or stomping and screaming like a crazy person. It was exhausting to be constantly needed — read me this book, play gin rummy, take me to the park, show me how to cook. She bored easily of every new toys, and always wanted to do something new and different. Lana placed her hand on her neck and pressed, trying to relax the muscles that were straining from her clenching her jaw and pursing her lips.

"Lana, are you listening to me?"

"I'm listening to you." Lana reread the same line of her bridge puzzle.

The girl grabbed the book out of Lana's hands and threw it across the room. "No, you're not."

Lana bent her index finger and brought it to her mouth. She bit on it for a moment as a vibrating moan wailed out of her. She sat up and swung her legs over the bed.

"What are you doing?" Bella asked, the spoilt child scowl on her face and in her pout.

Lana did not answer. She rummaged through her drawer and pulled out a small amber bottle. She removed the dropper and squeezed it over the glass of water by her bed. A line of droplets dove into the water, the light brown liquid dissolving into clarity as it hit the water. She stuck the dropper in once again, removed it and held it over her mouth as she tipped her head back. Three drops fell in. She put the bottle into her drawer and handed the glass to the girl. "Drink this."

"What is it?"

"It will help you calm down."

"I don't want to calm down." Bella pushed the glass away. "I want to be angry."

"Then I will drink it to calm down," Lana said, standing up as she drank her concoction.

"I don't want you to calm down. I want you to play with me." Bella smacked Lana's full bottom, then threw herself face down on the bed, screaming nonsensical ramblings. The muffled cries faded into the pounding of fist and thrashing of her legs. Candy leapt off the bed and ran to the corner of the room, her head held low, her body shaking as though she was going to get a beating.

"Stop it, Bella," Lana said. "You're scaring Candy."

Frenzied screaming continued to flood the room. Lana walked to the dresser, fumbling with a packet of cigarettes, trying to block out the demonic crying. She threw the packet on the counter. "Okay, you want my attention?" She opened Dima's drawers and grabbed his belt.

A slurp and thwack rang through the air. Lana froze, listening to the silence, a drug that chilled her anger. She looked at Bella who was twisted on the bed, clutching the back of her leg. The girl let out a wail, shattering Lana's momentary solace. Dima's wide, black leather belt slid off the little legs and whirred behind the angry matron.

"Why do you make me do this?" Lana shouted

This time, the almost-four-year-old turned around and put her hands out to shield her legs, only to pull them to her body when Dima's belt struck her palms like an angry snake. Her silent screams suddenly found their volume, and she screeched a sound her mother had never heard. She jumped off the bed.

"Stop. I'll be a good girl," she cried and cowered by Candy who scrambled to get away from the child.

"Why do you do this to me?" Lana sobbed. Bella crawled under the bed. A frightened sob mixed in with laughter escaped Bella's lips. Lana grabbed her foot. The girl tried to inch her body a little farther under the bed, to try and grab a leg, or the springs of the bed. She kicked; she twisted; but Lana, who usually could not pick up the growing girl, was able to pull the wiggling monster from under the bed and drag her into the center of the bedroom.

Lana stared at Bella, eyes glassy with tears or in a trance. Her lips were pursed together tightly, and moving agitatedly as though she were mashing live insects between them.

"Please, stop," Bella pleaded, backing towards the bedroom door. But her mother continued to advance on her, gathering the leather belt. The girl opened the door and screamed before the door was pushed shut, and her body twirled around so she was face to face with her mother.

"Why don't you listen to me?" the woman asked in a loud, hoarse whisper as she wrung the belt. "Why do I have to do this?"

The girl ran towards the corner where Candy was and wrapped her arms around the dog. Svetlana, whose movements were slow, lumbering at times, and resembled the unrushed movement of a hippo, took on the swiftness and smoothness of a gorilla with enormous power.

She pulled the girl off her sweet dog, and held her in front of her. "I can't stand your tantrums," she said through the grey streaks hanging messy and sweaty in her eyes. She threw her daughter on the bed and watched as the child took a breath to speak. No words came, just a scream as the belt cracked across her pink, cotton shorts and the back of her legs.

"I don't like to do this to you, but it's the only way you listen to me." An immediate calm overtook Lana, making her stare ghostly and eerie.

The child threw herself at her mother's legs, sitting on her feet and clinging to her. "I'll be a good girl," she said.

Lana dropped the belt, pushed the girl away and sat on the bed. Bella cried, her arms around her knees. It was in this detente that Lana heard the knocking on the door, and Ah Mui's voice.

"Miss Lana, please open door."

"What, Ah Mui?" Lana snapped.

"Miss Lana, please open door."

Lana pulled open the door angrily, startling Ah Mui. "What do you want?" Lana snapped. "I'm busy."

There was a pause as Ah Mui peered around Lana into the room. "You want Bella come with me?"

"No." Lana closed the door.

Ah Mui saw the girl's head rise, little sobs escaping from her tear-drenched mouth. "Miss Lana, your coffee ready. You come now?"

"Yes, just a minute." This time Lana closed the door and sat down on the bed. She fidgeted in her pockets, crackling paper and plastic until she pulled out a cigarette and a box of matches. There was a deep inhalation and a smoke-filled sigh. "You are so difficult. I don't know how to deal with you." Lana's body shook as one sob after another trembled from her contorted lips.

The child approached her mother, sat on the bed and leaned into her. The woman looked up with red, droopy eyes.

"You're impossible, but I'm sorry I had to do that." The ash from her cigarette fell on the floor.

"No." The child's reply threatened to become hysterical again. "I'm sorry." She looked up into the woman's dark, sad eyes and said, "I'm a bad girl."

The two sat side by side, clouded in cigarette

smoke, tears running. Bella lifted her mother's dead weight arm and draped it around her shoulders, where Lana let it hang as she stared at the floor, her thoughts already elsewhere.

That evening after dinner, as Dima, Lana and Bella sat with after dinner drinks, Dima noticed the marks on Bella's legs, as she leaned across the sofa to reach her doll. He picked up the child. Standing, he looked at Lana, his jaw tight, and walked out of the living room towards Bella's room.

"I couldn't stop her from screaming until I took the belt to her," Lana called after him. She stroked Candy's silky fur, pursed her lips and made kissing sounds in her face. She opened the silver box on the living room table and took a cigarette. "I told you I needed to get away," she said too softly to be heard. Her finger flicked the lighter on, and she pushed the tip into the flame. A sense of calm seeped into her body.

Dima walked back into the room and sat beside her. "You can't do that."

Lana exhaled a smoke cloud over their heads and put her cigarette in the ashtray. "I didn't hit her that hard. Just a smack or two like I do to stop Candy from barking."

"You left marks on her legs," Dima said, taking a deep breath, his eyes trained on Bella's room.

"She was screaming."

"She's three years old." His voice was strained, like he was trying not to scream, like he often did. That was another good thing about having a child in the house — he didn't want to frighten her by shouting.

Ice cubes clinked, as Lana took a sip of her gin and tonic. "I can't control her."

"No, you can't." He leaned back on the sofa, fingers raking through his shock of white hair.

"I need a break," Lana said, taking a sip of her drink.

"From what? A life of not working and being waited on by servants?"

"What do you know? You are at work all day." She

stared into the glass and exhaled. "I need more time."

"Yes, I see." Dima's shoulders slumped forward. They sat for a few moments without speaking with only the sounds of sloshing and clinking between them, as Lana swirled her drink. Dima leaned toward Lana. "How about we have Nina come here for a visit? You can go back to France with her on a holiday before you head to Israel."

Lana looked up at her husband and placed her free hand over her heart.

"Really?" Before he could answer, she committed him. "Yes, that would be nice, very nice." She would do well having time alone in Israel and being on holiday with the only other person she felt could truly understand her hell.

The Swimming Lesson

June 1971
  Hong Kong

Bella wiped her sandy hands on her sun-bronzed belly
and admired the sand piles she had just made. She
picked up her pail and held it out to her mother who
sat nearby, examining the myriad of broken shell
pieces around her feet. Summer was warming the
waters of Repulse Bay Beach.

"Lana, could you get me some more water, please?"

"Aren't you finished yet?" Lana asked.

"No. I want to put one more tower."

"Why don't you get some water then?"

"But, I'm not supposed to go near the water,
because I can't swim yet."

"Come, I'll show you how to swim," Lana said,
grabbing her floral swim cap and standing.

Bella looked at the water, then towards her
father. Dima was approaching after a jaunt towards
the towering statues of the Chinese gods at the edge
of the beach. Beside him was a younger woman. Bella
loved her strong voice, big smile and light blue
eyes that sparkled like the sunlit sea. Nina had
come from France to visit them and then travel
around Europe with Lana. Had the gods smiled upon
the twenty-seven-year-old two years ago, she would
have been their daughter-in-law; instead, she had
claimed the role as Bella's godmother.

Nina waved at Bella who waved back with both arms,
then pointed to herself before dropping the pail.
She took Lana's outstretched hand and they stood at

the water's edge. Lana pulled her cap onto her head. Bella let the water tickle her toes as it meandered in, and bury her feet as it rushed away, swirling and sucking away sand.

"Ready?"

Bella's face contorted as her sun-warmed body adjusted to the water's cool, almost cold, embrace. "What do I do?" Bella asked as the water rose around her with each step.

"Swim." Lana waded into the darkening green sea of the bay.

Bella tried to dodge the waves bouncing off Lana's body and wiped water from her face with her free hand.

"How do I swim?" Bella asked as a splash of water jumped into her mouth. She coughed it out and wiped her face one last time before grabbing Lana's arm with both hands and trying to scramble close enough to wrap her legs around her mother's. But, Lana straightened her arm, and Bella had to bounce-walk into the sea. As the water came closer to her ears, it grew louder. For a moment, Bella felt her feet lifting off the sand. The next moment, her face was submerged, her eyes were cold, and she was in a silent world of green and gold. Her feet touched sand, and she pushed against it. The water slapped against her ears for a moment before she saw the carpet of green stretching out towards the faraway mountains. Then, all went silent again and her feet once more felt the ground. She pushed off the bottom and burst through the water again.

I'm swimming, she thought to herself. She kicked her legs back and forth; her face was in the air and her eyes blinked rapidly. She opened her mouth to tell her mother. But, no sound came, just a burning in her lungs. Then she saw her mother's big, slow legs plodding in the moving light patterns of this quiet world.

Before Bella's feet could reach the ground, arms wrapped around her chest and pulled her quickly into the air. Nina was behind her, holding her close and screaming. A fountain of water poured from Bella's mouth, and she began to cough. Nina turned Bella and held her tightly against her.

"Oh my God, Svetlana." Nina patted the spluttering Bella on the back. "What are you doing?"

Lana continued to look at the horizon. "Giving her a swimming lesson," she said, tucking stray strands of hair into her swim cap.

"You could have drowned her," Nina said, leaning back to look at Bella, whose face was streaked with strands of hair that stuck to her like cooked rice vermicelli.

"Nonsense," Lana said, gliding her fingers through the water, "swimming is an automatic response."

"No, it's not." Nina moved the hair off Bella's face, held her tight again, rocking her.

"She was starting to swim."

"She was starting to drown." Nina's voice was high and fast. "Don't take my goddaughter from me. I've already lost Volodya. "She turned and splashed her way back to the beach.

Lana froze at the mention of her son's name, usually never said out loud. She stared after Nina and narrowed her eyes, then scooped water into cupped hands which she lifted over her head. She exhaled loudly, as the water ran down her face and neck and took a few steps forward. Stretching out her arms, she bent her knees until the water was above her shoulders. She kicked her legs, as the elegant elbows and hands of each arm alternately bent, lifted, reached out and dove into the deep green of the South China Sea.

As her head bounced on Nina's shoulder, Bella watched Lana swim away, and tried to memorize the movements for the next swimming lesson.

Stepping on Toes

Bella sat on the wooden chairs of the Peak Tram in her pale pink leotard and tights. Lana had left days earlier with Nina, so they could travel around France before Lana continued alone to Israel for her usual month-long pilgrimage. Dima and Bella would join her for her final two weeks in Israel. In the meantime, twenty-five-year-old Suyin had been hired to assist Ah Mui with Bella's many activities. This included taking the girl to her twice-weekly ballet class. However, Lana forgot to tell Suyin that on Tuesdays, Bella did not go to the Helena May on Garden Road, but to the old ballet school tucked away on Old Peak Road.

"Are you sure you know where you are going?" Bella asked, as the tram descended the steep hill. "I never took a tram there before."

"Yes, Mei Mei." Suyin patted the girl's hand.

"Are you sure my mother told you?" Bella's whine grew louder, as she felt a pain growing in her stomach.

Suyin continued to walk behind the blue walls of St. John's Church to the elegant entrance of the Helena May.

Bella looked at the doorway, her mouth open and tears welling. "This is the wrong place." She hit Suyin on the arm and stamped her foot. "Why didn't you listen to me? Now I'm going to be late."

Suyin patted Bella's arms, as if putting out a fire on her pink cardigan. "Okay, shh, shhh."

155

"You know where to go?" Suyin asked in Cantonese.

"It's on the way to the Jewish Club."

"Okay," Suyin said, waving her arm at a taxi coming down the hill. "We take taxi."

Bella stepped into the red vehicle, and Suyin scuttled in next to her.

"Go where she tells you," Suyin said.

"That way," Bella pointed up Garden Road.

The taxi driver looked at Bella, then at Suyin as he pulled out into the road and drove, following the child's pointed finger.

"Why does your daughter speak like she's a foreigner?" the driver asked.

"She's not my daughter," Suyin replied, her expression unchanged. "I'm her amah."

"Why does she speak English?"

"Why do you speak Chinese?" Bella shot back in English, irritated at the conversation.

"Oh," he said, smirking. "She understands me."

"Yes. She understands what she hears and notices." Suyin replied softly.

"What do you mean?" Bella asked. Suyin rubbed her eye and did not answer. Bella crumpled her face in a mixture of curiosity mingled with anger because it looked as though the partially-amputated third and fourth finger of Suyin's right hand had been sucked into her eye. Suyin quickly tucked her hand under her right thigh and gazed out of the window.

Bella's body relaxed. "Stop there," she told the driver, pointing to the school. "How long do I have?" she asked, turning to Suyin.

Suyin turned her wrist to show Bella her watch face and said, "Five minutes early."

"You are lucky I'm already dressed," Bella said.

Suyin took money out of her purse and placed it into the palm of the driver's hand.

"What happened to your fingers?" He stared at her missing digits.

Bella watched as a redness engulfed Suyin's face and said, "Mind your own beeswax." She tugged on Suyin's arm. "Let's go."

Suyin nodded to Bella, thanked the driver and

followed Bella. The driver looked at Bella and shook his head as he drove off.

"Come on, Suyin. We have to hurry."

Suyin nodded, following as she sniffled and again wiped her eye.

"You have a cold," Bella said weakly. "Drink ginger lemon tea when we get home, and you will be all better."

Suyin nodded again but said nothing. She pressed her lips together. Her eyes were moist and her pocked-marked cheeks were still red. The white blouse she wore today had a frilly collar, and she carried a black cloth handbag behind which hid her hand.

Had Suyin dressed up for this little outing? Bella wondered. For just the hour she was going to sit with other mothers and watch ballet in the big auditorium of the Helena May? Bella felt a huge ball of sadness press hard against her chest and a strange, squeezing in her belly made her feel sick.

"Suyin," the child said, her voice breaking as it flooded with shame and regret.

"Yes, Miss Bella."

Miss Bella? Usually she called her Mei Mei, like she was Suyin's little sister. Bella gently took Suyin's damaged hand and rubbed it against her cheek. She could feel Suyin's hidden tears pressing against her own heart. "Next time you have to listen to me, so I don't have to yell at you." She looked up and smiled at Suyin. "But, everything is okay now, right?"

Although Suyin smiled, Bella could feel the weight of what had passed between them, and knew that things were not okay. This, too, would not last.

Life with Ghosts

June 1971
  Israel

Bella lay on the bed and looked around the room. She folded her arms across her chest and huffed. She would not have a fun summer here.

This house was dirty and old. Long cracks stretched like a tree from the ground to the seam between the wall and ceiling, branching into small twigs that splintered across the wall. The grown-ups' books were yellowed and dusty, and there were no children's books or toys.

The other places she had gone to with Dima on her way here had been so much fun. At the Marco Polo Hotel in Singapore, she had ordered spaghetti bolognese in the restaurant both nights and played Marco Polo in the pool with other children.

When she and Dima lived at the house next to his office in Jakarta, Indonesia, she had eaten sweet coconut stew and played by the pool all day with the servants there. *Why did Lana want to come to this house? It was so hot and boring, and there was no one to do the work for them.*

Bella got up and stepped onto the balcony. She leaned against the thin railing and looked into the garden below. Deep yellow oval fruit peeked through the shiny, dark green leaves. She trudged into Lana's room. "Are you sure we can't reach those mangos?"

"No. I told you we will borrow the neighbour's ladder when they get home later." Lana was sitting on her bed wearing her long white nightie.

"Why are you going to bed? You said you would play Gin Rummy with me."

"After I rest."

"Why do you always need to rest?"

"Because you make me tired."

"No, I don't. That's not fair."

"Not everything in life is fair."

"What am I supposed to do?"

"You can nap with me or entertain yourself until I wake up," Lana said, patting Dima's side of the bed.

"But I'm not tired."

"So go downstairs and watch television with Dima." Lana stood and guided Bella towards the door.

"There's nothing on. And it's all in Hebrew or Russian."

"That's a good way to practice your languages." She nudged the child out of the room.

"Fiiiiiine," Bella shouted at the closing door.

Lana's bedroom door closed and there was a click as the door to the room across the hallway opened. Since her arrival one week ago, the room had been locked except for Lana moving in and out to open and close the windows and adjust the shuttered balcony doors. When Bella had asked if she could go in and see the room, Lana had brusquely told her to leave it alone. Bella had tried to peek through the long door shutters from the adjoining balcony of their rooms but couldn't see anything.

Bella took a deep breath and approached the partially open door. She stopped when Dima's chair creaked. She heard the dial on the television click once, twice, three times, as Dima switched channels until he settled on a show in Russian. This one had no people laughing, just spooky music. The chair creaked again, this time groaning as Dima fell into it with a sigh. As Bella touched the thin, metal door handle, its coolness moved through her body, and she shivered.

"Hello?" she said in a whisper she thought would be loud enough for someone inside the room to hear but quiet enough for her mother not to hear.

"Hello?" A jolt of excitement and fear danced

through her thin body as she remembered a story she had read about Bluebeard in *A Book of Russian Children's Stories*.

"Can I come in?" Bella asked almost imperceptibly.

No answer. She pushed the door and peeked in but only saw the wall. Moving no closer, she pushed the door once more and a little more until she pushed as much as her outstretched arm could reach without stepping forward. She took in a quick breath. This was not a storage room, or what her family called the "box room." There was no dehumidifier running to keep piles of blankets or shelves of books from getting mildewy. There were no coats with pockets filled with bags of mothballs. This was a bedroom. Not an empty room for visitors. This had been or maybe still was someone's bedroom.

Dust particles danced, swirling in streams of light that shot out from the angled blinds. Books and papers covered the desk in ordered piles. The top sheet of a yellowed notepad lifted in the cross-breeze, revealing scrawled notes in faded ink. There was no one in the room now. It looked as though someone had just left — gone to the bathroom or left to make a cup of tea, leaving the bed blanket thrown aside, a pillow with an indentation where the head would be, flip flops kicked off by the bed and a green windbreaker tossed over the desk chair.

Bella inched closer to the desk and peered at a small silver frame with a photo of two people with the same oval face. Lana and a young man. One arm relaxed around her shoulders, a large, homemade card with three candles below the number 23 in his other hand. His sparkling eyes looked straight at Bella. Lana looked like Lana — a cigarette in her hand, but there was something unfamiliar. She was looking over her shoulder, her body relaxed. She was smiling at the man who looked like her and holding a tin bucket of green-yellow mangos. Her eyes were shiny, so happy, so filled with love, that Bella realised what feeling unloved might feel like. Her throat felt scratchy and dry, the corners of her mouth turned downward and trembled, as she realized that this was a photograph of the son that died.

A sensation of boney, cold, fingers creeped along Bella's neck and arms. The familiar tingle wiggled through the child's body, this time, urging her out of the room and away from its secrets.

Learning How To Entertain

July 1971
  Hong Kong

Lana returned from her trip to Israel with her usual
pocketful of suffering, a souvenir that she had
acquired two years ago and could not — would not —
release. Although she had learned, on her flight
home, that Suyin quit her job as their amah, Lana
had an air of relief about her. As though she had
discarded a heavy coat. Her step was lighter, her
frowns less frequent, her attention span and focus
on Bella longer and more tolerant. This sense of
renewal came at the perfect time, as a party was in
order for Bella's fourth birthday party.

The Hoffman's parties were the talk of the
community and took weeks to plan. They involved
lists in Lana's lined legal pads, phone calls to
everyone to see which dates worked, handwritten
invitations, the servants' network to make sure the
event was staffed and a comprehensive menu. Bella
knew that the party ended with a freshet of gifts
from the guests.

Bella followed Lana from the piles of letters and
bills stacked on top of the dining room sideboard to
the bedroom bureau, watching as she pulled out pads
and curled pages over in search of a blank page.
Unsuccessful, she let the sheets of paper unroll,
rushing one over the other with a faint clapping
sound like cards being shuffled. She replaced the
pads into a pile and continued her search.

"I knew I had a blank pad here," she said,

hoisting a blank pad into the air, as though it were a flag of victory. "Now, where is my pen?" Lana rummaged through her handbag, picked out a packet of cigarettes, shook it, crumpled it, and dropped it back into the bag. She fished out her silver Parker pen, again with a triumphant wave, then situated herself at the dining table. Here, pen tapping against her lip as she pondered, she drew up the logistics for each elaborate dinner party. There was a list for the guests, one for the food to serve, another for the food to buy and yet another list for the helpers she would need and the dishes and glasses to use.

A spray of apple juice shot through the air as Bella bit into an apple. She sat across from the master planner, flipping back and forth between lists, listening to the mutterings and occasional comprehendible comments that made Bella uncertain if Lana was talking to her or to herself. "I can't invite Sophie if Renee is coming." Lana scratched out the top name and continued her formulations. "We have to have fish since Sophie doesn't eat meat."

Although Lana wrote in the name of each guest, the date and time on the invitations, Bella's job was filling in the telephone number on the RSVP line of each invitation. Each invitation was the possibility of a new doll or a game or a book from the guests. At very least, there would be a box of Quality Streets, the delicious and different-shaped chewy and crunchy chocolate and toffee combinations encased in bright foils and translucent wrappers. Sometimes, there would be a box with so many chocolate varieties that the box had its own little book and map that showed the flavour of the treat at each location within the box. At her first big party, where she met Lana and Dima's friends, she had received so many presents that Dima brought her back a white trunk from his trip to the Philippines to store them.

*****

Bella dodged the staff weaving in and out of the kitchen with plates, glasses and linens. She stood on her toes to peer at the trays on the counters. Thin, rolled up, sheets of orange smoked salmon were placed on white crackers and sprinkled with sprigs of dill. These filled the left side of the three sectioned crystal platter. In the center, oily fish, bigger than Bella's fingers, lay side by side. These had not come from the fish market or the Fish Man. Ah Mui had fished these out of a glass jar. Rings of red onion decorated their headless bodies. On the other end of the platter, the same circular white crackers balanced stacks of tiny, round orange balls of salmon roe. Before Ah Mui could wrap the platter and put it into the refrigerator, Bella picked up a several goopy, sticky balls and put it into her mouth. She rolled them around the back of her front teeth, feeling them warp, as she pressed on them gently. When they burst, she tasted a saltiness that reminded her of the sea spray at the beach.

Glass and crystal platters, dishes and plastic containers were stacked on top of one another in the refridgerator. Unable to fit her fingers into the bowl of deviled eggs without knocking over the dish of asparagus spears, Bella slid out an asparagus spear from underneath the plastic wrap and dropped it into her mouth, like a bird swallowing a word. Chewing, she searched for the pillameny, but realised that the small meat dumplings would probably be coming from Baba's house since she was the one who made those. Bella poked at the kholodetz. The translucent loaf of pieces of chicken, carrots and parsley suspended in gelatin wobbled. She turned her nose up and closed the door.

Steam rose from the rice cooker. Ah Mui's cleaver sliced through chicken breasts that Lana had bought from the store earlier that day. Four large cans of sliced button mushrooms stood unopened by the stove. Bella clapped and let out a 'Yay!'. They were having chicken stroganoff for dinner.

The front door opened.

"Dima." Bella ran to him with open arms. "Why are you home so early?"

He hugged Bella and looked at the chaos around them. "I came home to help Lana prepare for the guests," he said. "Please bring me a cup of tea," he said to Ah Mui, who was adding mushrooms to the large pot of stroganoff.

She muttered to the other amah in the kitchen, who put down a tea towel and glass and began filling up the kettle with water. Dima removed his jacket and threw it across the sofa. He walked to the other end and sat down with an extended, echoing exhale. "So, tell me about your day," he said.

The commotion continued around them as starched white linens flapped and fell onto make-shift tables made of sawhorse legs and long, wood boards, delicately-patterned plates, glistening stemware and rows of silverware embellished the tabletops.

Lana appeared and disappeared from the living room several times, her hair in curlers one time, uncombed another and finally set in the sticky hold of hair spray. When she finally appeared, fully dressed and accessorized in her favourite aqua dress and long strand of pearls, she tutted at Dima and Bella.

"Please put your jacket away." She picked up the jacket and handed it to Dima who had removed his shoes and placed his feet on the coffee table.

"Time to get ready," he said, winking to Bella who stood up with him.

"Bella, aren't you washed yet?" Lana put her hands on her hair, as though she was a magician trying to create a spell. "Ah Mui," she called, "Bella still needs to have a bath." There was no reply, and Lana tapped one of the helpers. The young woman stopped, an empty tray in her hands. "Could you please help my daughter wash?"

"No." Bella put her arms around Dima and hid her pouty face. "I don't know her."

"Come on, I'll see that you are washed. Just don't splash me," Dima said holding out his hand.

Candy barked each time the doorbell rang, and Bella ran to the front door. Guests entered, their custom-tailored suits and designer dresses accessorized with pocket handkerchiefs and sparkling broaches and necklaces. Bella hugged the guests that she knew and shook hands with those she did not, all the while deciphering the packages in their hands that held bottles of alcohol, or boxes of chocolates. The bags had the valuable treasure, like dolls, games and stuffed animals.

Dinner devoured and plates removed from the table, the guests sat against the backs of the dining chairs with a hand in their pockets or arms across their chests, relaxing. Dima stood up and tapped a dessert fork against his wine glass.

"Many of you were here last year when we toasted to Bella for the first time. Now, I ask you to toast her again and wish her a happy fourth birthday."

The room fell into darkness illuminated by the living room light. The tune of "Happy Birthday" summoned Ah Mui and her helper into the dining room with a cake, an arc of glowing candles above it. Ah Mui cleared a space in front of the birthday girl, whose warmed skin beamed in the candlelight. Bella joined in with the clapping and blew the flames out as she had seen Baba do for her birthday cake last month.

She pointed to the cake and read, "Happy Birthday, Bella." She raised her arms when she was done, commanding a round of applause and cheers from the guests. Taking unusual pleasure in being the center of attention, Bella decided to thank the guests for her gifts, which included another Barbie doll, a Lite Brite and a book about Queen Elizabeth. She lifted her right hand level to her face. Palm open and her thumb in front of her fingers, she performed the royal wave. Rotating herself to the left and right, she undulated her hand to the sea of Westerners around her, as she spoke. "I thank you all for your kindest wishes," she said with a precision and an accent that was becoming so British every day that it was hard for her to remember ever sounding like anyone else.

A Rose by Any Other Name

August 1971

It was an unusually grey morning. Bella, still in her pajamas and the gentle embrace of wakefulness, walked into the living room. She walked to the window, as she always did, before deciding what to wear that day.

Standing on her tippy-toes, she reached up for the window handle, which she could just reach with the end of her fingers. She stopped. Vibrations tingled from the cold steel. She placed her feet flat on the ground. She had a strange sensation but did not know what it meant. She reached up again, grasped the edge of the long handle and pulled down. The window opened forcefully, as though someone, something, had been on the other side and grabbed it and pulled it open wide, lifting Bella off the floor completely until her belly was resting on the window ledge.

Perched on the ledge, her fingers held onto the handle as the window shook in all directions. A small clear rectangle jerking itself free from the house to fly away like her mother's stationery pad, her father's newspaper and the cloth napkins that were being sucked out of the room into the hammering rain and grey abyss.

A flash of lightning splintered the grey, and a crashing of thunder bellowed but the child, still in a state of dreamy wakefulness, held onto the handle, watching as the top hinge of the window cracked. Strong, erratic vibrations shot through her hand. This time, she was jolted away, letting go as the window rocked in the wind, ripped free from the top hinge, then the bottom, and disappeared into the grey.

Balanced precariously on the window ledge, Bella gazed into the distance as the window spiraled away from her, into the mouth of a giant demon, that was inhaling everything around it. The child felt the pull of the great monster, but she also felt an invisible pull that set her feet back on the dining room floor. She stood in front of the gap where the window used to be, rain spitting in her face and her hair blowing around her face. Suddenly aware of the rush of activity in the house, she turned around slowly.

In a blink that snapped her into complete awareness, she saw the surrounding chaos. Sections of newspaper twirled around the house, the curtains in the far end of the living room were flapping in the air. The long, precious Asian silk scroll paintings held down by decorative ceramic weights slapped against the wall. The table cloth was askew, and the boxes of cereal and powdered skim milk had toppled to the ground, sprinkling bits of white granules and yellow flakes around the dining room.

Candy lay partially hidden under the coffee table. Her father stood immobile at the doorway to the dining room, his face drooped, like it was melting away in despair and horror. Ah Mui bumped him as she rushed past, startling him back to life. He moved towards the window, a folded chair in his left hand. He placed his right hand on Bella's shoulder, guiding her towards the corner of the room, into the sheltered space between the wall and the buffet, and pushed her down into a crouching position. He lay a folded deck chair over the bottom half of the window. It clanged, fighting like a fish gasping in air, until it was sucked flat against the window frame.

"Another chair. We need another chair," he yelled, the vortex outside the house, sucking away his voice.

Ah Mui appeared with another folded deck chair that they used on the boat and held it over the

168

second half of the window. Lana appeared with string and a large pair of scissors, and the three adults began to tie down the chairs against the open frame, looping the brown twine through the latches of all the other windows. Though wind still roared through the plastic slats of the window, Bella's hair, no longer whipping around her face, splayed slightly around her head in a static halo; the notepapers and playing cards that had been whirling around the room lay scattered on the floor.

As the grownups stepped back to check their handy work, Bella stood quietly, her body shivering. Ah Mui wrapped her in her pastel pink wool blanket and placed her in the cozy armchair a safe distance from all the activity. The little girl wanted to laugh and cry, but she just stared wide-eyed, her pupils large, her breathing shallow. The memories of the vibrations in her hand when she touched the window, her balancing perilously on the window ledge and looking into the mouth of a hungry demon lingered in her memory.

Dima's face appeared in front of hers. "Why did you open the window?" His fist was clenched, so was his jaw.

Bella thought for a moment, searching for an answer besides that it was what she did everyday.

"To see if it is hot or cold, so I know what clothes to wear."

Bella's father shook his head. "Why do you need to know what to wear? You're not going outside."

"Why?" she replied, more out of habit, than curiosity.

"There's a typhoon." He waved towards the window then threw his arms in the air. "How did you not know there was a typhoon? Can't you hear the wind? Don't you see that you can't see outside?" He raised his voice, in anger or his deafness from the previous whirlwind. "Don't ever open the window in a typhoon again."

"Dima . . .," Lana said softly from behind him. She stood perfectly still, as though she was trying not to attract the attention of a wild animal.

"Dima, nothing," he replied in Russian. "It's just my voice. It's just volume. That's not going to hurt her."

"She's just a child," she said in an unusual and quiet defense of the little girl.

He looked at Bella's lips, tightly squeezed together to restrain the quivering efforts of a cry. His tone softened. "She could have been killed," he muttered. He made a fist with his right hand. "Do we need that, again?" He pulled and pushed on the deck chairs to check that they were secure, then plonked himself down at the dining table. "God, almighty," he spat under his breath.

Lana patted Bella on the head, glanced towards Ah Mui and gently pushed the child towards the amah before joining Dima at the table.

Except for the growling and whistling through the chair slats, and Dima shaking the now-half-empty box of cereal into his bowl, there was no noise. As Ah Mui led Bella into the bedroom to get dressed, Bella looked at the remaining windows, crisscrossed with brown twine. She looked at her father, sitting with elbows on the table, hands fisted in one another as he stared into his meagre serving of cereal, the muscles in his jaw, clenching and releasing.

Once in her room, the young girl looked up at Ah Mui. "What is ty-phoon?" she asked in English.

Ah Mui tilted her head, as though processing the question. *"Toi fung,"* she answered in Cantonese. Still, the girl did not show any sign of understanding. Ah Mui picked up the little girl and they stood by the bedroom window. "A typhoon means a big wind that can blow and break things," she said, pointing towards the park below where tree branches shook violently. "And, see there," she said, tapping higher up on the window.

In the distance, the flag outside the residence of the Japanese Consul General's house waved erratically, flashing glimpses of the red circle at the center of the flag. "When there is a typhoon, everything moves — even people and trees — so you must be careful and stay inside."

"I didn't know it was a typhoon," Bella said softly, sniffling as she wrapped her arms around Ah Mui's neck.

"Don't cry," Ah Mui replied softly. "Now you know." She bounced the little girl gently in her arms, adding, in Cantonese, "After every storm, there is new growth."

Yom Kippur Diet

September 1971

It was almost seven o'clock when Bella hurried into the dining room, hungry for breakfast after the early dinner the night before. Instead of the usual elegant setting of cups, plates and platters of fruit, Parma ham, Gruyere cheese, toast, butter and jam, there was only a simple place setting for Bella and Svetlana, but no food. Bella hurried into the kitchen, hoping she had not somehow missed the meal.

"Where's breakfast?" she asked Ah Mui.

"Jo sun," the amah replied with a smile.

Bella stopped peering at the counters and looked at Ah Mui. "Good morning, Ah Mui,' she replied in English." She scanned the stove. "Where's breakfast?"

Ah Mui pulled out a dish of ham, sliced cheese and fruit from the refrigerator. "For you, hungry girl," she said as she led Bella back into the dining room. "Your mother said not to show your father the food today."

Bella nodded and scooted onto her chair. Her father's belly had been getting round again, so he was probably on another diet. She picked up her fork, stabbed a square of honeydew and placed it onto her plate. "No Special K and powdered milk for him?"

"No food for master. He only eat dinner today,"Ah Mui answered as she tidied the girl's hair. Bella tore a slice of ham in strips, lay them across the melon, licked her fingers, rolled up the morsel and placed it into her mouth. She turned when she heard her parents' bedroom door open.

"Hello, Ah Mui," said Lana, "a small cup of coffee and toast, please."

"Good morning," Dima said, patting Bella on the head before making a high-pitched warble as he wiggled his fingers down to her armpits.

Bella poked her father in his belly. "Are you on a diet again?"

"No," he said with a laugh. He watched Bella point to his empty place setting. "Didn't you learn about Yom Kippur at Sunday School yet?"

"What is it?" Bella asked, now busy tearing up more ham strips.

"It's a holy day which Jews observe by fasting or not eating for a whole day." Dima sat at the table, placed his bible, yarmulka and Tallit in front of him, taking care not to let the short bobby pin on his blue-toned yarmulka catch the fringe of the white shawl.

"Not eat for a whole day? That doesn't sound like a holiday."

"It's a *holy* day. And it's not a day to be happy," Lana said, as she buttered her toast."Why are you eating? " Bella, asked. "Don't you like to celebrate Yawn Keeper?"

Lana shook her head and bit into her toast resolutely. "No," she said nonchalantly through a full mouth, "I'm wasn't always Jewish."

"Really?" Bella turned to Dima. "How about me? Was I always Jewish?"

Dima paused and nodded slowly. "Of course you are Jewish," he replied, looking at Lana with a raised eyebrow.

"Then, I shouldn't have eaten breakfast," Bella said, bothered, as she put the last piece of melon in her mouth and pushed away her plate.

"You don't have to fast," Dima said with a chuckle. "You're only four." He looked at his watch and caught Lana's eye. She quickly drank a gulp of coffee as Dima stood up. "That's good because I think I would die if I couldn't eat all day," Bella replied, scooting off her chair to give her father a hug. "So, you're not even eating lunch at work?"

"Correct. There's no food and no work on Yom Kippur," Dima said, nodding as he kissed her head.

"No work, sounds like fun," Bella said. "But, where are you going then?"

"I'm going to the synagogue with Baba and Deda, to pray."

"For Yawn Keeper?"

Another laugh. "Yes, for Yom Kippur."

"And, you're not even going to have rice pilaf or coconut macaroons at the Jewish Club?"

"No," said Dima as Lana picked up her car keys and walked to the door.

"Really?" Bella said. "You are so brave and strong." She patted her father's arm. "Just don't think about food, and you will be okay."

"Sounds like a good idea," Dima said, bending down for another hug.

"I don't think I would be okay. I would be so hungry." Bella walked her parents to the door and waited for them to get into the lift. She waved to them. "Don't worry, Dima. You won't starve," she said brightly, "I'm going to eat your breakfast for you." And, with that, Bella closed the front door and resumed her spot at the dining table. "Ah Mui, breakfast please!"

Nannies and Monsters

October 1971

Months after Bella's tantrums had chased Suyin out of the Hoffman household, Ah Mui left the Hoffmans. She decided to work in Bertha and Boris' tranquil home. Although Ah Mui had said her decision was based on the amount of work in the Hoffman household, and that she did not want to take care of the dog, Lana was certain Bella's "unpleasant personality," was to blame.

Bella was enrolled in preschool, ballet class and spent many afternoons and weekends with her grandparents but Lana decided the girl needed more attention. So, this time Lana was determined that Bella had someone who could take care of her and be available to her — a firm, less sisterly servant who wouldn't be intimidated by the girl. However, when Lana met Gang and his wife, Bik, she was so bewitched by their quiet obedience, she decided they would be the perfect staff for her.

Bella did not like Gang from the start.

Maybe it was how the top of his freckled, almost-bald head shone or how the remaining strands of hair wrapped around the side of his head like greasy, black noodles. Maybe it was the way the brown mark on Bik's left cheekbone looked like a tea stain on a white tablecloth and reminded Bella of Suyin. Bik made the beds, did the laundry, vacuumed the rugs, cleaned the vegetables and cooked while Gang sat staring stupidly at the television in the back room until everything was done. He served the food and

175

cleared the table to get face time and practice English with Bella's parents.

Gang and Bik argued in the kitchen every afternoon while Lana napped. Gang raised his voice as he fired off a slew of emotional sentences, his pointed finger darting in the air like a zealous conductor while Bik — nose scrunched as though she smelled something putrid — took out her annoyances on whatever she was doing, like dropping the pot on the stove or pounding the chicken for schnitzel.

But, it wasn't these frequent, angst-filled exchanges that alarmed Bella. These were at once troubling and comforting, as they reminded Bella of the discussions between her own parents. The child discovered the reason for her uneasiness when her parents were at a dinner party. That night, the girl ate dinner in the back of the kitchen in front of the small black and white television. Bik seated between her and Gang. Gang muttered to his wife.

"No," Bik replied, not moving.

Gang turned to Bik as he straightened his shoulders and inhaled, giving the impression that his body had increased in size. Bella tensed and glanced at Bik. Gang poked her arm hard enough that she leaned into Bella. Gang protested louder and pointed out of the kitchen, towards the sleeping dog in the hallway. Bella stared at the television, the black and white comedy and slapstick routines not as amusing as they were moments earlier.

Gang sprang to his feet, knocking his stool behind him. Bik stood and flung her arms down. She spat out grains of rice as she screeched a slew of words. She stormed towards the front door,

"Candy!" Bik grabbed the dog's choke collar and rammed it over the groggy dog's head.

Bella stood to follow Bik.

"Bella." Gang's voice was normal, calm. His straight-lipped smile, slick. "Bik come back soon." He picked up the stools and straightened them. He tapped the stool next to his. "You sit here. Wait for Bik."

Bella looked at the stool. When she looked back for Bik, the front door slammed. Bik and the dog were gone. Gang pointed to the television and the stool again. Bella returned to the stool and sat down. Gang tapped her arm.

He pulled at the sleeve of her cotton pajamas. Bella looked at him. Something inside her stomach was rolling and squeezing; making her feel sick.

"Ve-ly soff." Gang showed off his English as he rubbed his fingers together on the fabric. He smoothed his fingers across her hand. "Your skin, also soff." He drew out the 'o' in "soft," and spoke in slow motion, his mouth held open, as he breathed out the word.

Bella moved her hand away from him. She picked up her bowl. He stroked her leg. She shifted her leg, pressed it closer to the other as she turned away from him. She shoveled rice grains and vegetables into her mouth. She stared at the television over her shoulder even though she couldn't hear anything except the pulsing inside her eyes and the sound of him gulping down his saliva between each word.

"Is the skin on your leg soft?" Gang asked her, now in Chinese. The child didn't answer or move. Gang repeated himself, louder. The child shrugged her shoulders.

"I will tell you," Gang said. He stroked and patted himself on the chest.

"No." Bella heard herself whisper, uncertain if the word actually came out.

"Come on. Just quickly show me your leg and I will know," he said and tugged her pants.

The child slid off the stool, her body feeling heavy and slow. She stood by the table just out of his reach.

Gang continued asking her to show him her leg. "Just a little?" He pouted and tipped his head sideways. "For Gang. I always look after you when your mother and father go out."

Bella's body sagged forward, trying to hide itself the way a snail shriveled into itself when it was touched. She took her foot out of her slipper and placed it on the chair. She began rolling up her pant leg.

"No." Gang put his hand on hers. "The other way."

The child did not understand.

Gang put his hands by his waist, pretended to grip the top of his pants and moved his hands towards his knees.

"Huh?"

Gang repeated the motion. He reached forward, took Bella's arm and moved her until she stood in front of him. He put her hands on her waist and pulled her pants down

"No." The child shook her head.

"Come on," Gang said, an edge in his voice now.

The child obeyed. She put her hands on the top of her pajama pants and pulled them down to her knees in one quick movement. Still clutching the elastic waistband, she started to pull up her pants.

Gang held out his hand to stop the child. "Wait."

She'd never seen his eyes like this before. So big and round. The white part so large and frightening. The child looked down, tugged at her tee-shirt and put her hands in front of her.

Gang put his hands on his pot belly.

He slid them down to his waistband. "You see my legs, now," he told her in broken English.

The child shook her head and yanked up her pants.

Without standing, Gang pulled down the front of his drawstring pants. The child's face froze in a contorted expression. Trying to understand what it was, she stared at the strange swollen shapes protruding from the mass of black hair. An explosion of sour vomit filled her throat. She swallowed it, making herself gag.

The front door opened, and Gang let go of the front of his pants. They snapped closed, swallowing the grotesque creature. The child ran out of the kitchen, past Bik, and into her bedroom. She shut the door but reopened it almost immediately.

"Candy. Candy." Bella's voice strained from the loud whisper. As the dog trotted towards the room, the child grabbed her by the scruff of the neck and tugged her into the room. She closed the door and sat onto the floor, her arms wrapped around Candy's neck.

Bella looked up through the windows at the almost-full moon above. She turned away when swirling shadows of clouds moved, contorting like deformed monsters with arms and tentacles that reached down to poke and grab her.

The child lay next to Candy, on the old rug stained with dog accidents, and fell asleep, hoping for better dreams.

*****

Lana sat at the dining table observing Bella's bad behaviour towards the servants. It was the girl's blatant disregard for them that had given the family a reputation among the servant network. That's why only a few applicants for the helper position. They were lucky that Gang and Bik took the position, even though Bella had scowled at them when they were interviewing for the job. The girl had a lot to learn about respecting those below her station in life.

"No. Thank. You." Bella said to Gang, who stood beside her, offering a serving of mashed potatoes. Her voice was tight and there was an obvious air of displeasure about her, anger even, as she looked at her plate.

As Gang stepped away from the sullen child, he smiled and nodded his head at Lana. She softened her frown. She returned his smile and dropped her shoulders for Bella's terseness. When Gang stood beside her, she sat up, looked him in the eye. "Oh, thank you, Gang," she twittered, as she scooped a spoon of creamy, yellow mash on her plate. "It looks delicious."

"Bik is the one who made it," Bella said, looking at Dima who leaned back in his seat, hands on his belly, watching the exchange unemotionally, as though he were watching a cricket practice. Lana's mouth remained open and the serving utensils remained in the air as she tried to collect herself. She looked at Dima for support but he simply motioned towards the suspended utensils to hurry her along. She replaced the utensils in the bowl and looked at Gang. He smiled and made several micro-nods as he scrunched up his nose, as if to shrug off the incident. Lana winced and tilted her head, dropping her shoulders again in appreciation of his understanding. She was always apologizing for the girl's behaviour. She turned back to the table and huffed, as she looked at Bella, whose head remained downcast, only glancing up every now and then.

"Bella. You can't be rude to the servants," Lana said as Gang left the dining room.

"I'm not," the girl said, looking over her shoulder to make sure Gang had left the room.

"Maybe you think I don't know everything, but I see how you talk to them," Lana said.

"I don't like him," Bella gritted her teeth and put down her fork noisily against the plate.

"Bella," Dima said before shoving a spoonful of beef stew into his mouth. He continued to speak as he dispersed particles of food over his plate. "Don't break the china."

"He is an old man," Lana said giving Dima a look of exasperation. "You must be nice to him."

"Even if *he*'s not nice to me?"

"You're talking nonsense. I see how he treats you. He is very nice to you."

Bella opened her mouth, but Lana raised her voice. "And, yes, you always have to be polite to those around you, especially if they work for you." Lana stopped, looked to her husband. He gulped his soda water and filled his fork with mashed potatoes.

Lana resumed her cause, talking over the girl's protests. "You are a rich, little girl who cannot treat people like the way you do. This is why nobody will keep working for us." She shook her finger at Bella the way she did when she told Candy off for defecating in the house. "Learn to respect your elders."

"I'm not rude to him because he is old," Bella's voice quivered.

"You're just rude to him to be rude." Lana interjected, hoping to squelch Bella's ebullition of rage and concomitant tantrum.

"No."

"You're just acting like you are a spoiled child."

"No, I'm not."

"You're impossible. You just say 'no' all the

time."

"No, I don't."

"You, see? You just want to argue." Lana waved a hand in the air as if flicking off a bug.

"Khvatit." Dima picked up the napkin from his lap and threw it down on the table. "Can't I just have a quiet dinner without all this arguing about nothing?" he said in Russian, pressing against the back of the chair; breathing like a bull ready to charge.

Lana wasn't sure who to glare at. "Nothing?" she wanted to yell at him, but she knew his volume and force was far greater than hers, or at the girl, for causing this trouble. But, she didn't want to incite Dima further, so she glared at Bella as she put a forkful of stew and mash into her mouth and chewed deliberately

Bella looked towards the entrance to the dining room, then leaned over her plate. "I have to tell you something about Gang."

Lana took a sip of her water as she regarded Bella with a sideways glance. Dima picked up his napkin and placed it on his lap.

"Well, Bella. What do you want to say?" Lana asked, putting another forkful of food into her mouth. But, she stopped chewing as she looked at the girl who was quite subdued.

"What do you want to tell us?" Lana asked, regarding Bella's sudden quiet with suspicion.

Bella paused. "They fight all the time."

"So?" Lana said, again surprised by this statement that was not a declaration, but almost a question. "Dima and I argue all the time."

Dima didn't lift his head from his plate as he rolled his eyes. Bella also offered no rebuttal, only continued to eat her dinner. Although Lana was not used to having the last word, she liked the feeling.

Lana did not have the chance to relish this sense of being right for very long. One week after her defense of Gang, Bik appeared at the dining table with Lana's morning coffee, sporting a timid smile and a black eye. Lana fired the altercating couple with some reluctance, not because she was particularly fond of them, or their service, but because she dreaded having to put out the word that the Hoffman family were without servants and were, once again, looking for help.

Cook Envy

Lana had every intention of being more selective
about the next set of servants. However, given their
bad track record for keeping staff and the rumors
through the households of the expatriate community
that they were a difficult family, only one couple
showed up for an interview.

Lana and Bella sat at the dining room table with the
stiff shouldered Kwan and his plump wife, Wong.
Lana, distracted from her next question by man's
overbite, tapped a cigarette against her lips.
"Kwan, you were a professional chef?" she finally
asked.

"Yes, I many year cook for a small hotel in
Mongkok." He licked his lips nervously. "I cook meat
and chicken, and my especially-ty is desserts. I
make cream blu-lay and lazbelly taht."

Lana wiggled her eyebrows. "Oh, brulée and
raspberry tarts?" She looked at Bella with wide
eyes, and Bella nodded enthusiastically.

"Just show me photo and I can make." Kwan said
proudly, smoothing down his oily hair. "I go to
market and buy what to cook."

"Wong can clean the house and look after the
little girl." He pointed at Wong, who looked at her
husband, then at Lana, and nodded as though she
understood what he had just said. Kwan smiled to
reveal three protruding teeth.

A wry smile appeared on Lana's lips as she

considered a schedule with no cooking or food shopping. No meal planning and carefree parties could be organized by her full-time, in-house chef. Who else had a full-time chef? Delighted, she hired the husband and wife team on the spot.

Lana was thrilled, not only to have a master chef in the house that completely removed her from menu and kitchen-related chores, but to have someone that helped entertain Bella. There was a lightness to her step, a boom in her hosted social gatherings, and a general rise in her spirits.

The girl helped Kwan choose the weights to measure the ingredients that he balanced ingredients on a metal plate and hung off a notched wooden stick. She rolled pastry and helped cut and stack dough to create double-layered cookies. She nibbled on fat steak fries, and fruit tarts, crepes and cake.

When Kwan served three-course meals at her bridge functions and dinner parties, everyone was in awe of the dainty, rice-paper, wrapped hors d'oeuvres, the variety of appetizers, the delicate flavours of the smooth sauces, the richness of the chocolate cake and the way the tea biscuits crumbled and dissolved in their mouths.

Lana could not stop gushing about Kwan's culinary prowess. "He's a genius in the kitchen," she marveled. "His eclairs are better than the Mandarin Oriental's," she oohed. "I give him basic requirements and he does all the planning and shopping," she purred, "so I have time to relax." "He chooses the tastiest fish and vegetables, or maybe it's his cooking that makes all the food so delicious as well as beautiful. I don't know how I managed without him," she said with a sigh.

*****

Bella sat in her bedroom playing cards with the ever-smiling Wong. She handed a card to the woman, who nodded thankfully as though she had just been given a treasure. Bella frowned. She wanted to be mean to the amah, just to stop her from plastic grin and always saying, "Yes, Miss Bella."

Bella picked up a card and listened to Kwan

laughing with Lana as they discussed the upcoming dinner party. She didn't want to help Kwan cook anymore, or watch Lana go into the kitchen because she "just couldn't wait until dinner" to get a taste of the "divine" food. Bella didn't want to help Kwan measure flour, look at his greasy hair or the way the top row of his teeth hung over his crooked bottom teeth. Bella began to detest the dinner parties; watching the gluttonous guests talking through mouthfuls of the gooey sauces, slurping spoonfuls of creamy and chocolate crème brulées and making 'oohing' sounds.

Bella missed the twice weekly visits to the Dairy Farm supermarket with Lana. where she could look at the bright vegetables and fruits, and choose Australian macadamia chocolate chip cookies, Chocolate Club bars and barbecue potato chips for her daily snacks. But it wasn't just the buying a treat in the store or to see what else was new in the shops, or maybe bumping in a friend there, Bella missed going for the short drive to the supermarket, maybe visiting one of Lana's friends on the way there or going to the park to swing while Lana had a cigarette. Bella was tired of how Kwan hogged her mother's time and attention. Lana already had so little time to spend with her.

Kwan's cooking started tasting too salty, too sweet, too watery, or too dry and Bella ate less and less of it. Meanwhile, her complaints, pouting and tantrums increased.

"You used to like Kwan very much," Lana said.

"I don't like him anymore."

"Why are you being so difficult?"

"I'm not."

"If you don't behave, and Kwan leaves, then you won't have Wong to play with you anymore."

"I don't care." Bella folded her arms across her chest and frowned. "She's too boring." Why didn't Lana understand anything?

"Too boring?" Lana eyes moved jerkily, as though she wasn't sure which way to look. "That's nonsense." She put the cigarette in her mouth, tightened her lips and sucked in until the end glowed bright red. She blew smoke into the air and stamped the cigarette out.

"No, it's not," Bella said, her arm swatting at the cloud of smoke around them. "She just smiles and does whatever I want. It's like playing with a happy robot. Not even Candy is so, so, mechanical."

Lana's annoyance gave way to a look of confusion mixed with pity. "What am I going to do with you?"

When it was time for Kwan and Wong to leave the Hoffman house, Bella hid under the bed in the guest room by the front door. She saw Lana's leather shoes move towards Kwan's cloth ones and thought she heard her mother's voice break a little as she said, "Thank you so much for all your wonderful cooking. I'm so sorry it did not work out."

Bella heard a rustle of paper and Lana said, "This is a little something for you." There was an edge to her voice as she added, "I think you will be very happy with the new family."

"Thank you." Kwan replied. He bent down and put a long white envelope into one of his wicker baskets. He took his straw hat from the top of the other basket and stood. Lana opened the front door, and Kwan and Wong's feet moved toward it. Kwan's stopped. His knees bent and he called out, "Goodbye, Miss Bella."

Bella's face warmed. He could see her. She pulled herself further under the bed. She didn't answer or come out of her hiding place until her mother closed the door. Bella felt a mix of happiness and sadness as she ran to her mother.

"Now we get to do the shopping together again," she said, taking Lana's arm.

Lana lifted her arm away and shook her head. She was frowning, and her lips were tightly pursed, even though she had no cigarette in them.

"Why, Bella? Why do you do this to me?"

Bella stood, mouth agape, as she watched her mother walk away and close the bedroom door. The girl walked to the window where she stood watching the two figures. Wong was round, short and bobbled down the hill in a roly-poly motion. The tall and slim Wong walked unevenly. Had he always limped so badly?

The ocean in Bella's stomach churned and rolled again. She felt seasick, like she was going to vomit. She looked away just before the two figures disappeared from sight. She wanted to eat something. She walked into the kitchen and felt a kick in her chest. There was a platter of raspberry Linzer cookies on the counter — the otherwise empty counter, with no scales, no containers of flour, no strangely shaped, shiny cooking utensils. She gently took a beautiful, round cookie with a dot of sticky, bright red jam in its perfect center, and bit into it.

As the sugar and jam tingled on her tongue, the sweetness seeped into her brain. A tear rolled down her cheek as she realised there would be no more of these yummy treats.

Although Bella had to suffer Lana's frozen profile, sideways glances and minimal conversation for several days, and the stash of designer dinners were gone, within weeks Bella was once more cheerily playing in the kitchen and eating rice dotted with dace and black beans. Ah Mui had moved back into the Hoffman home, where she now had a plush, new mattress and a shiny, 19-inch television set.

Playing with the Past

Bella's index finger pressed gingerly on the keys of her late birthday/early Chanukah present, a new piano. She ran her fingers up and down the black and white keys that were so much bigger than the little keyboard of her plastic lap piano.

"Maybe this is too extravagant a gift for a four-year-old," Lana said to her father-in-law.

"Nonsense! This is the perfect time for her to learn," Boris said. "She just needs a good teacher to spark her interest, and she will be playing in no time."

The following week, Dima sat at the breakfast table with a fruit knife in hand. He sliced through the tops of a stack of envelopes and sorted through the pile of letters in response to his advertisement in the South China Morning Post for a University-degreed piano instructor.

While they waited for the perfect piano teacher, Bella continued to tap different sequences of keys, listening to the sound they made and matching it to the tune she was singing.

"Twink," Bella winced. That wasn't the right note. "Twink." Nope. Not that either. She moved her finger to the next white key. "Twink," There it was. Bella smiled. "Twinkle, twinkle, lit-," she sang before stopping and shaking her head. That's not the right note. "Twinkle, twinkle, little." Yes, that was it. By the time she was rooting around for the notes to "How I wonder," Dima was massaging his temples and sighing loudly. "When is the piano teacher coming?"

he asked Svetlana.

"Mrs. Moore will be here on Thursday afternoon," Lana said.

"Thank God for that."

"Why?" Lana smirked. "Do you think she will sound like Vladimir Horowitz after the first lesson?"

"Anything will be better than this."

Dima was wrong. Bella's piano playing became more structured after the first lesson, but still the repetitions were a musical nagging that made him irritable. Bella wasn't too excited about the practices either and less about both the teachers that had shown up one after the other, each doing their best to relay the "importance of the fundamentals," encourage the girl through theory and insist on the scales and repetitious *Dozen-a-Day* exercises.

"Mrs. Moore is so boring." Bella ladled a spoon of warm borscht into her mouth.

"She went to a very famous music school," Lana retorted.

"So?"

"You said that Mrs. Johnston was boring, too," Dima said.

"She is. Maybe they went to the same school."

"I thought you wanted to play the piano, Bella," Lana said.

"I do. But those teachers are too boring." Bella slumped forward in her chair as though she were falling asleep.

"Yes. So you've said." Lana did not smile.

"I think they are too old," the girl added thoughtfully.

"They are here to teach you, not be your friend." She crossed her arms and looked at Dima. "You have to learn to get along with people — teachers and servants."

Bella watched as Dima gave Lana his 'look' that he usually accompanied with a terse, "Why do you have to say that?" Bella pouted. It wasn't her fault she didn't like the servants whom Lana chose. She took the last sweet bread roll and bit into it.

"Don't the Gordons' friends' children have a young piano teacher?" Dima asked Lana.

"Is she any fun?" Bella sat up quickly.

"This isn't about fun." Lana tapped her finger on the table. "It's about learning to play seriously."

"Oh. So is that's why piano lessons are so boring?"

The doorbell rang at precisely two o'clock on Tuesday afternoon. Bella pushed past Lana to see the new piano teacher, and squealed. This teacher had long, straight, black hair. It draped over her left shoulder like a silk blanket. Her flowing pants down to her ankles and a short denim jacket over her white shirt. She was pretty, young, *and* she was Chinese.

"I am Miss Ling Liu," she said, tilting her head slightly as she smiled.

"Hello. I'm Mrs. Hoffman." Lana smiled and stepped aside, nearly tripping on Bella. "Please come in."

"You're Chinese," Bella said, her voice high and crisp.

The young teacher smiled, her gaze intent on her new student, her lips apart, as though she wanted to say something.

"This is Bella, your student."

"Hello, Bella," Ling said. She bent over and extended her hand.

"You're Chinese," Bella said again, watching Ling like one adores a puppy.

"Yes, I am." Ling's voice was soft, the English words structured perfectly, albeit dotted with a slight Chinese accent.

"I used to be Chinese, too." Bella took the young teacher's hand and led her towards her bedroom housing the upright.

"How old are you?"

"Four and a quarter."

"All the piano books are in the bench," Lana said, as she stepped into the room. "Do you need anything else for now?"

"No, thank you," Ling replied.

"Bella, please listen to Miss. Lou."

"Please, call me Ling."

"Ling." Bella scooted closer to her teacher, gently batting at the strands of hair that hung down as Ling looked into her bag for a notebook.

"How old are you?" Bella asked.

"I'm twenty."

"Oh," Bella sat up straight and tapped her chin, hesitating before she said, "That's a little old."

Ling's laugh was like a chirruping sparrow and made Bella chuckle. When they stopped, the silence held student and teacher in a still observation of one another. Bella wanted to say something, but her brain and mouth weren't connecting with her heart. It was like catching water in her fingers.

Bella touched Ling's hair. "I used to have long hair, but my mother cut it off because I don't take care of it."

"Your mother . . ."

"Svetlana Hoffman is my mother. Dimitri Hoffman is my father." Bella recited one of the declarations she used to prevent more questions.

"They are lucky," Ling said, moving the girl's wayward strands off her face.

Bella looked at Ling. No one had ever said that to her before. She had only heard about what a lucky girl she was to have such a big house, so many toys, food on the table and people to clean up after her.

"I like you," Bella said. She opened her arms wide and leaned in to hug her teacher. "You are my favourite piano teacher."

She felt Ling's arms wrap around her and her long, jasmine-smelling hair fall across her face. "I wish you could be my sister."

A *Secret Resurfaces*

Mrs Wong sat in the dining room of Mei Hua's Repulse Bay penthouse. Twinkling above the circular rosewood table, the chandelier scattered a magical light over Mrs. Wong, her daughter Mei Hua, her son-in-law Benny and granddaughter Ling.

"Your mother told me you have several new piano students this month," Mrs. Wong said.

The young woman nodded in response but said nothing more as she brought the porcelain bowl to her lips and delicately used her chopsticks to push rice and fish into her mouth.

Mrs. Wong turned to Mei Hua who looked back at her and shrugged her shoulders.

"Yes, I do," Ling replied after a moment. She glanced around the table, took a sip of her tea and looked at her parents. When she looked at her grandmother, she paused.

"What happened to Ching Ha?"

The question squeezed out of her as a whisper. Yet, Mrs. Wong felt as though she had shouted it, hit her with those soft spoken words made of steel.

"What?" Benny's relaxed demeanor turned stiff as he sat up and glared at his wife and daughter.

"Did someone say something to you, about her?" Mei Hua leaned toward her daughter, voice high, strained.

Mrs. Wong placed her hand on her granddaughter's shoulder. "What happened?"

"I thought that problem was taken care of," Benny said to his wife.

Mrs. Wong winced at her son-in-law's words.

"It IS taken care of, Benny," Mei assured her husband. "Ling, what happened?" she asked again, her voice now shrill.

"Nothing," Ling said, eyes downcast. "I was just curious." She lifted the napkin from her lap and placed it on the table. As she stood, she glanced up and said, "Excuse me, for a moment." Mrs. Wong thought she saw the gleaming of tears in the corner of Ling's eyes as she left the room.

Mei Hua let out a little laugh. "Ling, you make me worry-lah," she said, switching to English as she shook her index finger at her daughter. "Don't get silly ideas about finding her. She is gone." She swooshed her hand through the air, as though batting away a fly. "Forgotten." With that, Mei Hua resumed an animated conversation in a mix of Cantonese and English with Benny, who had dribbled brown sauce down his shirt.

"Not forgotten," Ling's grandmother said to Benny and Mei Hua. They stopped laughing and looked at one another as Mrs. Wong stood and followed her granddaughter out of the dining room and onto the balcony.

It was true. Ching Ha was not forgotten. In fact, Mrs. Wong thought about the child every day, especially when she walked past the food stands on the way home from market day or when she saw children staring out of tram windows. Now, she wondered if Ling had also been thinking of the child — her child.

"Ling, wait." Mrs. Wong touched her granddaughter's arm.

"What's going on?" Mei Hua asked, approaching and directing her mother and daughter out of earshot of the servants and her husband.

"I've been thinking about her so much in the last few weeks," Ling said as she stepped onto the balcony. "My newest student is Chinese."

"So?" Mei Hua said, sliding the doors closed.

"Her family isn't."

Mrs. Wong covered her mouth. "Do you think it's Ching Ha?"

"No. How could it be? You and Mama told me that

she was sent to Britain for adoption." Ling pressed a finger into the corner of her eye and sniffled. "It just made me wonder about her."

Mrs. Wong lowered her head and took Ling's hand. "I must tell you something."

"No, Ma." Mei Hua grabbed her mother's arm.

"Yes, Mei Hua," Mrs. Wong said, pulling her arm away from her daughter. "It's time. Secrets will never stop chasing you until they are freed."

Mrs. Wong and Ling sat on the rattan peacock chairs, Mei Hua on the low bamboo armchair. The evening was clear and cool. The lights of the Repulse Bay Hotel and nearby buildings cast a golden light on the streets below. Mrs. Wong stared into the inky sky, as though she were telling a story of a faraway land, of a princess and a baby.

"It is true that your mother and father wanted to send Ching Ha to Britain with the other children from Hong Kong being adopted there. But, when I saw Ching Ha lying in the nursery of the hospital, I would not — could not — allow it." She pulled out her handkerchief from her pocket and dabbed her eyes. She looked over her shoulder at Ling and hoped that this confession would not destroy their relationship — the one she was trying to hold onto by letting Ching Ha go.

"So, what happened to her?" Ling's brows furrowed, her head cocked and her stare somewhere between frantic and fearful.

"I kept her."

"What?" Ling moved with the speed of a viper from the chair to her grandmother's feet. She closed her smooth, long fingers firmly around Mrs. Wong's hand. "Where is she?"

"She's gone, now." Mei Hua sniffed and motioned to the sky.

"Gone, where?" Ling continued to watch her grandmother. She squeezed her hand tightly. "Where is she?"

"She was adopted a year ago."

Ling stood up and backed away from her grandmother, her head shaking. "A year ago?" Her voice was high and rising. "Where was she until then?"

Mei Hua approached her, arms outstretched.

"No," said Ling, swatting at her mother's arms, her voice reverberating against the backdrop of the lights. "Where was she until last year?" she repeated, her voice thrown to the skies like an angry goddess.

Through broken sobs, Mrs. Wong answered. "Living. With. Me."

Ling put her hands over her ears then dragged them across her face, hiding it from those who had betrayed her. She fell to her knees, head falling forward.

"I'm so sorry, Ling." Mrs. Wong reached down to touch Ling, to hold her, to draw the pain away from her granddaughter.

"Don't touch me." Ling flinched and threw herself backwards.

"I just wanted to keep her in the family."

Ling scooted backwards until she was leaning against the balcony railing, her head rolling side to side. "Why didn't you tell me? Let me see her?"

The words she had said to herself for years finally escaped her lips in weak breaths. "I'm sorry, Ling." Mrs. Wong sat hunched, head bowed down. "I was wrong to keep this secret."

"I didn't want her to do it," Mei Hua said, pointing at her mother as she moved to kneel beside Ling, "but she insisted."

There was a strange and sudden silence, as though Ling's body had become an empty shell. It was only for seconds, but it felt like a long time. When Ling came to life and jerked her head up at her mother. Her sadness was gone, the dazed look of confusion had vanished. Instead, there was a shining darkness in her eyes, like an animal ready to attack. Ling looked at her mother and sat up so their faces were close. Mei Hua craned her neck back.

"Ling?" she extended an arm to keep her daughter away from her face

Ling advanced into her mother's space, and Mei Hua leaned back until she fell onto her bottom. "But, you knew, didn't you?" Ling's lips flinched slightly as she spoke, snarling her words to her mother like a hungry tiger. "That's why you and Ba sent me to study music in Europe." Ling pointed at her mother. "You kept me from my baby — again."

"She was the one who kept her." Mei Hua pointed at her own mother. "Your father and I wanted to get rid of her and spare you this pain." She held her arms out to her daughter, her voice gentle again, her lips in a childish pout.

"Get rid of her?" Ling swatted her mother's arms "Yes, I remember.'" Ling said, moving towards her grandmother. "Poh Poh, look at me." Ling lifted Mrs. Wong's head.

"I can't." Mrs. Wong freed her head from Ling's soft hands and looked down again. "I am ashamed for keeping Ching Ha a secret from you."

"No." Ling lifted her grandmother's head once more. "*You* tried to help me, to help Ching Ha."

"So, now *I* am wrong?" Mei Hua stood and brushed off her silk slacks. She plopped into the peacock chair, her arms flopped over the arms ungraciously.

"Poh Poh, do you think my student could be Ching Ha?"

"You are both crazy." Mei Hua sat up, her nose scrunched up as she pointed back and forth between the two of them. "Four million people in Hong Kong and you think Ching Ha is your new student?"

"There are four million *Chinese* people, not Westerners," Mrs. Wong said.

"Hah." Mei Hua laughed and let her head fall back. "You think all the gweilos know each other?" Mei Hua's smile did not make it to the edge of her lips before Ling stood in front of her mother.

"Yes, of course. They all go to the same clubs, and there are only seven schools in Hong Kong for their children. It was my current client, Mrs. Rosenberg who gave my name to her friend's friend."

Mei Hua straightened and fiddled with the strands at the back of her now-messy hairdo. She shrugged a shoulder as she cast a glance at Ling. "So? It doesn't mean the new student is Ching Ha."

"Poh Poh, what was the name of the family that adopted Ching Ha?" Ling asked, touching her grandmother's face as she kneeled in front of her.

"It doesn't matter." Mei's voice bubbled, ready to boil over. "There is nothing we can do, now."

Mrs. Wong tapped two fingers against her forehead. How could she forget something that important? Hoh fun, she kept thinking because Ching Ha had said, "*Hoh fun?*" when she heard the man's name at the wedding. Mrs. Wong chuckled, as she remembered the child's love for food. No doubt she was had hoped for a plate of rice noodles to appear. "Hoh-fun," Mrs. Wong said aloud.

Ling swallowed. "Hoff man?"

"Yes," Mrs. Wong said.

"I forbid it." Mei Hua pounded her fist on the armrest of the chair. She stood and slid open the balcony door. "Benny," she called as she stepped into the flat.

"Is Hoffman your new client?" Mrs. Wong asked, her lips trembling.

Ling nodded, leaning forward to embrace her grandmother. "Oh, Poh Poh. What can we do?"

"I don't know." Mrs. Wong buried her face in Ling's shoulder. "I don't know."

Dreaming of Possibilities

December 1971

Ling and her grandmother walked towards Ching Ha's new home. Expecting a glimpse of her beloved great-granddaughter distracted Mrs. Wong from the steep gradient of Mount Austin Road. She wondered if Ching Ha remembered coming here with their lanterns during moon festival. The child had wanted so much to go to the top of the mountain.

"Is it much farther?" she asked Ling.

"We are about halfway there. Are you tired?"

"No, excited." This opportunity to see Ching Ha a year after she had left was much more than coincidence. This was something fortuitous. Mrs. Wong linked her arm through her granddaughter's. Ling had forgiven her for keeping the secret; however her bitterness towards her parents, for forcing her to give Ching Ha up in the first place, had resurfaced and had yet to be resolved. But does one really ever forgive a betrayal?

"So, what will you do while I'm teaching?" asked Ling, distracting Mrs. Wong from her pondering.

"I'll wait for you, somewhere," Mrs. Wong answered. "Don't worry. I have my newspaper and my flask of hot tea. Just pretend I didn't even come with you."

"You probably won't see her. She rarely comes downstairs to see me off."

"I'll be happy knowing where she lives, being able to imagine where she is," Mrs. Wong said, leaning her face on Ling's shoulder.

"I know what you mean," Ling said, as she pressed her face against her grandmother's. "I must act normal, even though I'll want to hug her and tell her I'm her mother."

Mrs. Wong stopped walking and turned to Ling. "You must not say anything, or they might not let you back." She tapped her on the nose. "We agreed, Ling. We just want to be able to see her, to know she is alright. We cannot reverse the flow of the river. We can go with it."

Ling looked down as tears fell and her chest began to shake. Mrs. Wong put her arms around her. "I'm so sorry this is so hard, but this is the only way now. The only realistic way."

The two women stopped at a small park surrounded by several buildings. "That's it," Ling said, lifting her chin towards the grey, four-story.

"It's not such a fancy or big building." Mrs. Wong shrugged nonchalantly, trying to placate an uncommon surge of insecurity.

"There are only two flats on each floor."

"Oh," said Mrs. Wong, deflated as she visualized the expanse of each stretched across the length of one floor.

"See you in about an hour?" Ling said with a wave.

Mrs. Wong nodded and walked towards a bench near red hibiscus bushes that afforded her a view of the building. As she drank her tea, she imagined piano music floating out of the window on the third floor.

*****

Bella nodded her head as her fingers, showcasing bitten fingernails, ambled across the keys of the upright. She finished the "Ode to Joy," dropped her arms by her side and stuck out her tongue, like a tired dog. Bella looked at Ling, staring at her.

"I know." Bella sighed. "I need to practice more." She shook her head. "My mother already told me it's too jerky." She huffed, raising her shoulders to her ears and dropping them.

"Remember where you were last month, see where you are now, and you can see your playing has improved."

"And I can read some notes now." Bella's voice

bounced, and she sat up, pointing to her piano book. Her teacher gazed back at her. "Ling, are you okay?" Bella asked touching her shoulder.

Ling swallowed and lifted her hand to the girl's face. "Ching Ha?"

Bella watched the teacher's lips move, the name ringing in her ears, but in the voice of an older person whose face she couldn't make out in her dreams anymore.

"What did you say?" Bella leaned forward to hear her teacher whispering.

"Nothing." Ling pulled her hand away and shook her head, her cheeks reddening.

"No. Tell me. Please?"

Ling cast her gaze downward. "Ching Ha."

"What's that?"

"Just words I sing sometimes when I play." Ling's lips smiled as she looked back at Bella, but her eyes were not shiny anymore.

"Ching Ha, Ching Ha," Bella sang as she played two notes on the piano, trying to make Ling smile again. She moved her finger to the next octave and sang again. She repeated this until her eyes were opened in an exaggerated stare and her mouth was wide to release the high, broken notes.

Ling laughed, and Bella relaxed, satisfied that she had made her teacher happy.

"I'm going to sing that all the time because I don't like to practice."

Ling nodded and made a sound of agreement, her relaxed and easy demeanor restored. She put her hand on Bella's shoulder. "Do you know what my grandmother used to tell me?"

"No, what?" asked Bella as she reached up and placed her arm on her teacher's extended arm.

"Practicing is like life. It can be hard. But every lesson you learn makes the next step easier."

Bella wasn't sure what this meant exactly, but it made her feel good. The tiny stars in Ling's eyes twinkled, and that made Bella feel like she had puffy clouds floating in her heart. She realised that's how Lana's eyes shined when she played with Candy. Bella put out her other arm and drew her favourite piano teacher in for a hug and held tight, cherishing the feeling fluttering around her heart.

*****

Mrs. Wong's newspaper remained crisply folded on her lap. She sat on the bench, the chirping of birds lifting her spirits as she watched them flying around the park's flora. Birds were seldom heard over the traffic near her building. Her attention moved to a bald man opening the gate to the building grounds. He began to sweep the leaves into the nearby bushes. She placed the paper and thermos back into her basket and strolled towards the caretaker, a small notion blossoming into a plan with each step.

"Nay ho," she said to him with a quick nod.

"Ho ho," he replied warmly. "You visiting someone here?"

"No," Mrs. Wong said haltingly. "Do you know of anyone here looking for help?"

"What kind of help?"

"Cook, cleaner, Amah. Maybe someone has small children that they need help with?"

He looked skyward, leaning on his broom handle, and considered. "No," he said with a shake of the head. "Everyone has at least one servant working for them." He paused and added with a chuckle. "Even the family with the child that chases everyone away."

Mrs. Wong cocked her head. Perhaps she could get a job with that family, just to be closer to Ching Ha.

"Yes. They had so many servants come and go. They said the girl was very disrespectful and bossy — almost worse than the lady." He shook his head and resumed his sweeping as a hibiscus leaf blew under the gate towards him. "That's what happens when you take a child that does not belong to your culture."

Mrs. Wong put a hand to her heart in surprise. "The disrespectful girl is Chinese?" Surely Ching Ha was not that girl, she thought to herself.

"Yes." The caretaker stopped sweeping again. "Do you know them?"

"No," she replied quickly, "but maybe they need more help?" She could apply for a job as a servant or Ching Ha's private amah. She would see her daily.

Maybe there was a live-in position? She felt giddy with the hope of holding the girl once again, cooking for her, reading to her and telling stories like she used to when they were together. The caretaker turned his head away from Mrs. Wong, looking past her.

"You can ask for yourself." The caretaker pointed behind her.

Mrs. Wong turned to see the familiar peacock blue Chrysler pulling up the street. She saw a white haired man sitting in back, raising his hand in the air in greeting. Although she could not see his eyes behind his sunglasses, Mrs. Wong realized that he recognized her because the smile on his face dropped, as did his hand.

Mrs. Wong did not see the white-haired man grab his sunglasses off his face, because she had hurried down the hill, ducking behind a group of trees bordering the next building. By the time Benson stopped the car under the granite pillars of the building and Dima had rushed towards the gate, Mrs. Wong was out of sight. She stood, her body tense and pressed flat against the tree trunk, feeling its rough bark, scratching her back, peeling away layers of delusions and bringing her back to reality.

She breathed hard, not from her brisk walk, but the rush of coming to her senses. She put a hand against her forehead, pressing against her addled brain and ridiculous idea. How could she have thought she could work for them? They knew exactly who she was. What had she been thinking? How could she have forgotten such a crucial point?

When Ling found her, Mrs. Wong was standing quietly in the far end of the park, hidden behind a tree that faced away from Ching Ha's building. The rims of the old woman's eyes were red, her face flushed. There was an air of disquiet in her usually serene composure.

"Poh Poh. What's the matter?" Ling placed a hand on one of her grandmother's slumped shoulders.

Mrs. Wong stared towards the building. "I was so foolish."

"What happened?"

Shaking her head, Mrs. Wong put her face in her hands, unable to respond.

"You shouldn't have come." Ling shook her head. "This was too much for you." She linked her grandmother's arm through hers. "This is hard. I don't know what we are trying to do," she said, leading the weary woman down the hill.

"You know," Mrs. Wong said quietly through teary breaths, "it's wonderful to imagine possibilities, but so disappointing to realize not all possibilities are possible."

* * * * *

Bella's little voice floated through the air, two words repeatedly dancing through the layers of increasing tension at the dinner table. "Ching Ha, Ching Ha."

Lana looked at her husband, her lips and brows furrowed. Dima looked back at her, an eyebrow raised.

"Where did you hear that name?" he asked through a mouthful of chicken kotlets.

"It's not a name, Dima. It's a song." She sang it again, lifting and dropping each shoulder with each syllable.

"Who taught you the . . . song?" He took a sip of soda water.

"Ling, my piano teacher."

"I see." Dima shot Lana a shake of the head as he inhaled and didn't seem to breathe out.

"Why?" Bella stopped swaying and studied Lana and Dima's faces.

"What else did she say?" Lana asked, her voice wobbling.

"About what?'

"The. Song." Dima breathed out each word, like a dragon spat fire in the cartoons Bella watched in the afternoons.

"She says it when she plays music." The child looked at Lana, who looked down at her packet of cigarettes. "Why? What does it mean?"

Dima shrugged his shoulders. "It means nothing."

"So, I can say it?"

"No," Lana said. "Don't say something if you don't know what it means."

"But, I like how it sounds." She resumed her swaying, chanting, double time. "Ching Ha. Ching Ha," and watched the rippling motion in Dima's jawline.

"Have you finished eating, Bella?" he asked her.

"Yes."

"Then you may leave the table."

"I don't want to."

"You can watch television."

"What's on?"

"Sesame Street?"

"No. Sesame Street is on at two o'clock."

"Bella," Dima said, his fist pounding the table top, "Go help Ah Mui in the kitchen."

Bella's eyes widened. She didn't like when Dima was angry, although he usually shouted at Lana, not her. She hurrumphed softly, her lips vibrating with the sound. As she squished her lips together and stomped towards the kitchen, she heard Dima say in a low growl,

"Remind me, Lana. Where did we find this teacher?"

Crushing Dreams

A scratchy noise filled her bedroom, as Mrs. Wong placed the needle on the revolving record. Moments later, her own melodic voice rose and fell with the song that played. She walked to her kitchen table, the song wafting through the air after her, and sat down. Her heart tingled as she folded pale pink wrapping paper around a thin box of pink note paper and matching envelopes. She pushed away embarrassment about how irrational she had been in thinking she could become the Hoffman's amah to see Ching Ha. Hope and desperation so often led logic astray.

On their way home from the Hoffman's home that afternoon, she and Ling had devised a far more reasonable plan to allow Ling to see Ching Ha. Ling would develop her relationship with the Hoffmans as Ching Ha's trusted piano teacher. It was not uncommon for Westerners to allow their staff to take the children on trips. Perhaps, in time, Ling would be permitted to take Ching Ha on excursions and Mrs. Wong would meet them, see her beloved great granddaughter once more. Until then, Mrs. Wong could send gifts to Ching Ha through Ling. Maybe Ling could even take a photo of the child, so she could see how the child had grown.

Mrs. Wong laced a polka dotted ribbon around the paper and tied the two ends together into a simple bow. She inserted a black pencil through the ribbon and lifted the package to eye level to examine her handiwork. She nodded. *Yes, Ching Ha would like this.*

As her thoughts moved to Ling, Mrs. Wong's expression darkened with her. She and Ling had not discussed any other options than Ling only being Ching Ha's piano teacher. Mrs. Wong placed her elbows on the table and put her hands in her face. Would Ling want her daughter back? What would the Hoffmans do? Although they had only known Ching Ha for a year, and even though Ching Ha was Ling's baby, surely the Hoffmans loved Ching Ha and would be devastated if they lost her. Mrs. Wong would not wish that on anyone. She knew the pain of saying, "goodbye" especially to a child. But, would Ling be content to just visit her child? Would Ling want her baby back? What would Mei Hua do? Even this could get complicated.

Her heart heavy again, Mrs. Wong shuffled to the altar and lit three incense sticks. She looked at the photo of her husband, a mix of joy and stabbing sadness filling her mind and body. She held the incense in clasped fists and fanned them up and down, sending her questions and worries up in the wisps of sandalwood-scented smoke. Two knocks on her front door jolted her from her introspection. Mrs.Wong looked up and placed the sticks in the holder. Someone knocked on the door again, more loudly. Mrs. Wong turned her wrist to check the time. She hurried to the door calling, "Who's there?"

"It's me, Poh Poh," came Ling's muffled voice.

"Ling?" Mrs. Wong pulled the door and froze. Ling stood in front of her, shoulders rounded, neck drooped, face down, like a string puppet waiting for its master to give it life.

"Poh Poh," Ling blurted as she stepped forward and into her grandmother's arms, her chest collapsing forward, then heaving, as one sob after another tumbled from her slender body.

Mrs. Wong closed the door. "What's wrong?" she asked, lifting Ling's face as she looked her over. "Are you hurt?"

Ling shook her head and hid her face in her hands.

"Come, sit down and I'll make tea." She led Ling to the kitchen table, lit the stove and placed the kettle over the fire.

"Sorry, Poh Poh." Ling dabbed her eyes dry, the muted lilac trim of her cotton handkerchief turning dark with her tears. "I wanted to be with you. Ma and Ba wouldn't understand how I am feeling. They would just be happy."

"About what?" Mrs. Wong placed a small dish of candied ginger on the table. She sat next to Ling and placed a hand on her back.

Ling leaned on the table and put her face in her hands as her breath became staggered. She sat back and looked up at the ceiling. She took several deep breaths.

"What's happened, Ling?"

Ling looked at her grandmother and took her hand. "Mrs. Hoffman called me this evening. She doesn't want me to come back." Ling squeezed her eyes shut, her teeth gritted.

Mrs. Wong took a drawn out breath, a weight in her chest suffocating her. A fog in her head made the room spin and the music coming from her room sound like warped, slurred speech. "What did Mrs. Hoffman say?" She heard herself ask Ling.

"'Thank you, but please do not come back.'"

"I'm sorry, Ling." Mrs. Wong stood up and walked to the stove. Her body felt detached from her mind as she put two teaspoons of tea leaves into the strainer of her teapot and filled it from the kettle. Her hands trembled as she poured the tea. The books, pens and paper, the little mouse she wanted to make and all the other gifts she planned for Ching Ha floated in her vision and became translucent, dissolving into nothingness. She stared at the small, pink package on the table and brought the cup to her lips.

"Poh Poh. Are you okay?"

"Yes," Mrs. Wong said, sipping her tea, her focus returning to her kitchen, her home, Ling, reality. "Drink. Tea always makes you feel better."

Ling sipped her tea. "I don't feel better, Poh Poh."

"It needed to be stronger," Mrs. Wong said, lines forming around her lips, "much stronger." Leaning across the table, she picked up the gift she had wrapped, stood and carried it to the empty room that used to belong to Ching Ha. She set it down on the bedside table and sat on the edge of the bed.

"Poh Poh," Ling said from the doorway. "I'm sorry. I think I ruined our plan."

"No," Mrs. Wong said, looking up at Ling and patting the bed beside her. "It is no one's fault, just circumstances."

"So, what do we do now?" Ling asked, tears welling. She sat on the bed and leaned against her grandmother.

"What we must always do," Mrs. Wong said, remembering how she felt after her husband died and after she had said goodbye to Ching Ha - the first time. "We go on, listening to the music, singing when we know the words and humming when we don't." Mrs. Wong turned to Ling and lifted her face to look at her. "And we keep listening to music and learning new songs. That's how to live."

Tears rolled down Ling's cheeks, as she blinked. "You say such strange things, Poh Poh." She put an arm around her grandmother, pulled her close and pressed her head against hers. "You know what makes me really sad, Poh Poh?" Ling sat up. Her nostrils flared and her body shook as sobs fought their way out of her. "I feel like I lost my baby twice. And both times, I wasn't able to say goodbye."

Mrs. Wong held her granddaughter as they sat on Ching Ha's old bed, listening to the music that drifted in from the other room and invited them to sing.

Ghost of Christmas Past

21 December, 1971

Bella was bored. She had no school, no ballet and no piano because of the Christmas holidays. Instead of a fun holiday, there was a weight, a moroseness, in the air today. It made Bella feel like she was on the boat on a windy day, the waves high and turbulent. The rolling in her belly made her think of the ghost in Israel. She wondered if it had anything to do with the candle in the glass jar.

Lana and Dima had lit the short, white candle early this morning and placed on the tall bar it at the far end of the living room. They had whispered, as the flame glowed. They were acting so quiet and secretive that Bella had been afraid to interrupt them or ask, "What are you doing?" She knew by their furtive glances to one another, their lack of eye contact with her and vague answers that it was one of those things that she should not to talk about.

She decided to complain about something else to get Lana's attention. "I haven't gone to school or had a piano lesson for weeks." Bella tempered her whiny voice, uncertain if Lana would respond with the dreariness that she had been exhibiting the last few days or an explosion of fury.

"Yes. I know." Lana turned the page of her newspaper. "It feels like it has been weeks."

The last eight nights Bella had celebrated Chanukah, lighting candles, eating fried food and doughnuts with her grandparents. The nightly merriment and the gifts made the days feel mundane.

Even The more presents she received, the less time and interest she had in them.

"I kind of liked decorating the tree," Bella said, remembering the old, battered boxes of tangled lights, tinsel, glass balls and streamers. The wisps of string snow ended up on her arms and face, its invisible fibre glass needles making her itch and sneeze. The twisted strings of lights had to be painstakingly unraveled like her knotted hair after swimming class. She remembered how she, Lana and Dima had laid the lights along the carpet like fishing lines on a beach and replaced each dead bulb with a new one. Lana said nothing as she brushed Candy's fur.

"What should I do?" Bella said.

"Go practice piano?"

"When is Ling coming?"

"I"m not sure," Lana said, folding the newspaper crookedly. "But I have a headache so I need you to entertain yourself."

"Why don't you take your headache drops so we can play?"

"I don't want to play. I want to rest."She stood and tapped the side of her leg as she made a clicking noise at Candy. "I'm not feeling well." The dog stood and followed Lana towards the bedroom.

Bella pouted, arms across her chest. She was tired of entertaining herself and wished she had gone to Dima's office with him. His secretaries probably would have played with her, taken her out for dim sum and given her chocolate Santas to snack on while she clickety-clacked on their typewriters. "Can I go to Baba's house?".

Lana stopped, looked towards the ceiling, as though recalling something. She muttered and shook her head, stopped again and turned towards the telephone table. She sat down and dialed the phone. The rotary dial made a cluck, cluck, cluck sound, like a chicken as it rolled back into position after each number was dialed.

"Privyet, Bertha. Kak dyela?" Lana said, getting the pleasantries out of the way before asking if she could send Bella down to their flat.

Bella watched Lana's pinned on smile change to a relaxed one as she spoke, her voice modulating its lilt of sweet concern to gratitude as she signed off. Bella clapped and ran to the door as Lana called for Ah Mui to take her downstairs.

*****

"I look very Chinese today," Bella said, as she raked her grandmother's comb across the top of her straight black hair. "But I'm Jewish. Right, Baba?" The girl looked at her grandmother who was seated beside her at the low, rosewood vanity.

"Da, Bella, you're Jewish," Bertha confirmed with a nod. "And you are Chinese."

"No," Bella said with a shake of her head. "I'm not Chinese anymore, Baba." The child shook her head and frowned at her grandmother's reflection. "Now I am Jewish and Russian and British," she said.

"You can be all those things and Chinese, can't you?" Boris asked. He lay on his twin bed in grey pants and his sleeveless undershirt.

"No," Bella said to her grandfather in a sing-song lilt. "I don't speak Cantonese anymore."

"You can be Chinese and not speak Cantonese."

"I can?" Bella cocked her head, considering his words. "Well, it's not just that."

"What is it?" Boris asked, "You know that . . ." He stopped mid-sentence. His wife was blinking at him, her head shaking ever so slightly.

"What?" Bella asked, looking at her grandmother.

"You know, Bellach-ka," Boris said. "You do sound British." He stretched. "Maybe you can read the news on the radio soon."

"This is the BBC World Service." Bella heard that radio announcement every morning when Dima ate breakfast and listened to his shortwave. Boris chuckled, watching as Bertha attached pearl clip-on earrings and ornate combs to their granddaughter's hair.

"She learns English so quickly," Bertha said in Russian. "And she's only four."

"She learned faster than you," Boris said to his wife.

Bertha tsked at her husband and gave him a

sideways wink.

Bella continued to play with the baubles on her grandmother's vanity, as her grandparents talked. Even though they were speaking Russian, she knew what they were saying. She didn't know how it happened, only that in the haze of listening to the words around her, she began sorting them by the person who spoke, who they spoke to and how the words sounded. But, as Bella listened to all the words spoken at home, on the radio, on television, on the street, at dinner parties, at Mrs. Dobry's preschool and Sunday School, Bella found it easier and easier to speak in English. In fact, she was forgetting how to speak Cantonese. But, she didn't care. Ah Mui understood English, and Bella was English, now.

Bertha lay down on her twin bed, which lay parallel to her husband's. They watched Bella play dress up with Bertha's flowy night dresses and silk shawls. They drifted off to sleep as Bella perused the photo albums on the bookshelf.

Bella picked up a duster made of chicken feathers and wandered into the living room. She dusted the wooden trunk engraved with a scene with Chinese maidens in long gowns and wide sleeves sitting by a lake; the shiny, fake fruit made of a smooth, heavy stone and Baba's thick coffee table art books. Bella was heading back into the bedroom when she noticed a candle in a glass jar on the table of the enclosed verandah. She approached it cautiously, as though it were alive. She looked at the flame glowing around the white wick within it.

"Hello, Candle," she said. It jumped erratically in response. She spoke again, and it danced once more. She stepped back, wondering why both her parents and grandparents had a candle. What did it mean?

She stepped into the bedroom and leaned on her Baba's bed. "Baba?" she said, as she nudged her grandmother's arm. "Are you sleeping?"

Bertha opened her eyes. "Bella-chka. Hello, darling."

"Baba. Why do you have a candle? What's it for?"

Bertha's sleepy features vanished. She sat up, alert. "Boris. Boris," she said. "Wake up."

Bella sat at the table on the verandah with her grandparents, the candle in front of them.

"This candle is to remember someone very special," Boris said.

"Lana and Dima have a candle just like this, too." Bella tapped the glass.

"Yes, we know. We all knew the person who died," Bertha said.

Bella sat up. The twisting and confused way she felt this morning returned, as the memory of the Israel house popped into her head. "The person who died. Was it in Israel? Their boy?"

Bertha and Boris looked at one another, their wide eyes and raised eyebrows giving away their surprise.

"How do you know about this?" Boris asked lifting his granddaughter onto his lap.

"Ah Mui's friend told me," Bella said.

Bertha put a hand on her heart and another on her granddaughter's shoulder. "Oh, Bella."

"You know we love you," Boris said.

"I know," Bella said. She did know that she was loved. Just like she knew this candle was for someone her grandparents and Lana and Dima also loved. Someone who they would never forget and with whom she would always have to share Christmas.

Facing the Music

January 1972

Arrhymthic notes from "The Entertainer's" main chorus floundered through the air, like an injured fish trying to swim upstream. Bella, bored of the previous pieces that she had not perfected, was teaching herself a new melody. Images of Ling clapping, overjoyed by the surprise, dulled Bella's annoyance at her mistakes. She had practiced little over the Christmas and Chanukah holidays. Instead, she was at her grandparents with a yapping windup dog that somersaulted backwards and a screeching monkey in red-striped pants that banged on cymbals. Lana had banned both these gifts, given to Bella by her grandparents, from her home. As she tinkered with the new tune, impatience to see Ling distracted her.

"Lana," Bella called from the room. "It's been ages since I had a piano lesson, hasn't it?"

"I can't hear you," came Lana's voice from the other room. "Come here if you want to talk to me."

Bella skipped into the dining room table, where Lana sat, her bridge book and a cup of coffee in front of her. "What time is Ling coming?"

Lana scooped a teaspoon of Coffee-Mate creamer into her coffee blanketing the black liquid for a second before dark stains permeated the white powder. It disappeared into spirals, as Lana stirred it, turning the darkness into a milky brown. "Your piano teacher is coming at two o'clock."

Bella raised her wrist to check the time on her

new Mickey Mouse watch. "It is . . . five, ten, fifteen, twenty-two minutes after one o'clock." She looked at Lana. "So how long until she gets here?"

"Enough time for you to practice before your new teacher arrives." Lana paused, her eyes shifting towards Bella, then away. "Go practice your new song."

But, Bella had heard the slip. "What do you mean, 'new teacher'?"

"Nothing." Lana picked up her book, as she slurped the hot coffee.

"Not, nothing." Bella said as she moved closer to Lana. "Tell me. Do I have a new teacher?"

Lana put her cup down with a slight clatter. Coffee sloshed onto the green, cotton tablecloth, turning it an unappetizing shade of brown. She tossed her book on the table and made a sound that was somewhere between a snort and a growl. "Yes, you have a new teacher."

Bella stared at her, her mouth dropping open as her eyes grew wide and teary. "Why?" Her voice was a gasped whisper, like an escaping breath after being punched in the stomach.

"She wasn't a good teacher." Lana crossed her arms, her brows not furrowed, but lifted, as though she felt dispirited to have to burst Bella's bubble about Ling.

"She was *so* a good teacher." Bella's whine increased in volume and intensity.

"Dima and I didn't think so. We have a better teacher coming today."

"I don't want a better teacher," Bella's voice crescendoed. "I want Ling." Lana looked toward the open windows of the dining room.

"Stop your tantrums."

"No. I won't." Bella screamed, her lungs releasing fury-laced anger. "Not until you make Ling my piano teacher again." She stamped her feet and hammered her fists in the air.

Lana stood, her chair teetering back momentarily before it righted itself. She strode toward the front door. Bella followed, pulling at Lana's dress, pleading for Ling's reinstatement as her piano teacher. Lana opened the door to the closet and the chiming of the metal choke chain clinked at the end of the leather leash. Candy came running.

"I want Ling to be my piano teacher," Bella continued to wail, her small fist hitting her mother's fleshy bottom.

Lana let the choke collar fall to the ground, and waved the leather strap in the air. "Calm down, or I will have to help you," she said.

Bella's eyes widened and she repositioned herself. "No. No." Bella pressed her hands on Lana's elbows, so she could not bend them to bring the leash down.

"Stop screaming," Lana shouted, her arms extended in the air, as she tried to move around the girl.

"Please. Stop. I just want Ling. Please." Bella's ragged breaths jerked out of her body, her broken words stumbling out in the chaos of the entryway and her mind.

"Bella. You go play piano. Teacher come soon." Ah Mui stood in the kitchen doorway. She took Bella by the shoulders and pulled her back from Lana.

"I want Ling to be my teacher," Bella said, her voice still high and loud as she pressed her back against Ah Mui's legs. She gritted her teeth through tight lips as she pointed at Lana.

"Then you should have practiced more," Lana said, batting away Bella's condemning finger.

"What?" Bella's voice softened with her confusion. She shrugged away Ah Mui's attempts to shoo her into the piano room. "I did practice."

"Not well enough. Teachers don't want students who don't practice."

Bella was quiet for a moment. She placed her, hands on hips. "Did Ling say that?"

"Maybe."

"Tell me." Bella's voice screeched for a moment, until Ah Mui pressed on her shoulders. "Did she say that?" Bella reached to grab Lana's dress, but Ah Mui held her back.

"Please boil water to make tea for the new piano teacher," Lana said.

"Yes, Missy," Ah Mui said, taking the leash from Lana and placing it back in the closet before she returned to the kitchen.

"I *knew* she didn't say that," Bella said, shaking her head. "Ling would never say that. She's my friend."

"We aren't paying for her to be your friend." Lana tossed back as she walked into the dining room. "Your new teacher will be here soon," she added, walking towards her bedroom.

"I don't want a new teacher." Bella stopped by the dining table. Lana wasn't listening to her. She put her hands on either side of her head, pressing to staunch tears from coming again. She didn't know whether she needed to cry or shout. She only knew that she had to get Ling back.

"Lana," she said, running towards the bedroom. She bumped into Lana who was already walking out of her bedroom. "Please, Lana." Bella drew out each word. "I promise I will not talk so much, and I will practice all the time." Bella clasped her hands together, fingers intertwined and held them to her chin "begging" the way her friends did when they really, really wanted something. "Please, please, pretty, please with sugar on top, let Ling be my teacher."

Lana didn't respond. She was squeezing drops of clear liquid into Bella's glass of water. "I want you to drink this."

"Why are you giving me 'health drops'?" Bella dropped her pleading hands beside her, confused by the odd segue to hydration. "I don't have a headache."

"Well, I do."

"Then why don't you put them in your coffee?"

"Here," Lana said, handing the water to Bella. "You will feel better."

"I feel fine."

"Already you are arguing? Drink this if you want to discuss anything with me."

Bella huffed as her shoulders rose and fell. She drank the half-empty glass of water. "Now, can Ling be my teacher?"

The doorbell rang. "I'll tell you after you meet your new teacher."

"No," Bella crossed her arms and raised her voice to be heard over Candy's barking. "Tell me now."

Lines appeared around Lana's mouth as she tensed her lips. Her eyes were dark. "We haven't time for this now," she said as the deadbolt unlocked and Ah Mui opened the door.

"Missy, teacher here."

Bella stuck her head around from the dining room, so she could see the new teacher. A tall lady, with white hair pulled into a bun, wearing a knee-length brown and white geometrically-patterned dress and brown sandals entered the flat and waved to her. Bella waved back automatically. She didn't want to hurt the lady's feelings.

"Come, Bella. Meet your new teacher," Lana said with a smile and a singsong voice as she stepped towards the foyer.

Bella didn't want to hurt the new teacher's feelings, but a scream was building inside her body. It was in her finger tips. She made tight fists that squeezed the anger into trembling arms. A tightness in her chest was pushing a scream out. But, the headache medicine was working, making her feel like she was wearing goggles in the swimming pool, and could see even though everything underwater was all wavy.

"No." Bella muttered. "I want Ling." She thought she was shouting, but she wasn't sure. Her voice sounded she was underwater. She slumped on the floor, defeated by an onslaught of uncertainty, sadness and anger. Did Ling really not want to be her teacher? The patterns on the hardwood floor criss-crossed in her vision, making her feel dizzier as she listened to Lana talking to the white-haired teacher.

"I'm so sorry. Bella is not feeling well. Here is the payment for today, and I will call you to reschedule."

The front door clicked. Candy's nails clattered across the floor like raindrops on a tin roof. Lana's pointed leather shoes appeared in front of her. Bella looked up.

"You didn't meet the teacher, so Ling isn't coming

back," Lana said, leaning forward and hoisting Bella to her feet up by an arm

"Then I'm never going to play the piano again," Bella countered, her words slow and slurred as though she was dreaming.

Lana held Bella's hand, put an arm around her waist and guided the dazed child to the bedroom. "Well, we will have to get rid of the piano."

"I don't care," Bella said. And she didn't, because she was so tired, and her head felt like it was in a big bowl. Strange, she thought to herself, because Lana just gave her the headache medicine.

"Your grandfather will be very disappointed that you gave up learning how to play the piano he bought for you."

Bella didn't want to make Deda sad. She tried to say this, but only a humming-groaning sound escaped her throat. She crawled onto her bed. As her head sunk down into her pillow. Bella realized how to fix everything. If she practiced, she could make Deda happy, and Ling would come back. Bella closed her eyes and listened to the muffled piano music thrumming in the cloudiness of her mind.

Growing Up Asian

February 1972

Bella sat in the large dining room of the Jewish Club and waited for her mother to finish playing bridge. Lana rarely took Bella to her bridge games, but Bella had begged to go and promised to entertain herself. The child had her heart set on partaking in the ladies' tea event that afternoon.

Colours strayed further and further outside the lines, as Bella ennuied of the activity. She glanced at the clock on the wall. She wasn't sure when her mother was going to be done, but Bella hoped it would be soon. A staff member stood behind a bar, drying the glasses he had carried in from the kitchen. Bella put her colouring book in her bag and moved to the tall stool in front of the counter. She eyed the chocolate biscuits and macaroons behind him.
   "Two chocolate biscuits, please, she said."
   "You a member?" he asked in Cantonese.
   "Yes,"
   "OK," he said, scribbling on a chit. "Sign here." He put the pad in front of her, picked the cookies out of a glass jar, and put them into a paper bag.
   Bella wrote "B-e-l-l-a," adding a long squiggle at the end of the last letter. She picked up the snack bag and returned to the table, where she opened the latest library book by Enid Blyton.
   The sound of coughing and heavy feet coming down the stairs made Bella look up. A woman, with grey-

blue hair heaped atop her head, walked through the dining room. She looked to the left and right, peering up at the ceilings and down at the floors examining everything. Her eyes landed on Bella and she marched toward the table.

"Hello," she said.

"Hello," Bella said, sending several chocolate crumbs flying across her book.

"What are you doing here?"

"I'm waiting for my mother."

"Please eat in the back area."

"Huh?" Bella said. "My mother is upstairs."

"Well, bevakasha," the woman said, her deep voice resonating in Bella's ears. "You must wait in the kitchen." She circled a fat finger around the room. "This area is for members to enjoy." She leaned over the table and moved her finger like a metronome. "It is not for the staff or servants' families." When the woman straightened and walked towards the exit, her head and hair looked bigger and messier to Bella.

The child swallowed the piece of cookie that had become goo in her mouth. She opened her eyes wide and stared after the woman's fat, bouncy bottom, trying to make her tears go away. The woman turned around, and Bella looked down, closed her book and scrambled with her things, as though she was putting them away. Bella slumped in her chair as she packed her things. Her heart was a cauldron of feelings — sharp, painful stabs that made her want to scream and cry.

Her bag in hand, Bella walked out into the garden in search of Harriet, the Rabbi's dog. Together they sat on the grassy area in front of the clubhouse and shared Bella's last cookie.

The big-bottomed woman reappeared when Bella sat at the tea table with Lana and her bridge friends. The lines on the woman's face were softer, as was her voice. A smile plastered on her face, the woman approached Bella and Lana.

"Mrs. Hoffman, I must apologize to your daughter," the woman said. She placed her hand on Bella's shoulder.

Bella rolled her shoulder so the woman's hand fell away.

"Be polite to Mrs. Davidson," Lana said with a tsk. "She is very important. She the new Manager of the club," she said, nudging Bella.

"No, it's alright. I deserved that," Mrs. Davidson said, her lips curled; her cheeks reddening. "I didn't know she was your daughter. I was quite rude to her."

Bella grimaced as Mrs. Davidson and Lana spoke above her head. Although Bella stared down at her plate, she could see the women across the table were watching this exchange. Just go away. Stop talking, Bella thought, her elbows on the table and face pressed by her face as she, once again, tried not to cry in front of anyone.

When the woman left, Bella resumed her consumption of cucumber sandwiches, coconut macaroons and sweet milk tea. Most of the women at the table were friends of the family, came to the dinner parties at the house, and played bridge with Lana. Bella knew them all, except for the person sitting across from her. She was Chinese lady wearing big round glasses. Her shoulder-length hair draped around an ugly, lace-collared shirt. She smiled and laughed as she talked with everyone. Who was she? Why was she at the table?

Even though the woman looked plain, with no makeup, Bella knew a staff member would be wearing a uniform. She also now knew that staff would not sit at the table. Bella continued to eat the tiny square cucumber and egg sandwiches on her plate, observing the woman.

"I see you looking a little confused," said a voice. Bella looked at Lana's friend, Mrs. Freedman, who was sitting beside the Chinese woman. "This is Talia, my daughter," she said, putting her arm around the Chinese woman. "She's a nurse and lives in London."

Talia waved. Bella stopped mid-chew. Is this what Bella would look like when she got older? Bella looked at Talia and Mrs. Freedman again. They looked

just like Bella and her mother — nothing alike.
Bella looked at Lana for further explanation. There
was none. Lana lit her cigarette and turned her head
to speak to the woman sitting on her right. Bella
pushed the rest of the sandwich into her mouth and
slouched. She looked down at her ankle high socks,
decorated with laced edges like the one on Talia's
shirt. Bella wondered if all mothers picked out too-
frilly lace for their Chinese daughters. She looked
at Talia and decided she was ugly and her too-
perfect English voice sounded strange coming from
her Chinese mouth.

Bella held back tears as she looked down the
length of the table. Nobody looked like her, except
Talia and the people filling the teacups and taking
away the dirty plates. Bella looked at her mother
once more. Lana pursed her lips around a cigarette
and inhaled, squinting her eyes as she held her
breath for a second. She blew out a long cloud of
smoke. Bella reached for another egg sandwich and
pushed it into her mouth, wishing she had stayed
home with Ah Mui.

God VersusJunk

February 1972

Lana sat on the lounge chair in the garden of the Jewish Club, watching the last of the worshippers exit the historic Robinson Road synagogue, and stroll toward the Clubhouse. She looked at her husband, seated on a chair next to her. He kept turning to look over his shoulder at his father, seated on the other side of him.

The conversation had squirmed into existence this morning on the way to the club, when Dima hinted to his father that Sunday School was less beneficial to Bella than excursions on the junk he had just purchased. Lana was often indifferent to her in-laws, but she had a twinge of sympathy watching Boris persuade his son otherwise. If nothing else, Boris argued, it was time for him and Bertha to spend time with her.

Lana knew they loved Bella, but she also knew that when Dima wanted something, he fought for it like a willful child — even resorting to screaming at people. Although Dima dared not raise his voice to his father, this was going to be interesting. Lana sat back, happy to be a spectator rather than a participant. Her manicured nails pressed her cigarette to the side of her pouty lips, as though she were kissing it.

"A child needs spirituality to create a complete and strong sense of identity," Boris said. "She will need that, especially given her circumstances."

Dima was already sporting a full head of white

hair, just like his father. They also both had prominent, rectangular jaws that highlighted a fat, undulating muscle when they clenched. But that was the extent of their similarities. Except perhaps their obstinacy.

"Bella is happy, coming to Sunday School to learn Hebrew and be with other children. Is it wise to stop this?"

"What does she need Hebrew for?" Dima asked.

"It is her heritage," Boris replied. He sat up, leaning in as the volume of his voice grew. "You were born in Russia. You moved to China and Israel before coming to Hong Kong. You speak the language of all four cultures, but you won't give that opportunity to your daughter?"

"When will she need to speak Hebrew?"

"She needs it because she is Jewish, and it is her birthright."

"She won't use it."

"How do you know?"

"We live in Hong Kong, not Israel." Dima watched people making their way inside the Clubhouse for lunch.

"Life is about opportunities and chaos; doors open to unplanned places and doors close unexpectedly," Boris's voice faded, as he regarded his son's profile.

"Father," Dima said, turning. "I told you from the start that I'd let her come her to spend time with you and Mother, but not forever. She doesn't need all this," Dima said, momentarily elevating his voice, as he motioned to the synagogue and grounds. He looked at Lana. She glanced at him long enough to direct a raised eyebrow in his direction, then looked the opposite way, as if to say, "Don't drag me into this."

"It looks to me like she belongs here." Boris looked at the tennis courts, where the children played volleyball, using shuttlecocks from the badminton court. "Her sense of belonging will come with her sense of identity, self-confidence and being around people who have some commonalities with her."

"There are no other Chinese children here." Dima shrugged.

"Apparently, her appearance makes no difference to the children. They see her for who she is. That in itself is of great value."

"It's one day a week. She'll be fine without it." Dima swatted the air dismissively.

"Yes, it's once, sometimes twice, a week. Dima. Can you give her that, so she's not just *'fine'*?"

Lana saw Boris's fist clench. Ah, there was another similar mannerism between them.

"You have to help her discover, understand and accept her identity and make sense of her birth heritage and your heritage, which is now also going to be hers. Don't you understand that?"

"Of course, I understand that." Dima turned to face his father. "I'm not a fool."

Lana wondered where she could go, maybe excuse herself and go to the bathroom, where it was quiet. She imagined Dima's raised voice, re-staging this very conversation when they got home. She opened her handbag for a cigarette and closed it, not wanting to annoy her father-in-law with her smoking. He was agitated enough.

"That child is not a distraction, a toy. You would be wise to give that girl the knowledge and the confidence to answer questions — her own and those of others. Understanding her diverse background, and being proud of it — *that's* what will give her a sense of belonging, wherever she is."

"Well, I am giving her the experience of boating in fresh sea air. She can learn to swim, sail, fish and . . . and other marine-related things."

"She could do that and still come to the Jewish Club," Dima's father said. He paused, still looking at his son's profile. "But this discussion is not about Bella, is it?"

Lana pulled out a handkerchief and pretended to wipe her nose to hide her smirk. It was rarely about anyone but Dima. This time it was about making the most of his latest investment — a 52-foot junk.

"There's no point of her wasting her time with this community. She will never need it."

"But, a person always needs community," Boris said. "But, I see there is no point wasting the rest of our day with this." He sat back in his armchair. "You have obviously made your decision."

Boris watched Bella across the lawn in her grandmother's lap, eating a cookie. The child looked up at that moment and nudged her grandmother. They both looked at the debating men, smiled and waved.

"Do me a favour, and be the one to tell your mother," Boris said. "She looks forward to Bella's time with us here, talking to the other members of the congregation and treating her to lunch." Boris chuckled as he crossed his arms. "Good luck telling Bella that she won't be having rice pilaf and cookies every weekend."

"She will be happy to be on the boat," Dima repeated.

"What about Purim? Bella's playing Queen Esther. Your mother made a costume for her."

"I don't know. . ." Dima said, his lips screwing together. "I really wanted to start next weekend . . . "

Lana, fed up of her husband's bullheadedness, glowered at him.

"Fine," Dima exhaled. "She can keep coming until Purim is over."

"Thank you, son. I'm sure your mother, and Bella, will appreciate your . . . Consideration."

Dima gritted his teeth. He stood, motioned for Lana to rise and gestured to his mother and Bella to make their way into the club for lunch. Boris stood and patted his son on the back.

"Just remember that an understanding of Bella's religion will also give her a foundation and philosophy for living."

"Is this really her religion?" Dima asked.

Boris looked at his son and raised his eyebrows. "You'd better figure that out quickly," he said, "because if you don't know who Bella is, how will she?"

Revisiting Ghosts

August 1972
  Israel

Squinting against the sunlight, Bella followed Lana
out of the taxi. Dima paid the driver and took the
bags as Bella stared at the two storied duplex, in
the small suburb outside Tel Aviv, that she had
visited last summer.

The mango tree had grown since the last visit, its
branches and leaves reaching up to the top
balconies. The windows were dusty and lined with
silvery cobwebs. The shutters had been raised on all
the windows and doors, except one upstairs room.
Bella knew that was the ghost's room — the one that
she wanted to visit again this trip.

The three Hoffmans walked up the cobblestone
pathway towards the ornate, heavy front door that
creaked as it opened. A mustiness wafted out. Bella
followed Dima from the foyer into the main part of
the house. The stone floors and white concrete walls
blanketed the house in a chill that was unaffected
by the summer heat.

Bella pattered behind Dima up the curved marble
stairs onto the upstairs landing. Recognizing her
room, she ran to the left, excitedly snatching up
the thin book that she had left behind on the
bookcase last summer. She sounded out the words,
warmed by the familiarity of the mouse and musical
instrument on the cover. "Trubloff: The Mouse Who
Wanted to Play the Balalaika." She nodded,
congratulating herself on how much better she could

read this year.

A warm breeze and the swishing of the branches of the mango tree called to Bella, and she turned to see Dima pulling open the balcony doors. She tossed the book on the bed and stepped out and leaned over the rail, peering down at the garden. She walked to the room at the other end of the balcony.

This was the room that was still shuttered. This was the room with the picture of the boy smiling out at her from a small frame. She heard a *click* from inside the house. The metal shutters rattled and crinkled, dried leaves danced near on the ground as the doors to the secret bedroom opened. The shutters rattled again, sending debris and falling spiders scurrying across the doors. Bella cried out and leapt backwards, as beetle carcasses rolled out from beneath the moving shutters.

Lana's long nails appeared beneath the bottom bar of the shutters, and Bella heard a small grunt as the metal rolled up into a bin at the top of the door. She waited impatiently to run in, determined to spend more time looking for the secrets that made Lana lock up this room. This time, she would not be afraid.

But the shutters stopped below Bella's knee, and Lana's fingers disappeared. Bella placed her hands on the bar to lift it but pulled them away quickly when she felt the dirt and spiderwebs. She wiped her hands on her dress and replaced her small fingers along the bottom ledge. Groaning, she tried to straighten her legs, but the shutters would not move.

She looked at the ground and dusted an area with her shoe before kneeling and looking under the space. She saw Lana's swollen, bare feet padding around the room as she picked up papers that were on the floor.

"Lana, the door is stuck."

"No, it's not."

"Yes, it is. It won't open anymore."

"I want it that way."

"Why?"

"Just leave it."

Bella saw the chair slide quickly towards the desk, thumping when it hit the desk. She watched the feet leave the room, the door to the room closing behind them with a click. Growling, Bella huffed, sending sand into her eye. She rubbed her eye and stomped back to her room, her exploration delayed. Opening the suitcase that Dima had laid on a chair, she decided to put on a bathing suit and dig a hole under the mango tree and fill it with water.

It was toward the end of the visit when Bella finally made it into the room. She, Dima and Lana had been to Bialik Street for a falafel lunch. The outing had exhausted Dima and Lana, who came home and took a nap. Bella, who had been drawing with the colour pencils they bought at the stationery store, had been invited into the room by the ghost in the same manner as the first time.

The door to the ghost's room had been closed when she walked past it to go to the bathroom. When she pulled open the door to leave the bathroom, she heard a light, quick *clack* and saw that the door had opened a crack.

She could feel a draft through the space and imagined it was the ghost's voice calling to her silently.

Iciness tickled down her arms and spine.

But she had thought about this room many times since her last visit, and this time she was going to explore it, find out its secrets, not just run in and out as she had done last time. This was her brother's room, she told herself. It was his ghost speaking to her. She didn't need to be afraid, and so she stole into the room.

It looked exactly the same as the last time she had snuck in. It was empty, but alive with activity. The rays of sunshine tumbled in through the slats of the shutter, and the window and curtains sailed up and down in the air. Sheets of paper on the desk struggled to break free of a stone paperweight, dancing to the music of the leaves of neighbourhood mango, orange and eucalyptus trees. The air was dusty, perfumed by the scent of the jasmine flower hedges below.

The wardrobe doors and drawers were open and displayed green uniforms and caps and a matching jacket. There was an army backpack crumpled on the floor next to the high, black lace-up boots. The bed was still unmade, as though the ghost had just woken up and was returning to bed shortly.

The shuffle of the moving papers on the desk beckoned Bella to look once again at the photo of the young man, her brother, smiling at her.

"Hello, brother," she said. She picked up the book laying on the desk, a pen sticking out of it. She flipped through the handwritten pages and doodles of patterns inside different shapes, sketches of trees, the house, and Mack - their old dog. *Mack knew her brother?* Bella frowned, feeling left out. She took the book to the bed and sat down. She could not read the writing. It was partly in English and partly in Hebrew, and the letters had too many curly, messy lines.

Bella yawned as the sunshine warmed her back. Her embroidered slippers fell as she placed her feet on the bed. As Bella's head sank into the pillow, she smelled a mix of perfume and mothballs. It smelled like an old person's sweater. She yawned again, lay the book on her belly, and closed her eyes. Imagining her big brother reading to her from his storybook, she considered the success of this adventure.

Bella screamed. A pressure clutched her hand, and she was pulled up and off the bed. Her hand reached to the ground to stop from falling, as her other arm was held in the air, suspending her body. She tried to stand up.

"What are you doing?" Lana was shouting, her body unusually strong and scary. Bella, still dazed from her restful state and dizzy from the jostling, was unable to answer.

"I told you to never to come into this room." Bella heard the shrill scream followed by a smack and felt a burning on her thigh. She tumbled onto the hard, stone floor. Cowering, Bella saw Lana's narrow feet and curled up toes, stalking around her like a wild animal ready to spring. Bella put up her hands to protect herself as crawled towards the door. She was lifted into the air again.

This time, the scream she heard was her own. She landed in Dima's arms. He turned his body, so he stood between her and Svetlana.

"What are you doing?" His voice was low and slow, almost snarling, as he chastised her in Russian.

Bella peeked out from Dima's chest, her arms clasped around his neck. Lana spoke quickly, her tone and volume rising and falling as she picked up the book and placed it on the table.

Lana gingerly patted the bed and sat on it and let out a sob. She looked up and stretched out a hand to Bella, who instinctively moved her leg away. Lana let out another cry and put her face in her hands.

Dima kissed Bella's head and stepped out of the ghost's room that was flooding with the sound of Lana's uneven cries and mutterings.

Her bottom lip trembling and her breath shaky, Bella looked at Dimitri.

"I'm sorry, Bella." His voice was less than a whisper, just a puff of air coordinated with a slow blink of his dull, droopy eyes.

Overwhelmed by the chaos she had unleashed by revisiting her ghost, Bella let out a wail and squashed her face into the side of Dima's neck. He walked down the stairs and out of the cold house.

For many moments, they remained in the garden, Bella in Dima's arms. They listened to the crash of furniture, and Lana's inhuman howls that sailed into the air and hung on the glossy leaves of the thick trunked tree and its heavy, ripening mangos.

No one spoke of the incident. Lana did not leave the door unlocked again. But, for the next two nights, when everyone was supposed to be asleep, Bella lay in the adjoining room to the ghost's room and listened to Lana crinkling paper, shuffling objects around and packing boxes. Her lamenting moans seeped through the locked glass door, into the hallway and into Bella's room.

Though the skin around her eyes drooped, Lana wore a brave new smile on her face each of those next mornings. She made cooing sounds at Bella, as she called her "darling."

But all these antics made Bella uncomfortable. The girl didn't know what to say or how to respond to it. To hug Lana whenever she saw her, and cover her face in kisses like she did with Dima, seemed alien. It wasn't that she didn't love Lana or like the attention. There was just something missing in Lana's sudden rise in affection and awareness of her. It was like a house with no floor. Bella decided, however, that she was going to make an effort to match Lana's adoration.

Bella walked into Lana's bedroom. It smelled like lemon. Her face looked oily. A spot of yellow cream clung to her ear. She was hunched over a bent knee, cutting her toenails.

"Do you want me to start calling you 'Mummy?'" Bella asked.

Lana looked up and put her leg down. She straightened. "Why?"

"I don't know," Bella said, raising her shoulders to her ears and holding them there for a second. "I thought it would be nice for you."

Lana shrugged. "Call me what you like, darling." She said the last word as though it was a foreign word and difficult to pronounce.

Bella cringed imperceptibly.

"There's nothing wrong with calling me 'Lana'. That's my name."

Bella thought about this as she tapped her finger on her cheek, as she had seen in the Pink Panther cartoon. "Okay," she said and raised her hands in the air nonchalantly. "I'll just keep calling you, 'Lana.' And you can just call me 'Bella.'"

"Okay, Bella." There was a lightness in Lana's voice.

The child leaned forward and gave her mother a hug. It didn't feel strange this time. Lana patted her back.

"Now, go entertain yourself, Bella." Lana put her foot back on the bed, hunched over her knee, proceeding with her pedicure.

Bella skipped out of the room with a smile, content that everything with Lana was back to normal.

Channukah-mas

December 1972

Bella leaned on her grandparents' dining table and stared at the nine candles in the brass chanukiah. Tonight was the eighth night of the special Jewish holiday. And, tonight, Bella was going to eat her grandmother's delicious potato latkes. Her mouth watered thinking about crispy outer layers and the warm gooeyness inside.

Although it was weeks until Christmas, Dairy Farm sold chocolate santas and boxes of Christmas chocolates, *The Sound of Music* and other Christmas specials were on television, and sections of large parking lots were filled with fresh-smelling evergreen trees of all sizes for sale.

For the last seven nights though, Bella, Lana and Dimitri had been celebrating Chanukah. She had visited her grandparents each night, to light candles on the chanukiah, say prayers, sing and, of course, eat.

As Boris recited the blessings, Bertha helped Bella bring the match to the shamash, then lift the shamash out of the chanukiah, using it to light each of the other candles. The soft glow of sunset filtered through the linen curtains, adding to the rosy glimmer of the candlelight.

After Deda chanted the blessings over the warm, yellow flame of the fat, white candles, the family clapped, singing, "Sivivon sov sov sov," followed by "Dreidel, Dreidel, Dreidel." Bella smelled the latkes and knew they would soon be eating. First, though, she had to win all the gelt from her father and grandfather in a dreidel challenge.

Bella let out a hearty laugh, worthy of a pirate, as she gathered her winnings. Despite the shiny, pretty gold foil, that was fun to peel off, the chocolate tasted stale.

"These are yucky." Bella furrowed her brow playfully at her grandmother. "Are these coins from last year, Baba?"

Bertha widened her eyes and put her hands on her face, imitating Edvard Munch's, *The Scream*.

"Oy. Such a cheeky Bella," Bertha said and tapped Bella's nose as she scrunched her own. Even Lana laughed in that moment of pure, relaxed joy that made Bella feel like she was watching a Christmas movie. Dima leaned in to steal a chocolate.

Bertha left the room, returning with a gold-trimmed platter holding latkes and two dishes — one with applesauce, one with sour cream. "Chag Sameach."

"Chag Sameach," Bella repeated, joining the applause greeting the food. She watched as Lana placed a latke on her plate.

"I want sour cream, please," Bella said, rubbing her belly as Lana placed a dollop on the lattice of potatoes. Bella spread white cream across the latke and pushed a fork full of the goopy mess into her mouth. She made a low moaning sound as she slumped, melting from the yumminess. "Baba, these are so good," she said with her mouth full. "I wish you made them every day, not just for Chanukah."

"Save room for the other treat," Bertha said

Bella's eyes widened, and she looked at her parents, then at her grandfather.

"What's coming?" she asked.

"It's a surprise," said Bertha.

"First tell me, Bella," her grandfather said, "are you looking forward to Christmas?"

Bella refilled her mouth as she thought back to last Christmas and the preparations this year."

"I don't know which one I like better." She wiped her mouth on a cloth napkin. "I liked opening all my Christmas presents," she said, even though couldn't

remember what she had received because there had
been so many presents.

She did like the sparkling Christmas lights on the
tree, but it was fun to light the shamash with a
hot, flickering flame. Using the shamash to light
the other candles in the Chanukah menorah with
actual fire was more fun than plugging in strings of
lights. "I like lighting the candles," she said. The
recollection of the ghost's candle popped into her
mind, and how both Dima and Lana brooded the day
they lit it.

"I like that Chanukah celebrates something from
history, like Passover but better food and more
fun."

"Some people think Christmas also celebrates
something from history," Boris said.

"It does?" Bella said. She ate the last bite of
her latke as she wondered what Santa Claus's history
celebrated.

Bertha left the dining room again. This time she
returned with a crystal dish of assorted, round
doughnuts.

"Souvganiot," Bella said loudly, kneeling on her
chair and leaning over the table to inspect the
puffy pastry.

Bertha placed the doughnuts in front of Bella and
pointed to them. "These have strawberry jam; these
have marmalade; and these are plain."

"They are so pretty, Baba," Bella said, taking a
strawberry one with no hole. "Did you make these,
too?"

"No," Bertha chuckled. "These are from the
Mandarin Hotel."

Bella paused mid-bite, remembering the beautiful
lobby of the downtown hotel, where her grandparents
had introduced her to afternoon tea, served on
three-tiered, flower-decorated trays filled with
small, square sandwiches on white bread, and
colorful, creamy mini-cakes.

"That's so fancy, Baba." She bit into the
souvganiot, jerking her head forward. The jam that
oozed out dripped onto her plate. She bent down and

licked her plate.

"No," said Svetlana. "Where are your manners?"

Bertha laughed. "It's all right. I'm glad she is enjoying it so much."

Lana cut into her doughnut while Dima bit into his, sending jam gushing out the side. Boris took a bite from his souvganiot and watched Bella.

"I think Chanukah is better than Christmas," said Bella. She licked the jam out of the doughnut, pressed it until more jam oozed out and licked it again.

"Taking down all the Christmas decorations is so boring," she said, remembering the tree undressing that was so much longer and unexciting than choosing an ornament and deciding where it should go. She looked at her grandmother. "I like coming here for Chanukah, to eat Baba's cooking."

Bertha winked at Bella who took the last bite of her doughnut and sighed.

"Well, you are lucky," said Boris with a nod of his head. "You don't have to choose. You can have both."

"That's good, because I can't even decide if I want another latke or souvganiot."

Bella alternately bit the jam-filled doughnut and the crispy tenderness of the potato latkes. She hummed the Dreidel song, happy to have so many holidays and good food to celebrate.

Finding Ching Ha

February 1973

Two years passed before Ah Kain returned to the house on Mount Austin Road to fulfill her promise to visit Bella. The child did not have any clear recollections of her former nanny, yet there was a familiarity about Ah Kain's mole, dimpled smile and tender voice that comforted her. So, the five-year-old joyfully accepted the invitation to go into the city to watch the dragon dance celebration and bring in the Chinese New Year.

The street tram rattled along Johnston Road, the ding ding of its loud metal bell warning impatient jaywalkers to cross quickly. Bella sat on Ah Kain's lap, looking out of the window and sniffing the smoky air. She could hear the rapid click-clacking as fireworks cracked in the distance. Bella leaned against Ah Kain as the tram shuddered to a stop in front of a large park with tall lampposts. The yellow lights shone over the people gathering around market stands filled with baskets of seeds and dried fruit, red licee packages and bright red and gold decorations to commemorate the new year.

"We get out here." Ah Kain tightened her hand around Bella's, and they joined the huddle of people pushing forward to descend the tram. As they approached the park, Bella looked up at a metal sign reflecting the yellow, red and green glow of street signs.

"Southorn Playground." Her small voice dissolved in the hollow sound drummed in the distance. A tinny sound rang through the air. Clang! Clang! Clang!

"What's happening?"

Ah Kain did not respond. They kept walking, stopping, bumping and swerving with the people around them. Bella caught glimpses of the park and the food stalls through the legs and bodies jostling around her. They zigged and zagged through the crowd.

"Hold on," Ah Kain said. Bella felt herself rise off the ground and land on the narrow ledge of the light's base. She wrapped an arm around the pole, her other hand still touching Ah Kain's shoulder.

Bella straightened and smiled as she scanned the park. Now that she was almost taller than everyone around her, she could see that people were gathering in two lines, leaving a path in between them.

Crack! Pop! Pop! Pop! The sounds grew louder. Clang! Bella's heart boomed as a skinny man dressed in a bright orange shirt and baggy, red and purple pants banged on golden, round, flat discs that sounded like kitchen pots and pans. Bam! More musicians appeared down the path, dressed in the same vivid costumes that billowed as they moved. More dancers followed, wearing giant costume heads with big eyes and painted smiles. Waving their arms, they swayed with onlookers and threw down strings of red firecrackers. The exploding bangers jumped and jerked around as they flashed and flickered noisily, releasing dark smoke into the air. A huge, furry head with a green and red face poked up in the distance and disappeared in the crowd.

"Ah Kain, Ah Kain." Bella's high, quick call was barely audible as she shook Ah Kain's shoulder. "The lion is coming." The procession grew louder as it moved along the path towards them. When the lion's mouth opened, Bella saw the face of the lead dancer. His arms held the bamboo cane frame of the lion's head that moved it up and down, left and right, to the sound of the music.

The lion shook its white, fluffy mane as it twisted and lurched in time with the music, opening and closing its painted eyelids. Under the gold and red cloth of the lion's body, dancers' feet, adorned with bright red and yellow shoes, tapped the ground and kicked high into the air. Together with the firecrackers, they were scaring away evil spirits and clearing the way for the new year — the year of the water ox.

Even in the chilly winter air, dots of sweat beaded above Bella's lip as she danced on her perch. Although the chaos and crowds subsided as people followed the parade past Bella and through the playground, the boom and clang of the music still played in her chest and head.

She held onto Ah Kain's hands and counted, "Yut, yee, saaaaahm," as she jumped to the ground.

As the burning, chemical smokiness of the firecrackers dissipated into the air, a yummy sweetness filled its place. Bella tugged on Ah Kain.

"Do you smell that?" she asked. She sniffed the air and rubbed her stomach, just in case Ah Kain couldn't hear.

"Siu lot jee,"Ah Kain said, inhaling the fragrance. "You want roasted chestnuts?"

Bella bobbed her head up and down quickly. "I've loved roasted chestnuts since I was a little girl."

Ah Kain laughed and pinched Bella's cheek gingerly. "You are still a little girl," she said affectionately.

Bella's mouth watered as she hopped-skipped towards the aroma. She opened her mouth in a silent shriek of joy when she saw the chestnut stand. A man in a long-sleeve shirt stirred a huge, black wok filled with dark coals and shiny brown chestnuts. He used his gloved hand to pick out chestnuts and place them into a brown paper bag which he handed to a young woman in a coat.

Two pretty ladies were in queue, their red cheongsams stuck out from underneath their grey and white coat. They looked like walking mermaids.

"Fai dee lah," Bella said to Ah Kain, intoxicated by the moment to repeat the Cantonese words that she heard many times this evening as they hopped on and off the trams and buses. Bella and Ah Kain stood in line behind the two mermaids and watched the old man, sweat glistening on his forehead as he stirred the shiny coals. The rough black lumps made a scratching sound, as they tumbled around the big paddle and bumped against the oversize metal wok that Bella was sure was big enough for her to bathe in.

"Gung Hei Fat Choi," two voices said behind Bella.

"Happy New Year," Bella chimed in Cantonese with Ah Kain as they turned around to the old man and woman now in line behind them.

The old woman with silvery hair gave Bella a wide smile, which dropped into an expression of shock. She put her hand to her heart and nudged the man beside her. He looked at the old woman, then followed her gaze to Bella. He squinted as he bent forward slightly. He straightened, then bent down again. He looked back at the old woman. Her lips curled up and down as though she were deciding whether to laugh or cry.

The mermaid ladies walked away, each holding a bag of chestnuts. Ah Kain and Bella turned and stepped forward. Ah Kain held up her index finger.

"Yut bao siu lot jee," She looked in her handbag for her coin purse.

Bella watched the chestnut vendor take a paper bag from a box, shake it open and put chestnuts in it.

"Your daughter is beautiful," the old man said to Ah Kain.

"Thank you. But, not my daughter," Ah Kain said, turning. She patted Bella's back tenderly.

The old woman tapped Bella's shoulder and asked in Cantonese, "How old are you?"

Bella turned. "Five," she answered in English. She held out an open palm with outstretched fingers. "And a half," she added, holding up her other hand as she tried to decide which finger to bend. She looked at the woman's large, dark brown eyes, and an image of her staring into the watery obscurity of fish eyes popped into her head.

Ah Kain pressed the bag of chestnuts into Bella's hands and turned back to the vendor to pay. Bella held up the bag to show the old man and woman the great treasure.

"Ching Ha?" the old woman said.

Bella looked up at the woman in line, and the center of their eyes met in a laser focus; their gaze in one another's eyes holding like a magnetic bond.

When Bella heard, "Ching Ha," the pandemonium around her fell away into a mist-like dream, and a sense of something she had once known rained over her. She could feel the flat and rounded sides of the chestnuts through the warm, paper bag. The buttery, sweet smell rose in white steam that danced from the bag and evaporated into the air. Silver strands of the old woman's hair sparkled as they reflected the street light. Bella thought she had seen those teary eyes and whispering lips sometime in a dream, in a picture frame that floated in her heart.

"Okay, Bella. Let's go home," Ah Kain said.

The images that drifted in that dreamy space of her chest dispersed and disappeared. Bella gasped, as though she had been holding her breath.

"Thank you," Bella said, not looking at Ah Kain. Her voice wobbled as her brain tried to remember and understand the pictures and feelings that had just inundated her core. The silver-haired lady leaned forward, stretched out a hand. She gently tugged on the girl's pink jacket. Bella felt something fall into her front pocket.

"Goodbye" hung in the air until the old woman waved.

Bella could not wave back as Ah Kain led her away, nor could she check her pocket. One hand was in Ah Kain's firm grip, and the other clutched the precious snack to her chest. She continued to look back at the old woman whose stare mesmerized her even as people walked into their view of one another and the distance between them grew. Before Bella turned away, she thought she saw the old woman's lips move as her hand sailed into the air in a farewell.

Bella was too far to hear, or read the message from the old woman's lips, "See you tomorrow."

Tucked in bed that night, her belly filled with

roasted chestnuts, Bella thought about the old grandmother-looking woman. *Who was she? One of her Baba's friends? One of the servants that worked for them at the big parties?* She remembered the tug on her jacket. Throwing off her covers, she ran to the closet. She reached up and felt around her jacket pocket. She eased the flat disc into her palm. Returning to bed, she propped herself on her elbows and examined the coin in the moonlight streaming in from her window. It was a fifty-cent coin. Its silver shininess had worn off Queen Elizabeth's face, and the words around the edges were hard to see, but Bella let an ahhh, linger in the magical moment.

Bella tapped the coin on her headboard and rolled it up and down. It made a tuk-tuk sound in the silence of her room. She pressed the coin against the dark surface, accidentally scraping a short, vertical line into the wood. She studied the contrast of the slim, white line against the dark grain and smiled.

"I," she said. She pushed the coin against the wood again, this time carving out, "am." She remembered what the old woman had called her.

Bella didn't know anybody who called her "Ching Ha," but she was sure that she had heard that name before. She wondered why it made her feel like swaying her shoulders and singing.

Once more, the coin rasped across the headboard as Bella sounded out words from her picture dictionary.

"Ch, cheese. Ch, chocolate. Ch, chat." She scraped out more letters. "S, ing." "R, ing." "L, ing." She paused. "Ling. Was that a word?" She touched the headboard. Her fingers traced the words as she read, "I am Ching Ha."

Satisfied with her work, the little girl flipped onto her back, her hand reaching above her head to feel the engraving.

She yawned and closed her fingers around the coin.

Her breathing grew steadily deeper and peaceful as her mind filled with the vibrant colors of the lion dance.

She imagined blurry movies of the old woman

feeding her noodles, and the sound of shoes clicking as a Chinese woman walked down the hallway, singing in a fuzzy language, in an almost-forgotten dream of a faraway place and time.

Epilogue

February 2012
  Tel Aviv, Israel
  Bnei Brak Cemetery

Bella stood next to a raised slab of brown crystalline-patterned marble. Wisps of fragrant smoke floated into the sky as she fanned the incense up and down. She pushed the sticks into a tin can half-filled with sand and pebbles that she had set by a dish of three oranges. Bella sat down at the edge of the slab. She sighed, imagining Lana and Dima's voices saying, "So the prodigal child returns."

"I know. I know. It has taken me a few years to get back here to visit both of you. I've always had a love-hate relationship with Israel; a country to which I do and do not belong. It's like Hong Kong, except that I can blend in more easily in Hong Kong, even though I also don't speak the language there." Bella paused. She had practiced what she wanted to say. Did she even need to speak? Couldn't they just hear her thoughts? Maybe so, but she needed to say this aloud so she could hear it.

"I am finally here to say, 'goodbye,' in person. I probably won't be back." She stopped again, as though waiting for an argument from them. There was none. "Ken retired from the military last October, and we moved to an island just outside Seattle. Only Mitch lives at home now. He heads to university next year. In anticipation of an empty nest, I started playing the piano again." Bella tilted her head as if listening to something. "Why, after all these years? Well, thanks to your loyal secretary in Hong Kong and all her connections, I was reunited with my old piano teacher. Ling Liu, as you probably know, and knew all those years ago, is my biological mother. She lives in Seattle with her other daughter, who is twelve years younger than me." Bella stopped. She thought about the part of her speech that retold her reunion with Ling and decided to leave it out. She had told that story so many times. Lana and Dima probably knew all about it. Were ghosts omniscient, like God? "Seeing Ling brought back visions that I'm not sure whether I remembered or imagined. Her reappearance has helped me to fill some of the potholes beneath my feet, where the past tripped me up with questions and wonderings, sadness and strange longings."

Bella looked up and smiled at the groundskeeper, who waved as he drove by in his golf cart. She waited a moment and looked around self-consciously before continuing to speak.

"I hope that you are at peace now, with Volodya — that space in your lives and soul, that I, only partially and always impermanently, could fill. Thank you for your rich history and all the stories that you gave me. I now blend them with my Chinese roots — a birthright that I learned to cherish. I have embraced this vivid, complex, heritage of mine and.have the confidence, strength and understanding to share with my children."

Bella's chest felt tight. A surge of emotion? Grief? Sadness? Heatstroke? No. She breathed deeply. It was just the surfacing of those few, rarely spoken words that never flowed freely with Lana and Dima, or anyone else for that matter. Bella swallowed and exhaled the three little words; each one heavy with as much burden as blessing. "I. Love. You."

Emotions and sensations engulfed her; her swelling heart, bumps tingling over her arms, high humidity, and the Israeli sunshine drowning her, cleansing her, freeing her. The energy of this place and moment mingled with hers for one final time. "Just because I won't be here, it doesn't mean that I don't remember you," she said as she stooped and picked up three stones from the ground.

Bella kissed the largest, speckled stone and conjured memories of Dima singing Waltzing Matilda with her on the bough of their Chinese junk. She placed it on the grave next to his name. As Bella brought the second stone to her lips, she glanced at the glow of the incense sticks. It reminded her of Lana's face vignetted in cigarette smoke. Bella placed the stone next to Lana's name. The third stone was the smallest of the three. Bella kissed it and closed her fingers around it. She moved to the adjacent grave. Its cracked headstone had faded. Its epitaph was almost rubbed away by the limbs of the sycamore tree that grew around it and held it in an endless embrace. Bella placed the stone on the grave. She opened her mouth to say something, but no words came; only the memory of her brother smiling back at her from a picture frame in his ghostly room.

Bella stood. She looked at Dima's name gleaming in the granite like a big smile and pressed her hand against his name. The coolness of the marble seeped through her skin. She felt a pinch in her heart as she brushed her fingers against the stone's smoothness. Her chest quivered, and she smiled the sorrow away.

"Goodbye," Bella said. She straightened and took a visual snapshot of the graves, set against the sun-bleached walls of the overcrowded cemetery. She turned and walked down the dusty path, leaving behind a final whisper, "See you tomorrow."

Acknowledgments

Writing and completing *Finding Ching Ha* has been a long and difficult process for me. Many people were part of my journey. Some are mentioned here.

Huge thanks to my reader and writer friends and peers who have, over the years, read various parts of this evolving project. I deeply appreciate all your time and diverse, insightful feedback.

Glenn and Julie Morey, thank you for *Given Away*. It gave me a sense of grounding and belonging I didn't know existed. The heartbreaking comfort that I was not alone with my hologram past, encouraged me in the last stages of this endeavour. Glenn, your moving and bittersweet foreword makes me smile and cry every time I read it. I feel fortunate that our paths have crossed.

Mike, thanks for constant reminders that a writer's existence can be hard, but not following the compulsion is harder.

Thank you, Jenny and Cindy, for your help with the Cantonese, and Chinese customs.

Paul, thanks for sharing your journey with *Sorrow*, a work that mirrored so many of *Finding Ching Ha*'s themes and inspired me to finish my manuscript.

Nina, Thank you for fishing Ching Ha out of Repulse Bay. I love you.

Thank you, my parents, for all the opportunities you gave me and the invaluable lessons about authenticity, making joy, and raising myself and my children.

Claude, thank you for your patience with my solitary and strange writing schedule, and, most importantly, keeping the fridge stocked, and taking over the cooking.

Thank you, Alister, Natasha, and Makai for weathering my tough parenting, giving me insight into this story and always making me laugh. Natasha, special thanks to you for the pep talks and brainstorming sessions.

And thank you, dear reader, for picking up this book. I hope my story resonates with you and encourages your journey to find truth and joy with your ever-unfolding identity.

With gratitude, peace and love,

Maya.

Discussion Questions

1. Did Mrs. Wong do the right thing by keeping Ching Ha and, later, giving her away?
2. Was Ching Ha lucky to have been adopted by the Hoffmans?
3. How many families are in this story and how do the dynamics, directly or indirectly, impact Ching Ha?
4. What are the strengths and weaknesses of the female protagonists?
5. What aspects of this novel could you most relate to, if any?
6. Did any parts of the novel make you emotional? If so, which ones and ones?
7. How do the characters evolve through the course of the story?
8. Did your feelings for any of the characters change from the start to the end of the novel?
9. If you could hear this story from another character's point of view, who would you choose?
10. How does Ching Ha's perception of her identity change during the story?
11. Is one's heritage linked to one's genetics, biological or adoptive family, or other?
12. Who is searching for their identity in this novel? What drives/satiates this journey and has it become a more complicated issue since the 1970s?
13. What is your most important takeaway from this novel?
14. What gives you a sense of belonging to a

group?

15. What is the significance of food in this novel?

16. Would Ling have been forced to give up Ching Ha in today's society?

17. What was unique about the setting of the novel? How did it enhance or take away from the story?

18. At what point do conversational questions become prying ones?

19. Was the ending of this story satisfying for you? Why/why not?

20. If you were making a movie of this novel, who would you cast in the leading roles?

www.ingramcontent.com/pod-product-compliance
Lightning Source LLC
Chambersburg PA
CBHW021232250626
47155CB00008B/2981